BARGAIN BRIDE

She married as a business deal – but can she find love?

Young Charlotte Mortimer is content with her lot. She loves her job teaching the poor and destitute at the local school and is happy with her strong, steadfast fiancé, Luke. Then one day a terrible mining explosion rocks the town, and suddenly everything Charlotte thinks she knows is thrown into doubt. The arrival of wealthy businessman Justin Harvard complicates things further. Charlotte must marry him to save the school she loves. Can she keep to her side of the deal, as she enters a seemingly loveless marriage? Will she ever love the austere man who saved her beloved school from certain destruction?

BARGAIN BRIDE

BARGAIN BRIDE

by

Iris Gower

Magna Large Print Books
Long Preston, North Yorkshire,
BD23 4ND, England.

MAGNA 11 07 08 MH

British Library Cataloguing in Publication Data.

Ke 6 08

Gower, Iris
    Bargain bride.

    A catalogue record of this book is
    available from the British Library

    ISBN   978-0-7505-2949-5

First published in Great Britain in 2007 by Bantam Press
an imprint of Transworld Publishers

Copyright © Iris Gower 2007

Cover illustration © Nigel Chamberlain by arrangement with
Alison Eldred

Iris Gower has asserted her right under the Copyright, Designs
and Patents Act, 1988 to be identified as the author of this work

Published in Large Print 2008 by arrangement with
Transworld Publishers

Magna Large Print is an imprint of Library Magna Books Ltd.

Printed and bound in Great Britain by
T.J. (International) Ltd., Cornwall, PL28 8RW

To my editor, Linda, for not only being a brilliant, conscientious editor but for always being there for me.

FOREWORD

A heartfelt thank-you to my readers who have taken an interest in my personal life, who have spoken and written to me with best wishes saying how much they like the small messages included in my books. Readers have sent me sympathy cards and helpful advice on coping with the loss, four years ago, of my dear husband, Tudor. He was my constant support, while happily staying in the background at the many events we attended together. When he died I felt crushed and lost.

And then when I met Peter, two years ago, and fell in love again, something I thought would never happen, the congratulations from my readers were heartfelt and warm, pleased to know I was happy. Peter fed me, worrying because I was so thin and small. He made me laugh, making me feel like a beautiful and talented woman, and showed me that even past sixty, life was not over yet.

Many, many thanks to you all.

Love

Iris

Iris can be contacted on her email address:
igower57@hotmail.co.uk
Website: www.iris-gower.co.uk

CHAPTER ONE

Charlotte stood on the quayside at Liverpool docks and tried not to cry as she hugged her stepmother tightly. 'Look after yourself, Ella,' she said, her throat constricting as she spoke, 'and thank you for all you've done for the family, loving us as if we were your own.'

'It was easy to love you, my darling. I've loved you girls as if you'd been born to me and it's hard to go away and leave one of you alone.' She hesitated. 'Fate does have a way of changing your life for ever – the Palace, the theatre that your dear father owned, changed my life completely. But anyway, you just go home to your Luke, he's a good man and I'm sure he'll make you happy.'

Charlotte wasn't so sure herself. Luke, the headmaster at the school, was sometimes proud and arrogant, and there was no passion in him when he kissed her. Charlotte wanted passion; she wanted to be excited by him. She wanted an all-consuming love such as her stepmother had with her second husband, Anthony.

'Go now,' Charlotte urged. 'I'll be all right.' She watched as Ella bustled along behind the children like a mother hen with

13

her chicks, and a pain of longing tightened her heart. She looked up at the massive ship towering above the dock; the twin screw *Carpathia* stood in majesty at the quayside and, already, travellers were boarding, heading for the long sea journey to America, a land Charlotte had only heard of.

The bullish sound from the ship's funnel rent the air and reluctantly Charlotte stepped back, watching as her family was shepherded towards the gangway by Anthony, who had rushed to their side having seen their luggage on board. He raised his hand and blew her a kiss, and Charlotte responded, aware that the tears were running unchecked down her cheeks.

At the last minute before boarding the ship, Ella paused on the gangway and waved her hand in farewell. Charlotte longed to run after them all, to go to the new land with them, but her feet remained rooted to the ground: she had to return to Swansea. She was teaching the children of the workers and she wouldn't desert them, she couldn't.

She thought again of Luke, of how he was worried about her travelling all the way to Liverpool without him. Luke Lester was a fine man, a good man. He was steady and reliable, a man who would always look after her. She respected Luke and she loved him. Of course she did hope he would change when they were married – he would be as warm and passionate as she wanted. Now, he was just being a gentleman and treating her like a lady.

Another blast came from the funnel of the big ship. The gangway had been drawn back like a snail into its shell, and fussy tugs kept close to the huge *Carpathia* like infants clinging to their mother.

Smoke billowed into the sky as the majestic vessel steamed slowly out to sea. The figures of her family were tiny now, barely distinguishable from the press of other passengers crowding the rails.

Charlotte watched until there was just a smudge of steam on the horizon to mark the passage of the ship. Then even that vanished from sight. Looking around, Charlotte realized she was the only one left on the quay, and loneliness gripped her, a new and horrible feeling of being alone in the world. She breathed in the smells of the docks, the salt blown in by the fresh wind, the fishiness, the coal tip just beyond the quay. It was all foreign to her and she wanted nothing more than to be at home among all that was familiar.

She picked up her bags and, with tears running down her cheeks and into her mouth, she made her way out of the docks and into the unfamiliar town, where people spoke with a strange mixture of accents, some Irish, some with the rich Liverpool twang, some Chinese. Liverpool was a place of rare colour and richness, of races mingling easily, all drawn by the industry of the docks.

As Charlotte made her way through the grimy streets, beautified by the spring sunshine, she blessed Anthony's thoughtfulness in booking a room for her at one of the boarding houses a short way from the docklands. Feeling weary and beaten, she was glad of his kindness and longed to shut herself away in private and cry her heart out.

The boarding house was squat and ugly but clean and respectable and Charlotte had a room at the front of the building overlooking the docks, giving her a glimpse of the sea. She loved the sea: she had grown up close to the ocean, watched its ebb and flow while picking shells from the sand, teasing the clinging barnacles from the underbelly of beached sailing boats. But now even the sea seemed like her enemy. It was forbidding and restless, and it had carried away the people she loved, leaving her empty and feeling so alone.

The bell rang for dinner and, wiping her eyes hastily, Charlotte made her way down the narrow stairway, suddenly feeling hungry. The savoury smell of boiled ham floated up to Charlotte as she negotiated the narrow, twisting passage, so different to the small but elegant hall of the house she'd lived in with her father since her birth.

'So there you are, young lady.' Mrs

Murphy spoke with the softness of the Irish lilt, a lilt Charlotte was familiar with – it was a language spoken in Swansea by the Irish folk who had come over the sea many years ago to make their home in Greenhill, just outside the town.

Mrs Murphy was a rotund woman swathed in a voluminous apron. She wiped her hands on it as she smiled at Charlotte. 'All your kin got away safely, by the grace of the blessed Virgin then?'

Charlotte nodded, meeting her kindly eyes but unable to stem the sudden tears that started to brim in her own.

'Poor little chick.' Mrs Murphy held out her arms and drew Charlotte close, patting her back. 'Cry you, darlin', cry it all out. It's only natural you'll miss your lovely family.' She hesitated. 'Are you sure you've made the right decision by staying here alone?'

'I don't know,' Charlotte said. 'I don't know anything any more.' She gently drew away from Mrs Murphy's motherly grasp. 'Thank you for being so kind. When I've eaten I'll get an early night, I must start on my way back home first thing in the morning.'

Charlotte ate sparingly, listening to the lively chatter that went on around Mrs Murphy's well-laden table. Her appetite seemed to have deserted her now she was faced with a full plate. By the time she'd drunk the glass of wine the kindly Irishwoman had poured, she was so tired she had to force her eyes to stay open.

Later, she was glad to fall into the clean but lumpy bed. Her head ached but, in spite of this and her loneliness, she slept well.

In the morning Charlotte bade goodbye to Mrs Murphy, feeling she was losing her only friend, and began her journey back to Wales. She walked to the station with quick steps, anxious now to return to the little house that came with the job of teaching the children of St John's parish.

She looked forward to seeing the kitchen, with its big window which looked out across the river Tawe to where the Red Rock copperworks lit up the sky at night and fumes and smoke coloured the water red-gold. The works had lots of chimneys, pointing like fingers to the sky. The Red Rock had been there for many years and Charlotte was so used to it now she rarely saw it in stark detail. Now, as she thought about it, she knew that, although it might be an ugly sight to outsiders, it was all familiar to her now, part of her life in Swansea.

Travelling by train was a new experience. On the outward journey she'd had her family to distract her. Now, she gazed through the windows seeing red-glowing cinders burst from the train to light pyres in the grass at the side of the tracks. She settled back and tried to sleep, but the journey seemed end-

18

less, and by the time she'd changed trains and waited on cold platforms, she was thoroughly dispirited and sick at heart.

At last, though, she was on the final leg of her journey, seated in the small compartment of the train looking out at the dun-coloured skies. The river Tawe was eerily still in the evening light, dark and menacing in a way she'd never seen it before.

There were only a few passengers on the train now. Sitting close to her was a thin woman clutching a bag to her small chest as if she feared someone would take it from her. On the seat opposite sat a girl about Charlotte's own age and an older woman, who kept her elbow pressed into the side of a young boy who took delight in making faces at Charlotte.

'If the wind changes you'll stay like that.' Charlotte leaned towards him and the boy subsided, puzzled, against the back of the seat.

'He doesn't mean any harm,' his mother said. 'Apologize, Timmy.'

He mumbled an apology and, too tired to respond, Charlotte closed her eyes, shutting herself off from any human contact. She must have dozed because when she woke the woman and her unruly son were gone.

Charlotte met the gaze of the young woman, the only other passenger remaining in the carriage with her. Charlotte nodded politely. Becoming aware of her bedraggled appearance, she straightened her shoulders, brushed back her hair and did her best to smile.

They travelled a little way without speaking. The only sound was the clickety-clack of the wheels on the rails and the occasional whistle. Suddenly, the other girl spoke.

'I did admire the way you handled that little beast of a boy. I should have been tempted to give him a slap.'

'I'm used to young children,' Charlotte said. 'I have four sisters and a brother and, as well as all that, I'm a teacher.'

'How interesting, tell me more.' The girl leaned forward, waiting, and reluctantly at first but with growing enthusiasm, Charlotte talked about her life.

'My father was a lovely man – everyone liked Jolly Mortimer. He was the owner of the Palace Theatre, well brought up, well educated, and he saw to it that we were too.' She shrugged deprecatingly. 'I was considered the scholar of the family, just because I could absorb books, remember detail; my sister Letty was the real talent, she became a writer.'

At the next stop, the girl left the train and Charlotte was sorry – just for a time she had brought her family back into her life, had enjoyed talking of happier times.

As the train curved towards Swansea,

Charlotte peered through the grimy window and saw, her heart giving a happy beat, the rise of Kilvey hill and the ribbon of water that was the river Tawe winding its way towards the sea.

At a place called the Loop, the train slowed. Charlotte wondered why – a tricky bend, a mail-collection point? It didn't matter, she was nearly home. She sat back in her seat and closed her eyes; she was tired but content now that she was back on familiar territory. The trip to Liverpool had been an adventure of sorts, albeit a sad one, but Charlotte was glad the adventure was over.

At the Loop the door of the train was flung open and a thin, poorly dressed boy tumbled in on to the floor, his unruly hair falling over his face. Charlotte recognized him at once.

'John! Lord above us, what on earth are you doing?' She grabbed the boy, who was in danger of falling back out on to the track as the train picked up speed. He scrambled to cross his legs and lean against the seat, staring at her with a mixture of apology and defiance in his clear eyes.

'John Merriman, what on earth d'you think you're doing? You could have been killed!'

He looked up at her, sheepish now. 'The other boys dared me, miss, said I didn't have the belly for it, but they were wrong, weren't they?'

21

'So you could be right and dead or mortally injured. That's not bravery, John, that's simply foolishness. Sometimes it takes more courage to say no than to accept a challenge. I hope you'll remember that.'

When the train pulled into the station, billowing smoke into the already murky sky above the town, John, with an apologetic look at Charlotte, jumped from the train before it had come to a stop. Charlotte peered after him anxiously and was relieved to see him walk away unhurt. She would have a sharp word to say to him tomorrow at school. She half smiled: it wouldn't do any good – boys were always taking dares, it was part of growing up.

When she alighted from the train, Charlotte stood for a moment looking round her, breathing in the stink-laden air that drifted through the town like a plague, but she was happy. She was back where she belonged.

In the morning, when Charlotte walked into the little schoolroom, which smelled pleasantly of newly sharpened pencils, she found a temporary master in Luke's place. Luke had gone away to a meeting in Chepstow and would not be back till the beginning of the following week. She felt a sense of relief – she was fond of Luke, of course, but sometimes, in his efforts to excel in his chosen profession, he could be just a teeny bit overbearing.

In the classroom, she looked at her pupils with new eyes, the girls sitting on one side of the room, the boys on the other. Some of the children were dressed in heavily patched clothes, others in what were obviously hand-me-downs from an older sibling. A quick look at the boys assured her that John Merriman seemed none the worse for his adventure on the train.

He was older than most of the other pupils, the cleverest and her favourite. John had the sort of build that promised he would soon grow tall, like a young sapling, and the lines of manhood were already forming in his features. John's father had been killed in an accident at the Red Rock a long time ago, and his mother worked tirelessly, washing and ironing and taking in mending. Scrubby hens pecked in her square of a garden but the eggs were good enough to sell. The ones that appeared in Charlotte's kitchen from time to time were a gift and Charlotte accepted them as such. Like John's mother, Charlotte meant John to have the best education a boy of his intelligence and background could, and she'd insisted on taking him on at the school, though Luke had protested loudly, calling it favouritism on her part. Still, she'd had her way in the end.

'Bore dda plant.' She said good morning in Welsh, and John Merriman looked up at her, sharp-eyed, hungry to learn. She felt

settled and happy to be back in her own school. Except, of course, it wasn't really her school. St John's was owned by the Red Rock copper company, and the parents of pupils were charged a penny a week for the privilege of their being given an education. Unfortunately, not many parents could afford to pay. Most had large families and inevitably one child was favoured at the expense of the others.

Charlotte loved her work, but her long journey had tired her, and when the bell rang out, echoing through the small building at the close of school, she sighed with relief.

She took the ferry across the river to Foxhole. From there she didn't have very far to walk, as her home now was a little house facing the school on the opposite bank.

The stone cottage was dry and warm and pleasant enough, except in its proximity to the Red Rock copperworks. As she approached the house, she saw the wraith of noxious smoke drifting above the water, yellow and lethal and bearing the stench of the works across the whole of the east side of town. The hills that rose above Swansea were barren except for a few camomile flowers, and they were bleached white from the smoke. But she loved it all: it was her town, her home.

Once indoors, Charlotte dropped her satchel of books and sank into her rocking chair. It was the one item of furniture she'd salvaged from the sale of her family home. She rested her hands on the smooth wooden arms, running her fingers over the grain as if caressing it. She pictured her father sitting in this very chair reading his Bible.

Charlotte sighed, it was time she lit the fire and made a meal for herself. She shouldn't be wallowing in memories, especially memories that smacked of self-pity. She smiled ruefully as she bent to the coals. Her life now was a whole world away from what it had been. Having lived fairly comfortably in her father's house, at first she'd found her schoolteacher's house plain. Her dining room was a space set off from the kitchen holding a simple table of seasoned wood. Little daylight penetrated the tiny window. Her bedroom was also small, its deep windows always grimed with copper dust. Still, it was a space of her own.

It was almost dark now, and Charlotte lit the lamp, disregarding a tug of guilt at squandering the precious oil. Across Swansea, good electric lamps lit the streets, but the Red Rock Company had more to do with their massive profits than spend them on a lowly teacher who lived in the house only by their grace and favour.

In the larder, Charlotte saw that her supplies were getting low. The flour bag was almost empty – just as well, because the coarse grains were infested with weevils. Shuddering, she took the bag outside and put it on the compost heap. She sighed as she looked at the flowerbed. Nothing seemed to grow in the soil; everything was choked by copper smoke.

She was hungry and tired and didn't know if she should eat or fall into bed. In the end, her hunger won and she toasted some cheese in the frying pan and laced it with fried onions. The lovely aroma of food filled the kitchen. When she'd eaten the cheese, she wiped the grease from her lips with relish – at least living alone had one advantage; she could forget her table manners and eat like a pig.

Following this thought, she opened the larder door and took out an egg custard tart. Smacking her lips in anticipation, she poked her index fingers into the soft creamy custard, scooped it up and carried it to her mouth.

The tart, another occasional treat, had been made for her by Mrs Merriman, who was grateful that her growing son was able to tot up how much she made washing clothes and selling eggs so no one could gyp her out of a penny. Mrs Merriman was a stick-thin woman with lines of strain etched into her face, but beautiful. Sometimes, she washed some of Charlotte's delicate under-clothes and, in exchange, Charlotte gave extra lessons to John.

Charlotte assured Mrs Merriman that she would teach John for nothing, it would be her pleasure, but the local people were proud: if they took, they made sure to give in return.

Charlotte cleared away the dishes, shook out the tablecloth and folded it back into a neat square before putting it away. At last she could relax. She selected a book from the small bookcase and sank back into the rocking chair. She was reading from Virgil's *Aeneid*, the story of Aeneas, who meant to win a kingdom in Italy as the Prince of Destiny. It had been written in a language Charlotte didn't understand but Luke had painstakingly copied the poems into English for her. As with everything, he had given the work his unstinting attention.

Luke had 'come down in the world', as he put it. His father had been a successful banker and the house Luke had lived in as a child was a huge structure built of good stone that stood on a promontory overlooking the sea. Luke had attended an excellent college – he was far brighter than Charlotte; she admired him so much. And now, she was relaxing with the book he had given her, even though she knew he meant it as a step forward in her education.

She was shocked yet titillated by the story of Aeneas's scandalous affair with Dido, the widowed queen of Carthage. It enchanted Charlotte and she turned the pages rapidly. She wanted a happy outcome for Dido, who was swamped with love for Aeneas – but all to no avail. As she read on, Charlotte gasped in horror as the hero abandoned poor Dido, leaving her desolate, and continued merrily pursuing his dream.

Her eyes began to ache and with a sigh she closed the book and put it back in the bookcase. The characters in the *Aeneid* were not life-like at all: real women were hard-working and had no time left over for indulging themselves with illicit love affairs. Still, such goings on were very thrilling to read about. She wondered if she should discuss it with Luke when he returned and rejected the idea. Luke was a deacon of the chapel as well as an excellent teacher and, though he knew the work was praiseworthy, he would baulk at reading it with her.

She looked at the clock and realized it was long past her bedtime. She stood for a while looking out of the window. The darkness was intense, the lights from the road smothered by the copper smoke that hung low over the rooftops. Sounds from the forest of works on both banks of the river penetrated the night, but Charlotte was used to the noise by now and almost welcomed it as company in her solitude.

The wind was rising, blowing away the

clouds and the yellow smoke; the brilliant copper-coloured lights from the tapped furnaces illuminated the night with an attractive aurora which turned the river to gold. It was a beautiful and yet savage aspect of the fabric of life in Swansea, and it was all in her bones, ingrained into her being, part of her heritage.

Charlotte went to bed and cuddled herself beneath the quilt, hugging her pillow close. Swansea, in all its beauty and ugliness, belonged to her, and she would never want to leave it. Content with her lot, she slept and dreamed of lovers and passion and woke refreshed in the morning, happy to face a new day.

CHAPTER TWO

Charlotte stood as the children filed out of the classroom, eager to be released into the fresh air. She watched them go, her little family, her children, at least for the hours they spent at school. She glanced with affection at the thin figure of John Merriman and saw with concern that his eyes were ringed with dark circles. His mother must be unwell again or working late doing her ironing and he would have had to sit up minding his baby brother. She felt a tug at her heartstrings. She would like to take the lines of strain from his face, buy him a good pair of new boots, but his mother would take offence and the other children would find out the truth, as children often did, and ridicule John.

She shook her head as if to rid herself of the sadness, she shouldn't stand there idle, she had a meeting to attend. She hurried to the staff room and, removing a pin that was fast sliding from her hair, replaced it as firmly as she could. There was no mirror in the room, but she rubbed at her lips, infusing a little colour into them. She was too pale, she knew that.

Luke had tried to impress on her that she needed to take more walks, in the sun when possible, and take her nose out of her books at least for a little while, but then even Luke didn't understand the thirst for knowledge that infused Charlotte day and night.

Luke was waiting for her in the corridor.

'Right then,' she said, catching his arm, 'let's go and speak to this terribly important school governor.'

Luke, fresh from an earlier meeting with the man, had eulogized about him that morning before classes began. He frowned. 'Please don't be facetious. Justin Harvard is a rich and powerful man. He's a widower who lives with his family at Thornhill, a fabulous house on the peak of Mumbles Head. He's got two little girls, as I understand.' He squeezed Charlotte's hand. 'At least he's made the effort to come to the school to see us – you have to give him some credit for that.'

Charlotte was unwilling to give him credit for anything; it was clear he'd called a meeting regardless of any plans she or Luke might have made. Well, Justin Harvard would find he had more to deal with than he'd thought. She wouldn't let him order her around. In spite of her brave thoughts, though, she felt a shiver of fear: what if he decided he'd close the school? Charlotte knew there was no profit in running the school – it was probably a liability – but at least the rich owners of the Red Rock were giving something back for the stink and fumes the works produced.

Then her heart lifted. The day was nearly over and soon she would go home. Luke would come with her, they would eat together and talk endlessly through the evening. He would take her arm, place a kiss on her cheek and make his way home to his small house on the slopes of the Kilvey hilltop which guarded the sea at the dock's entrance. In the meantime, there was a good impression to make on this Mr Harvard. However antagonistic she felt towards him, she must remember he would donate much-needed funds to the school.

'Let's get this meeting over and done with.' Luke echoed her thoughts almost exactly, and she smiled at him.

'Don't worry, I'll be at my most charming.' He relaxed then and returned her smile fondly, but she wondered if he was a little *too* fond – sometimes she thought he treated her almost like a sister, not a future wife.

Now, with the story of the love between Aeneas and Dido ringing in her mind, she was studying her feelings for Luke in a new light. She shook the doubts away: stories were all very well but, she reminded herself, real life was not as it was portrayed within the covers of a book.

'Remember, Charlotte,' Luke said, sensing he'd lost her attention, 'this meeting is important for the continued running of the school. Without him, and with our last governor and patron dead and gone, there's a real threat we'll have to close the school indefinitely.'

She felt her fears return. 'Are things as bad as that?' But she knew he was right, Luke was usually right when it came to matters relating to the funding of the school of St John.

He looked grave. 'It is a real possibility.'

'And this man Harvard, the power lies in his hands?' She trembled. How would she fill her days? And on a more personal, selfish level, if the school were closed, where would she live?

'I'll go on ahead,' Luke said. 'Give me five minutes and then join us.'

She spent those minutes pondering the power of this stranger, this Mr Harvard, who didn't know the school or what valuable work she and Luke were doing there. When she judged that sufficient time had elapsed, she made her way to Luke's little room, tucked in behind the shallow staircase leading to the small balcony area where the children attended choir practice.

She paused for a moment, twitching her skirts into place, touching her hair in an effort to tuck away a few unruly curls which insisted on feathering on to her neck. From inside the head's room a voice spoke, a deep, masculine voice.

'I assure you, sir, I'll listen as you suggest to what Miss Mortimer has to say, but I must tell you right away, the opinions of a mere girl, a newly trained teacher at that, won't influence my decision one way or another.'

A rush of anger tightened Charlotte's mouth. She lifted her hand and rapped angrily on the door.

'Ah, Miss Mortimer, do come in.' Luke appeared nervous. 'Come and meet the gentleman who we hope will be our beneficent new school governor.' He gestured with his hand at a very tall, big-shouldered man, a handsome man, his hair the colour of a new-struck penny. 'Mr Justin Harvard.'

Charlotte didn't smile and neither did Mr Harvard. She wondered if she should offer

33

her hand but, in defiance of the thought, she folded her hands in front of her.

'Good day to you, Miss Mortimer.' His eyes were a deep, moody green and she felt an unwelcome stirring of her senses. He was attractive enough, but he was looking at her with such a superior tilt to his head that she wanted suddenly to hit him.

She mumbled a vague response and remained silent, uncomfortable in the company of the man, who stared at her now with a puzzled expression.

'Tell the governor how well the children are doing,' Luke said anxiously, and for his sake, she relented.

'We have several very bright children in the school,' she said. 'One boy in particular, John Merriman, is exceptionally clever. He should go on to college, he has an eager mind, he wants to learn and he applies himself to his studies in a most admirable way.' She heard the formality of her tone and knew she sounded pompous, but it was too late to worry about that. In any case, Mr Harvard seemed unimpressed. Luke broke the awkward silence.

'Please, Miss Mortimer, take a seat. This is an informal meeting, an exchange of views, that's all.'

Reluctantly and only out of respect for Luke's superior standing, Charlotte sat down, but her back was stiff and she held her head high, her eyes not quite meeting those strangely penetrating eyes of Mr Harvard.

'I'm sure the boy is a very worthy case for consideration–' his voice had softened a little '–but an entire school cannot remain open for just one pupil.'

Charlotte's worst fears had been realized: the school was in danger of closure. 'There are others just as deserving,' she said quickly, 'just as eager to learn.' She paused. The governor didn't respond. She rushed on. 'The school is all the hope these children have of improving their lot in life. Surely you can understand that?'

'Of course I understand, I've children of my own, but the school has to be self-supporting financially.'

'Why?' Charlotte challenged. 'Surely the owners of Red Rock can afford to subsidize the school?'

'Red Rock is not a charity, Miss Mortimer.' Mr Harvard sighed and shook his head, as if at her naively. 'And surely you didn't think the few paltry pennies the parents of these children bring in is enough to fund a school, and a teacher living in a grace-and-favour house?'

Charlotte had been put firmly in her place; she felt foolish and she didn't like the feeling. In her family she'd been the clever one, the scholar, but now she felt anything but clever. In fact, she felt ashamed, ashamed to be reminded that she was obliged to the people of the Red Rock Company for providing her with the food in her belly and a roof over her head.

She looked down at her hands, feeling the rich colour that had rushed into her face spreading to her neck. It felt as though the blush were covering her entire body. Shame crawled like snakes through her head. Suddenly angry, she stared defiantly at Mr Harvard. 'How would you feel if your children were denied a decent education? The upkeep of the school must be a small drop in the ocean compared to the profits the Red Rock Company are making.' She saw him suppress a smile and became even angrier. 'Yes, go on, laugh!' She waited, but he didn't reply. 'Look, if it will help, I'll rent a room somewhere, you can sell the schoolteacher's house. That should help, shouldn't it?'

Mr Harvard shook his head in disbelief. 'No, it wouldn't help. Your ideas of financing are lacking common sense, but I like your spirit.' He turned to Luke. 'I'll take over the governorship, we'll give it a month or two, see how things go, and then we'll talk again.'

He shook Luke by the hand and then turned to Charlotte. 'Will you shake hands with me, Miss Mortimer? I'm not really an ogre, I promise you.'

Reluctantly, she took his hand. His grip was firm, his fingers curled around hers and she felt a flame of feeling she didn't recognize run through her veins. She withdrew her hand swiftly.

'That's so good of you, Mr Harvard.' Luke opened the door. 'We'll do our best to bring in more students and thus a little more revenue for the school.' They were empty words and everyone in the room knew it. Charlotte felt her courage fail as she watched the tall figure of Mr Harvard leave the room and stride along the corridor, his broad shoulders straight, his head held high. 'No doubt Mr Harvard could fund the school out of his own pocket if he had a mind,' she said bitterly.

'You know what it means if he doesn't stay on as governor, don't you?' Luke asked.

'Yes, of course I know what it means,' Charlotte said hoarsely. 'It means the end of all we're trying to do here, the end of our hopes and dreams and those of our pupils.' She made a wry attempt at humour. 'And I'll be without a home again. I should be getting used to it, shouldn't I?'

Luke reached out and touched her hand in an unexpected gesture of warmth. 'We could marry straight away instead of waiting, so you'd at least have a roof over your head.'

'But we can't live on love alone.' She felt panicky, she didn't want to be married – not yet, she was far too young.

'If it comes to the worst, I'll soon find a

job,' he said gently. 'If the Red Rock Company doesn't want my skills, there are other schools that will gladly take me on.'

Charlotte knew he was right. He was highly regarded in Swansea. Even if he didn't teach, he was talented enough to find employment in some other field.

'Let's just wait and see what happens over the next couple of months, shall we?' she said. 'Come on, we'll get the ferry across to Foxhole and I'll make us a nice hot cup of tea.'

Walking with Luke towards the banks of the river, Charlotte caught sight of Justin Harvard just ahead of them. The pale sunshine struck gold from his hair and her heart beat unaccountably fast. It was fear at what he might do to the school, she told herself, nothing more than that.

She saw him bend over one of the boys from the school, and she realized with a shock that it was John Merriman. His neck was straining backwards so that he could look up into Justin Harvard's face, which he was doing with rapt attention.

Charlotte wondered what the school governor had to say to one of the pupils. Perhaps he was suffering a large fit of conscience. She hoped so.

As they drew level with the pair, Charlotte slipped her arm through Luke's, feeling him glance down at her in surprise. She wasn't usually so tactile a person, but for some reason she wanted Justin Harvard to know she was spoken for.

'Evening to you, Mr Harvard.' Luke lifted his hat, and his voice was even, but Charlotte felt the guarded undertones beneath the polite words. So did Mr Harvard by the quizzical look on his face.

'Evening to you both.' Justin Harvard straightened his shoulders. The greeting was returned politely enough, but there was an echoing undertone of anger that matched Luke's both in his voice and in his remarkable green eyes.

Luke helped Charlotte down the slippery steps leading to the ferry and then climbed aboard the boat, which rocked dangerously on the choppy river. He held out his hand to Charlotte and she swayed a little as she seated herself beside him.

The ferryman made to cast off the line, but a clear, masculine voice called out to tell the man to wait. With a long stride Justin Harvard was aboard, and he sat down abruptly on the other side of Charlotte.

She felt his nearness as an almost physical shock as his hand rested briefly on her knee.

'I do apologize.' Justin Harvard smiled at her, and the effect enhanced his good looks so much that he appeared like a god from the book she was reading. 'I didn't mean to be disrespectful, it was just that the erratic movement of the boat caught me unawares.'

At her side, Luke was coiled like a spring. 'It's dangerous to go leaping on a boat when it's in motion.' His voice was cold and hard, and his eyes narrowed as he leaned around Charlotte and looked at Justin Harvard.

'Point taken,' Justin replied, sounding sheepish but not looking it at all. 'I would not dream of being familiar with a lady I'd only just met.' Now, his eyes innocent of expression, he seemed so sincere that Charlotte almost believed him – almost, but not quite. Luke, however, seemed mollified and resumed his normal position, leaning back against the shallow side of the boat. Justin Harvard turned away and watched the slippery bank of the river recede.

On the east side of the river there was a pantomime of leaving the boat to be gone through. Justin was first to step ashore, and he held his hand to Charlotte, smiling innocently. After a moment's hesitation, she took it and was hoisted by strong arms out on to the steps, aware that her hand was being held far longer than necessary.

Luke took possession of her hand once he was ashore and mumbled a word of grudging thanks to Justin, who climbed the steps before them and waited on the grassy verge, his eyes sparkling.

'Can we help you, Mr Harvard?' Luke's tone was wary, and Charlotte understood how he felt. He was antagonized by the man's effrontery in tagging along with them and yet conscious that Justin Harvard held the power of life or death over the future of St John's school.

'I believe you can or, at least, Miss Mortimer can.' He did not look at her but directed his words to Luke. 'Perhaps I could come into the house and have a word, if the good lady has no objections.'

'School is over for today, Mr Harvard,' Luke said firmly and caught Charlotte's arm, hustling her across the road so fast she felt as if her feet were not touching the ground.

'I'll be no trouble.' Justin was persistent, and the whole situation was becoming so ridiculous that Charlotte was hard put not to laugh. The two men were acting like children, each wanting their own way, each too pigheaded to give ground.

'Come inside, Mr Harvard,' Charlotte said, pushing open the front door. She ignored Luke's baleful look and gestured to a chair. 'Please, gentlemen, sit down. I'll rake up the stove and make us all some tea.'

Luke practically pushed her out of the way and, with more force than was necessary, raked up the coals. Charlotte read him well: he was establishing his familiarity with Charlotte and her home. Justin also read him well.

'Quite domesticated,' he murmured. 'I can

see Miss Mortimer has you well trained, Mr Lester.'

His tone implied that Luke was nothing more than a doormat, and Charlotte hid a smile. She could see Luke's hackles rising from where he was bent over, attending to the stove.

'That's very kind of you, Luke,' she said quickly. 'You know what a difficult day I've had.'

He looked at her in surprise – the day had been difficult only because of Justin Harvard. He caught the glint in her eye and she saw him relax.

'Yes, it has been fairly taxing, especially the latter part of the day.'

Justin stared at him, sparks coming from his mesmerizing eyes, and Charlotte wondered if he was going to resort to fisticuffs, but then he seemed to sink back in his chair. 'Touché,' he said. 'Now let's get down to business.'

CHAPTER THREE

Charlotte read the missive from Luke with a feeling of great relief. It confirmed that St John's school was to be reprieved for six months. With the letter from Luke was a thick page of writing paper embossed with the name of Justin Harvard, a document promising a sum of money to the school for the period of six months. Somehow just holding a letter Justin had written gave Charlotte a shiver of ... of what? She really didn't know.

She sat in her sun-bright kitchen – for once, the pall of copper smoke was thin, stirred by a brisk breeze – and stared at the letter, a sense of hope lightening her spirits. Everything would be all right, she could depend on Justin to see that it was. Once he saw the excellent results the school was achieving, he would want to stay with the project, she was sure of it.

A sense of ownership seemed to warm her, she was so proud of the school, so certain that, between them, she and Luke could improve the lives of the children they taught, children like John Merriman, old before his time, taking the place in the family of the father he'd lost to the Red Rock copper-works.

She looked down at the letter again, admiring Justin's penmanship. She scanned through the words and was impressed with the governor's good command of the English language. Perhaps there was someone who took care of such things for him, a woman, perhaps, catering to his every whim. The thought gave her a strange feeling in her stomach and she put the letter down abruptly.

The sudden clanging of the school bell startled her. It rang out across the river, sometimes clear, then muffled by the thick water mist created by the warmth of the sun shining on the cold of the water. She ran to the window, frozen with fear as the urgent sound of the bell continued to echo across, louder, more insistent. Something was wrong – the only reason the school bell would be ringing so persistently and so early was if some tragedy had occurred.

Not waiting to pick up her coat, Charlotte hurried outside and stood for a moment filled with dread as she realized it was not mist she could see over the river but a thick, heavy smoke belching into the air like the breath of some vengeful god.

The ferry boat was still tied at the landing stage. It was full of men going to start their day's toil at the works, but they made way for Charlotte, sharing her anxiety at the bell's warning. Their faces, to a man, were pale and drawn. The evil smoke interfered with the blood, tainting it in some dreadful way. The men who worked the copper would have short lives, she knew it and they knew it, but there were families to be fed and rent to pay.

'What's up, do you think, Miss Mortimer?'

Charlotte turned to the man sitting alongside her, both of them swaying as the boat was rocked by the incoming tide. He was one of the workers and looked even paler than usual in the morning light.

'I don't know, Tomos, but something's badly wrong.'

'I hope it's the Red Rock,' Tomos said laconically. 'We'd be well shot of that stinking monster and with a good pay-off from the insurance to live on.'

The river ran swiftly, driven by the stiff breeze, the waves slapping against the sides of the frail craft. At the opposite bank the men jumped ashore and stood staring indecisively in the direction of the school.

'Do you think we should go on to work, miss, or come to find out what's going on?' Tomos said.

Charlotte was touched. If the men took time off, the owners would condone it in the face of a serious accident but, nevertheless, they would lose a day's pay and that meant less food in the larder.

'Wait here,' she said. 'I'll run up to find out what's wrong, and if you can help I'll run back and tell you. If you don't see me in, say, five minutes, you go on to work.'

'No, we'll come with you, that all right, boys?' Tomos made up his mind and the men began to follow him as he strode up the bank.

Luke was in the yard, white-faced, the large bell in his hand. When he saw Charlotte he pushed his fingers in the bell to stop the ringing and came towards her.

'There's been an accident at Red Rock,' he said, his face strained. 'Many injured, some dead.' He looked over Charlotte's head at the men bunched around her.

'You'll help.' It was a statement.

Charlotte's hands trembled, and she pressed them close to her skirt so that no one would see. She looked at Luke. 'I wonder if Mr Harvard was there when it happened? He often has meetings there.'

'Perhaps. But many others besides. You stay here with the pupils who come into school early, keep them away from the fire. I'll go along the river bank and see if I can help with the rescue.' He caught her hands as she shook her head.

'I can't stay here, Luke, you know as well as I do that none of the children will come to school. They'll be with the crowds over at Red Rock.'

'Please, Charlotte, I don't want you to see sights that might haunt you for the rest of your life.'

'I have to come with you.' She drew her hands away and set off at a smart pace along the bank of the river.

With a sigh of resignation, Luke fell into step beside her. 'You can be so stubborn at times,' he grumbled. 'I only want to protect you, but you won't let me.'

She didn't reply, she had no answer for Luke; all she knew was she had to see what was happening and if the school would be affected. As she drew nearer the jutting chimneys of the massed works along the bank, Charlotte saw that the waters of the Tawe were washed with a ruddy glow. 'The Red Rock works is burning to the ground. Oh my good Lord, I wonder what's happened.' Fear rose within her like an icicle running up her spine.

The mist drifting from the river was lifting, exposing a scene out of hell. The roof of the works had gone, ripped through by the blast from what appeared to have been an exploding furnace. One ragged stack stood crazily at an angle like a blackened tooth, loose and waiting to be pulled.

Figures bathed in a red glow teemed about like frenzied ants. The fire brigade directed feeble jets of water into the blaze only for them to be devoured by the leaping flames. Charlotte wanted to put her hands over her ears to shut out the screams of the injured. She almost tripped over a man who was lying in the dew-wet grass moaning, trying to ease his horrific burns.

Charlotte knelt beside him. His eyes so blistered that he could barely open them, he pleaded with her to help. 'Hot, burning up, I'm in hell, missis, get me water, please get me water.' His lips were one big black blister, so he could hardly speak.

Luke had gone on ahead of her and

Charlotte looked round desperately. Where would she get clean water? It would take her at least ten minutes to reach one of the houses, which were set well back from the string of works. The only immediate source of water was the river, brackish with the plethora of chemicals spilled into its flow from the works along the bank, but it would cool the man's throat and, in any case, she judged, the poor creature would die, his burns too horrific, too deeply seared into his flesh for him to recover.

'I'll be back in just a minute,' she promised, in a voice already hoarse with smoke. Giving up the unequal battle to keep his damaged eyes open, he lay moaning pitifully at her feet.

Charlotte ran down to the river, careless of the mud that clung to the hem of her good skirt. She kicked off her boots and waded into the water, dragging off her petticoat and dousing it in the river.

It dripped rivulets of water as she returned to the injured man. He was still lying where she had left him, still moaning, more quietly now.

Kneeling beside him, she squeezed the water into his mouth. It dribbled away, leaving a silvery trail against his blackened face. She spread her petticoat over his body and felt him shudder. 'Pray God I'm doing the right thing.'

His eyes opened, thin, glittering strips. He could not speak, the burns had transfixed his face, melded the flesh into a tight, dreadful mask. And then he died. No fuss, no last declaration, nor even a shudder, he was just gone from this world. Kneeling there in the mud, Charlotte grieved for this unknown man who had given his life to the copper, for the copper to snatch it from him in the end.

Charlotte felt a pull on her arm. 'Come on, miss.' A young voice penetrated her sense of shock, and she focused her eyes with an effort and looked into John Merriman's face, his jutting cheekbones highlighted by the glare of the flames.

'We can't do any good by yer, miss, see, the walls are falling in. Let's move back from the fire, it's only sensible, mind.'

She looked into the roaring, monstrous flames. They were reaching higher now, prodding the sky, putting to shame the early morning sun. Still she hesitated.

'Come on, miss,' John urged. 'Me mam is here with the baby, you got to help me find her, take her home, where she'll be safe.'

Charlotte drew her knees away from the sucking mud. 'Your mother?' she asked, bewildered. 'Why would she be here, John?'

'She came to get the money,' he said breathlessly. 'She'll be by the pay office, that's where she'll be.'

'But why would your mother be getting

49

pay from the Red Rock?'

'Well, Mr Harvard decided to pay her for me dad, see, Mam being a widow woman and all that.'

She felt a flare of pride. Justin Harvard had a heart then. She allowed John to pull her along past the seat of the fire towards the pay office, which stood among the growing moonscape of clinker from the copper smelting.

The office was still intact; the fire hadn't reached it yet. Charlotte pushed the door and it swung open. She stepped inside and gasped as she saw that papers had been taken from files and flung on the floor. The drawers of the desk had been jerked from their housing and lay scattered about the room. Any money there might have been was long gone.

'Oh, Jesus!' John's voice penetrated her sense of unreality. Automatically, Charlotte remonstrated with him.

'Don't blaspheme, John Merriman.' As soon as the words were spoken, she realized how ludicrous she must sound in the face of such a disaster.

'Sorry, miss,' he responded, 'but me mam would never make this mess, would she?' His lips trembled. 'Some swine got yer before her.'

'Try and stay calm, John.'

'But what will Mam do? Without any

money she won't be able to buy milk or bread or feed for the baby.'

'I'll stay and look for the money, John, don't you worry about it now. We'll sort something out, you won't go hungry, I promise.'

'All right, miss, I'll go up the road and look, I expect me mam is gone up by there gossiping with the neighbours.'

'Aye, you go, John. I'll come after you. I won't be long.'

'But, miss,' John shook his head, his young heart torn between Charlotte finding the money and her safety, 'you can't stay in yer, the fire will get you. See, it's spreading to the outbuildings, it's not safe.'

'I'm going to look for that money, John. You go ahead, do as I tell you, there's a good boy.'

He took one last look round and pointed to the heavy door leading to the back room of the office. 'There's a safe in there, miss, I've seen it when I've come with me mam for the money.' He hesitated. 'I won't be too long, Miss Charlotte.' His eyes were clouded with tears. 'Soon as I find me mam I'll be back.'

'Go on!' She shooed him with her hands. He nodded and disappeared, leaving the door open. Charlotte heard the terrible noises from outside, the cries of the women-folk anguished, desperate, and the groans of men low, muted, beyond pain.

51

Stirring herself, she pushed open the dividing door and at once saw the safe crouched against the door as though hiding from the carnage outside. She knelt on the boards and smelled the polish – bees' wax fragranced with honeysuckle – and the aroma was so reminiscent of her childhood that, almost without noticing, she began to cry.

The safe was imposing, strongly built, requiring both a key and a tap to open it. She realized at once there was nothing she could do; she had neither the strength nor the skill to try to open the heavy cast-iron door.

Suddenly, there was a whoosh from the open door and flames shot across the room, curling along the ceiling like a living creature from hell. Charlotte pressed flat against the boards, trying to gather her wits, knowing she must find a way out of the office. Smoke, acrid, dense, all-enveloping, obscured her vision, making her cough violently as she dragged in a breath that seemed to burn her lungs.

Instinctively, she remained low on the wooden floor, crawling carefully towards the door. Every little bit of progress was an effort; she dragged herself forward inch by inch. She closed her eyes for a moment, trying to gather her strength and her courage to face the last dash to the outside, where she could breathe again.

As she neared the door to the outer office,

there was a terrible crash and the beams from the ceiling hung like broken limbs above her. She cowered back as huge burning timbers slowly, inexorably, crashed to the floor, barring her way.

There was no way out. The front office was burning fiercely, the heat forcing Charlotte to edge her way from the inferno and back into the smoke-filled office.

Her strength was failing and so was her courage. She rested her head on her arms for a moment, trying to think rationally. There was no window in the back room and the whole structure was made of timber; it was food for the flames, they would devour the place. It would all burn and she with it.

'Miss Charlotte!' She dimly heard the voice from outside. John Merriman was calling her. 'Miss Charlotte! I've brought Mr Harvard to help us. Don't be dead, please don't be dead.'

The heat was all around her now and her eyes stung with tears as she withdrew against the back wall. She was coughing in the thick, poisonous smoke, it was slowly filling her lungs, and she prayed she would die soon.

She felt the wall behind her shudder, her head drooped and she felt the rough wood of the floor against her face. It didn't matter, nothing mattered, not now. Her life was over.

'Lie flat, Charlotte.' She heard the voice dimly, but it was strong and commanding and she rallied, the will to live flooded within her and she did as she was told. The wooden wall behind her crashed inward, scattering splinters of timber all around. She heard the wood scream as the planks were prised apart. Then arms were around her, lifting her free, and she gasped like a drowning man at the blessing of cool, clean air.

'Charlotte, Miss Mortimer, breathe slowly, small breaths. It will be painful for a time but you are going to be all right.'

She opened her sore eyes and realized that she was being held in Justin Harvard's arms, and it all seemed perfectly right as she laid her head against his shoulder and gave herself up to the welcome darkness.

CHAPTER FOUR

After a week off work recovering from the effects of the smoke that had filled her lungs on the night of the accident, it was strange to return to her normal daily routine, to teach her children to spell, to add figures, to hear them at choir practice. It was all ordinary, familiar, yet in her heart Charlotte knew nothing would ever be normal again.

Every morning when she crossed the Tawe in the frail ferry boat, she saw the stark, burnt-out ruins of the Red Rock copper-works jutting from the scorched earth like grey, misty tombstones, but she thought not of the wounded and dying but of the wonder of being in Justin Harvard's arms. And every day she felt shame sweep through her being.

'You are very quiet today, Charlotte.' Luke's voice made her jump and she looked around the tiny staff room, then at Luke's anxious face, and took a deep breath.

'I was thinking of the fire,' she said, evading his searching eyes. 'How lucky we were that the flames were quenched before they reached the school.' She drew her hand over her brows. 'I'm sorry I'm such bad company, but I suppose I'm just tired. It's the end of another day. The children are restless, they've not settled back to the routine of school yet and most of them are going back home to face injured fathers, or their fathers have died.'

'I know how devastated they must feel.' Luke moved a shade closer to her and reached out his hand to cover hers. 'When I saw you being brought out of the flames and smoke of the fire, my heart nearly stopped beating. I realized how much I care for you – even though you can be difficult at times.'

Charlotte didn't know how to answer, so she shook her head and looked down at her hands.

'Charlotte.' Luke's hand was under her

chin, forcing her to look at him. 'Charlotte, let's get married as soon as possible.' He smiled and he was earnest, so familiar, and she knew he would be a good husband.

'But, Luke, we've never really talked very much about marriage, I need time to think about it.' She smiled. 'I know that's a silly, coquettish answer, and as a teacher I should choose a more original response, but really, Luke, this is so sudden.'

'We've had an understanding, though, haven't we, Charlotte? More than that, we are betrothed.'

She hesitated. 'Of course, Luke, but you know I don't want to marry for a long time. I can't give up teaching and be a homebody, not yet, we have so much to do here still.'

He saw the sense of her words and nodded slowly. 'I understand, you are young, too young perhaps to take on the responsibilities of children of your own.'

She sighed in relief. She loved Luke, in her own way. He was a good man, a fine, handsome, upstanding man, and yet and yet... She let her thoughts drift away and, as always when she thought of love, they centred on Justin Harvard, as they had done ever since he'd held her close in his arms and she'd let her head snuggle into the hollow and warmth of his neck.

She knew it was foolish: Justin Harvard was rich; he owned several substantial properties;

he was from a long line of influential forebears, one of whom had been made Lord of Swansea. No, she didn't belong in that world, and the sooner she took that to heart, the sooner she would get over the nonsense of fancying herself as Justin's bride.

When Justin married again, he would choose a rich, sophisticated woman, one who would grace the glittering events of the town with him, would shine at supper parties, even at the occasional event graced by folk of royal blood. Charlotte could never fit into that sort of society.

'What are you thinking?' Luke's gentle, loving voice interrupted her reverie and she shook herself mentally.

'Nothing worth repeating.'

'You looked desperately sad for a moment there.' Luke was perceptive, and she smiled at him.

'Don't worry about my silly thoughts,' she said. 'Now, I know we are both worn out, but we said we'd take some necessities round to a few of the families worst affected by the fire at Red Rock.'

'So we did.' Luke's voice was brisk now, his attention called back to his immediate duties. He rose and picked up the bag of food, tinned goods, mostly, and some carefully wrapped fresh cheese and a batch of eggs – all good nourishment for the injured and the grieving.

Charlotte took up her own bag. She had managed to get some fresh vegetables – good, rich, green cabbage, carrots with the fertile dirt of the fields in which they grew still among the leaves – all donated by the good folk of Swansea market.

'Our families will eat well tonight,' Charlotte said, and Luke laughed in fond derision.

'Oh, now we aren't only related to the children we teach but we've taken on their families, too! Don't you think that's a bit too ambitious, even for you?'

Charlotte pushed open the school door with her foot. 'You know what I mean and, in a way, they are our family. I feel for them as if they were blood of my blood. They are the folk I grew up with, they're a proud lot, hard-working and honest, and if the men get a little drunk on good beer every Saturday, who can blame them?' She became serious. 'My sisters, my little brother, they've all gone to live in a distant land, and sometimes I'm lonely without them.'

'So you've adopted the whole of Swansea in compensation.'

She shrugged. 'If you like.'

Luke sighed. 'And I come very far down the list of folk you care for, don't I?'

Charlotte looked at his downcast face and smiled. 'No, don't be silly, you are very dear to me.' And he was, in some ways.

As they made their way round the small

terraced houses that had sprung up years ago as dwellings for the coppermen and their families, Charlotte was horrified at some of the severe wounds the workers had sustained. Dai the fiddle would never play music again, his arm was set and bound in an unnatural curve, the flesh pulled, the muscles tortured out of shape by the intensity of the fire. He saw her face and read her well.

'It's all gone now, *merchi*.' With a nod of his head, he indicated his twisted arm. 'No more playing music in the cool of the summer's nights, no dancing to my tunes, no...' His voice trailed away and Charlotte knew there was nothing she could say to cheer him. She offered the only comfort she was able to give.

'In my pocket there's a nice flask of brandy.'

Dai raised a half-hearted smile. 'Ease my spirits with spirits, is it? Come on then, give it yer, I've never been averse to a drop of good stuff, be it brandy or whisky – even mother's ruin, at a push.'

Charlotte frowned. 'Mother's ruin?'

'Gin, Miss Mortimer, gin, but then I doubt you ever saw it in your father's house. Jolly Mortimer was a clean-living man.'

Dai's wife came in from the kitchen. Kathleen's hands were on her plump hips, but Charlotte could see a stout rolling pin tucked in her elbow waving about like the tail of an excited dog.

'Enough of your blather, good boy, you're keeping these decent people from their task. You're not the only one they have to visit the day.' She shifted her gaze from her husband's good-natured face and followed Charlotte to the door.

'Not going to see that Poppy Merriman, are you?' She didn't wait for a reply. 'A bad lot is that one, she 'as no man working in the copper, her, but many in her bed.'

Charlotte had to bite her tongue, and Luke, after a moment's hesitation, spoke for her.

'We will see everyone we can, and don't forget that Mrs Merriman has been a widow for years, thanks to the copperworks. She will have our help the same as everyone else.'

Luke managed to deliver the gentle rebuke without causing offence and, after a brief pause, Kathleen nodded.

'Aye, sure enough. Bad though she may be, she's a poor widow woman for all that.'

Dai was quietly sipping the brandy, sucking it out of the bottle like a baby its milk, hoping his wife wouldn't notice. His hopes were quickly dashed as his wife turned back to him. She waved the rolling pin, still covered with flour, dangerously close to his nose.

'That's enough, Dai.' There was a touch of humour in her gaze. 'It's early yet.'

Dai jerked the bottle towards the window, *'Duw,* girl, see how dark it is? It's surely time for a drink.'

Charlotte suppressed a smile. 'We'd better be going then,' she said, 'or we'll never get home.'

It was cool and dark outside. The moon was half-concealed by cloud and, below the roadway, the river moved sleepily towards the sea. On the east bank the houses were half-hidden by shadows, the occasional light burning briefly like the body of a firefly. Charlotte was tired, but there were others to visit before she could go home to her own cosy fireside.

The last house on her list was the house where the widow Merriman was living. Charlotte found the door ajar. Mrs Merriman was a beautiful woman and, against the squalor in which she lived, she stood out like a living Madonna. Her dark hair and the delicacy of her features all added to her air of innocence. In her arms was her baby, a crop of ginger hair protruding from the all-encompassing shawl in which he was swaddled. Charlotte wondered fleetingly about the unknown father. And yet, she didn't have it in her heart to condemn the woman for her loose morals, she probably needed love and thought the way to it was in a man's arms, any man's.

'Sit down, Miss Mortimer, there's lovely of you to call.' Her voice was low and lilting. She swept a bundle of clothing on to the floor and, obligingly, Charlotte sat on the stained, faded seat of the chair she had cleared.

'Our John is out playing with his friends,' she said. 'It's good for the boy to get some fresh air, mind.' There was a wry twist to her lips as she looked outside. She knew as well as Charlotte did that John was too old for childish games, he was probably flirting with some girl or other. In any case, there was a lack of fresh air anywhere about the copperworks, the smoke billowed around the houses, low today because of the clouds, the abrasive copper dust scratching the glass panes like witches' nails.

Charlotte removed the white cloth from her basket. 'We've brought some goodies. There's some cheese and some delicious fresh produce from the market.'

She saw the fleeting expression of pride on Mrs Merriman's face and added quickly, 'We've been to all the houses affected by the accident at Red Rock so, if you don't mind, we'll empty our baskets here.' She smiled. 'My arms are hurting like toothache, I can tell you.'

Before Mrs Merriman could say anything, Charlotte unpacked the food and put it on the table, nodding to Luke to follow suit. Charlotte had kept the best of the meat till last, and she laid it down now with due ceremony. 'You should get a couple of good meals from that piece of Welsh lamb.'

'It isn't true, you know,' Mrs Merriman said flatly.

Charlotte looked at her quickly. 'Sorry? What isn't true?'

'What folks say of me.'

Charlotte felt the slow colour climb into her cheeks. She looked at Luke, a quick glance that silently begged him to intervene. He turned away, equally embarrassed, and she took a deep breath.

'I'm not sure I understand.' The words came out shakily and Mrs Merriman wasn't fooled for one moment.

'They say I'm a trollop.' She lifted her chin. 'It's true that men come to my house, and it's true I got a nice man friend, but the others, they don't come to my bed.'

'Oh?' Charlotte was deep in unexplored territory; she pressed her lips together, hoping she didn't appear as embarrassed as she felt.

In the silence, she searched for something to say. She looked at Luke again, and she could see the beginnings of a frown cloud his brow. She felt like hitting him. Why didn't he say something and help her out of a difficult situation?

'I'm a soothsayer and a healer,' Mrs Merriman said, as if that explained everything. 'I cured one man of the sickness he feared because of his bad ways with the women. I told him to abstain from all feminine contact for at least a week and to bathe his ... his affected parts in a pan of hot salt water.' She smiled. 'All the man had was a common boil, and I dare say the salt and hot water helped heal him a bit. At the same time, his poor wife didn't have to put up with his half-hearted fumblings when he couldn't visit his mistresses. Since then, my fame has spread, but none of the men dare tell their wives what they do when they come here.' She shrugged eloquently. 'And there you have it.'

'And what about the soothsaying?' Charlotte asked, fascinated in spite of herself.

'I tell these men what their future will be.' She didn't look up but hugged her baby closer in her arms. 'A few want to know if their chosen one is faithful, most want to be assured they 'aven't got the pox. Men are such fools sometimes.'

Charlotte was shocked by Mrs Merriman's blunt language and her own tone when she replied was, for her, almost brusque. 'I'm not sure if I believe in all that, Mrs Merriman. My father was a staunch believer in the Church... Did you foresee the fire at the works?'

Mrs Merriman's heavy lids drooped over her strange, deep brown eyes and she shook her head. 'I did, but no one listened. I told Dai the fiddle he should stay home that day or he'd play his music no more, but that harridan of a wife of his told him not to be taken in by such nonsense, that they needed the money and he had to go to work if he liked it or no.'

Charlotte was shaken by the woman's words, unable to give credence to what she said. Charlotte's father had been a good Christian, he had read his Bible to his children whenever they would listen, and Charlotte offered up a prayer that the good Lord would spare Mrs Merriman his vengeance at her blasphemy.

Mrs Merriman's eyes opened wide and she stared at Charlotte with a sudden intensity. 'You, miss, your course in life is not the peaceful happy marriage most ladies want, oh, no – it's turmoil and pain and failure for you.' She relaxed, the intense gaze fading. She smiled at Charlotte. 'You will win through in the end, your sort always do.'

'And what about Luke? What is his life to be?' Instantly, Charlotte regretted her challenge and lifted her hand to stop Mrs Merriman's words, but they would not be stopped.

'I can't tell that, it's not my place to... I don't know. Now, you'd best be going, but thank you for the food.'

Outside, Luke looked doubtfully at Charlotte. 'You don't believe any of that foolish talk, do you?' He seemed genuinely troubled.

'Of course not,' Charlotte said emphatically. 'The woman is fey, lovely to look at, and I should say that her reputation as a whore is well justified.'

'Still, she was very convincing, especially

about Dai the fiddle.'

'A lucky guess,' Charlotte said. 'In a manufactory such as Red Rock, there is always the chance of an accident. You know that as well as I do.'

'I suppose you're right.' He shivered. 'Let's get home, it's damp and misty and the smoke is lowering under the clouds. We'll be more comfortable by a fire with a hot drink in our hands, and we deserve a rest. We've not had an easy day.'

Charlotte nodded agreement. Her hair was already curling in the fine mist that swirled around her. 'I suppose we've done all we can to help.' She looked up at Luke. His hair was darkened by the dampness of the air but he still looked strong and handsome in spite of the droplets of moisture clinging to his square jaw like tears.

'Miss, miss!' She heard the slap of bare feet on the slimy cobbles of the street. She looked round to see John Merriman running towards her, his arms full of the produce she had just left at his house.

'Here, miss.' He thrust the food back into her empty basket and stared up at her, his face tight with tension, only his eyes betraying his vulnerability. 'We won't need charity, miss, thank you kindly, me and me mam can manage on our own.'

'I'm sure you can, John, but we're taking food to everyone who was affected by the fire at the copperworks.'

'Me mam wasn't afflected, though, not this time.' Unaware he'd pronounced the word wrongly, he went on, 'We're all right. Give the food to those who need it more than us.'

Charlotte thought quickly. 'I would be obliged if you would take the stuff from me,' she said. 'It's surplus. I mean, it's all that's left now we've visited the people we wanted to see. I didn't know what to do with it all so I asked your mother would she kindly take it off my hands, she a widow because of an earlier accident.'

When he hesitated, she pressed home her point. 'Please keep it, John, it would be doing me a favour, I do assure you.'

She held out the basket. 'Take this as well, if you will, and bring it into school for me, will you do that?'

After a moment, John nodded. 'All right then, if it's a favour you're asking, I'll take it, just to help, mind.'

'And it'll be a great help. Thank you, John.'

She watched him turn back towards his house, his feet touchingly bare, the feet of a young man, long and well-formed, and a lump rose to Charlotte's throat as she saw how dirty and begrimed they were, splashing in the puddles of rain that had gathered between the cobbles. But I *will* make life better for him. She glanced at Luke.

'Come on,' she said, 'let's get home.'

CHAPTER FIVE

John Merriman looked up at his mother as she sat, hands clasped together, in the worn rocking chair near the fire. He was struggling not to break down and cry. His mother, too, was filled with emotion.

'Our baby is gone from us, dead and buried in only a week.' Her voice was full of the tears she was trying hard to hold back. 'At least Mr Harvard gave me enough money to pay for the funeral.'

John tried to be brave. He was fourteen years old and big for his age. Mr Harvard had been good to the family since he'd been governor at the school. He had seen John's mother all right for money, which meant John could continue to attend school, and now he'd provided the wherewithal to pay for the simple burial in St John's consecrated ground.

John knew his lip was trembling. He'd had little to do with the baby but he'd grown used to seeing the little fellow in his mother's arms.

'I've more news to tell you, John, and you'll have to be a man and take it well.'

John felt suddenly cold. 'What news is

that, Mammy?'

His mother sighed heavily 'It's no good hiding the truth from you, boy. I've worked with natural medicines since I was a child, John. I've treated folks for everything under the sun and I know all the bad signs.'

'What signs, Mammy, what are you trying to tell me?'

'I'm going to die before my time and that's an end to it.' Her voice broke a little but she looked him straight in the eye. 'The worst of it is, I'll be leaving you alone.'

John rubbed his chin, wishing that his beard had started to grow, then everyone would take him for the sensible man he was. He swallowed hard, knowing what he was about to sacrifice was the hardest thing he'd had to do in his life.

'Don't worry, Mammy, I'll leave school and find proper work. I'll go into the copper like my dad did. We'll get a doctor to tend you proper like.' He paused as his mother shook her head.

'And let the copper kill you like it did your father? No, you'll go into no copperworks, my boy.'

'But you could be wrong, Mammy, you've never cured women, have you? It's always men who come to have the healing, perhaps everything is different for women.'

His mother paused. 'That's true, John. Women have babies and all sorts of problems men don't have, but they're not ones to complain. The women of Swansea are toughened like steel, they 'ave to be to look after men and babies. But I know I've not got long on this earth and soon I'll join my little lad in heaven, so don't you go grieving over me, understand?'

'But, Mammy, if you see a doctor he could cure you. Perhaps things are not as bad as you think.'

'I'm really sick, John, it's the consumption. It works the same way for men and women. It eats up the lungs and...'

John couldn't bear any more. 'Don't say it, Mam, don't tell me you're going to die and leave me alone.'

'I can't help it, son, I'm going to meet my maker and, to tell you the truth, I'll be glad to give up the struggle for life, it's become too difficult.'

As his mother put her head in her hands, John flung open the door and rushed out into the darkness. He looked up at the sky and shook his fists at the stars.

'I hate you, God, I bloody well hate you!' He didn't know if there was a god and, if there was, was he the faraway god the Bible described or could it be one of the Greek or Roman gods Miss Mortimer told him about? Either way, nothing happened. The sky was silent, the stars still shone brightly and the moon looked down at him with its lopsided face.

Slowly, John sank to the ground, careless of the mud under his bony knees, and let the scalding tears run from his eyes. 'Mammy, what will I do without you?'

It was there, lying in the mud of the street, that Justin Harvard found him. He lifted the boy to his feet and, big as he was, the boy stood curled into his arms, his eyes shut. His tears had left streaks down his grubby cheeks and his hair was matted with the cruel rain.

Justin looked around at the small houses crouched beneath the towering chimney stacks, from which billowed deadly, smothering smoke. 'Let me take you home, John.'

John's eyes remained tightly closed, though stubborn tears forced a way between the lids. Justin pushed back his damp hair. 'John Merriman, talk to me. It's your mother, isn't it? She's told you the bad news?'

John's eyes opened at last. 'I don't want to go home.' His voice was small, frightened, and Justin frowned.

'You have to face your responsibilities, John. No point in hiding your head in the sand.'

John sighed a heavy, weary sigh. 'She says she's going to die.' His young voice shook. 'She's got some lung sickness, funny name, con something.'

Justin tightened his lips, knowing there

was nothing that would cure the curse of the creeping disease that tainted the blood and bones of its victims. 'And you're frightened, lad, well, don't worry about that. Sickness frightens all of us.'

John peered out from the folds of Justin's coat, his eyes gleaming like those of a small feral animal. 'Would you be afraid of it?'

'Of course I would. Come, now, let me come home with you and talk to your mother. Is that all right?'

John snuggled back into the folds of the coat. 'Please, I don't want to go back. I know I'm a coward but I can't bear to see my mam die.'

Justin thought quickly. He knew that with a little help the boy would have a good future ahead of him. He made up his mind. 'You won't have to go home for ever, just for tonight. I'll get a nurse to stay with your mother.' He said softly, 'I've got the need of a good stablehand. Are you willing? Of course, you'll have time off for your studies.'

'So I can still go to school?'

Justin nodded, still holding the boy close to him. 'Of course. Would I deprive Miss Mortimer of her brightest pupil?'

John wasn't quite convinced. 'What about my mam? I will have to be with her at the ... the end.'

Justin thought about his big house, with its endless corridors and spacious rooms. 'I think we can find a place for her too.'

John's face crumpled and tears sprang from his tightly closed eyes, again in spite of his efforts to hold them trapped behind his damp lashes.

'Well, we can't stand here all night, my good boy.' Justin began to walk. John looked up, startled.

'Wait. I can't go. I mean, I'll take you to see my mam and I'll stay with her till other things can be arranged.'

Justin smiled. 'That's what I hoped you'd say.'

Mrs Merriman was crouched near the empty fireplace, her head still sunk in her hands. She looked no more than a living skeleton, except that her eyes sparked with relief when she saw her son come through the door. Justin nodded reassuringly to her.

'Come by yer, *boy bach*.' She held out her arms and John went to her side and let her fold him in an embrace.

'Mam, I'm not a little boy.' John untangled himself from her hands. 'We are going to be all right. I'm to work for Mr Harvard as a stablehand. You're to come as well, and Mam–' his voice brightened with excitement '–I can still go to school.'

'Is this true, Mr Harvard?' Her voice held more than an element of doubt.

Justin nodded. 'Pack your things, Mrs

Merriman. I'm going ahead to prepare, and you wait here. I'll be sending a pony and trap to fetch you.'

Mrs Merriman looked around her and grimaced. 'I haven't got many things to pack, got no luggage bag, for that matter.' She sighed. 'And what am I going to do about the landlord? I owe him rent, you see.'

'Don't worry about any of that now, it will all be sorted out.' He moved to the door and saw the flash of fear that darkened John's face. 'I swear that I won't be any longer than half an hour or so, and that's a promise.'

John squared his shoulders, obviously calling on all his reserves of courage. 'I'll be all right, sir. I'll help Mam while I wait.'

Justin rested his hand on the boy's shoulder for a moment and felt the bones jutting through the skin. A wave of pity mingled with anger: no boy of John's age should be saddled with such a burden of grief. 'Sooner I go, the sooner I'll be back,' he said, mustering as much cheer as he could. He glanced at Mrs Merriman and saw the raw gratitude in her eyes and coughed to hide his own helpless feelings. The poor lady was doomed and there was nothing anyone could do for her. She read his face well.

'You can take good care of my son,' she said in a low voice.

Justin gave instructions to his servants as

soon as he got home. He sent two of the maids, Bessie and Bertha, to make up the beds and dispatched Leon, his master of stables, to fetch Mrs Merriman home to Thornhill.

He stood in the hall. He'd promised to return for John himself, but then he would be better occupied giving orders to Cook to prepare a hot meal for the boy and his mother.

He stood for a moment, the sounds of his house breathing and living around him, and realized in that moment how privileged he was. He had lived all his life in comfortable surroundings, eating well-cooked food. How could he understand the hardships endured by the people who lived in the town of Swansea? He couldn't solve all their troubles, but at least he could help little John Merriman and provide some comfort to his mother. He had heard her request to look after her son, and that he would do with all of his strength.

Decided now, he left the house and hurried down the hill. He knew deep within that John Merriman needed him now more than ever, and he would do all in his power to ensure that John had the best start in life that money could give him.

John looked at his mother in concern. Her skin was so pale, so thin, he could see her veins like blue threadworms. She was propped up in bed in the bright room Mr Harvard had given her at the front of the house overlooking the sea. As though aware of his scrutiny, his mother opened her eyes and held out her hand to him. 'Come here, my son.'

He sat on the floor beside the bed and, feeling foolish, held both her hands in his. She was still as the night, her breath hardly stirring the folds of her blouse beneath her shawl.

'You'll do fine, my son,' she said. 'Mr Harvard will take good care of you, I know he will.'

'He'll have a doctor to look at you again, Mammy.'

His mother shook her head. 'I won't be with you for many more days now, John, you will have to learn to manage without me.'

'Yes, Mam, but not yet, is it?'

'Soon, John, very soon, and I told you I'd be glad to be out of it, so don't grieve for me too much.'

John felt a chill settle over his limbs; she spoke the truth with such dignity and smiled at him so sweetly, a lump came into his throat. She bent and kissed his hair, her lips resting against him for a long moment. 'I'll always love you, my son,' she said. 'I'll be up there in the sky looking out for you. Just stare up at the stars, and the one that twinkles the brightest is me, your mother loving you always, however far away I am.'

She closed her eyes and drew his head on to her thin chest. He could feel her breath on his cheek. His hand was around her shoulder, rubbing her back as if he could take the disease away from her frail body.

Slowly, so slowly that he was taken by surprise, he felt his mother slip from his arms. He tried to hold her but, thin and gaunt though she was, her body was limp, too heavy to support.

He pulled the blankets up the bed and wrapped them round his mother. Her eyes fluttered. 'Be good for Mr Harvard now, and God in His mercy go with you.'

With her last words blood bubbled from between her colourless lips. In horror John stared at his mother. 'Mam, Mam!' He fetched a towel and wiped the blood from her chin, but the fresh blood would not be stopped. His mother coughed, a hollow sound, and more blood spurted from her mouth.

'I'll clear it up now, Mam,' he said, pressing the towel over her slack mouth. 'You'll be all right, just hold on. Mr Harvard is coming.'

The blood dwindled to a trickle, her eyes rolled back in her head and then she fell back, staring sightlessly upward. He knew she was dead. He wanted to close her eyes; it didn't seem right that they were still open.

He lifted her head and cradled her in his arms as though she was his child not his mother, the burning tears falling thick and fast.

The door opened, and he was taken up in warm, comforting arms. 'Come away, John, there's nothing to be done.' Justin Harvard spoke gently as he led him to the door. John ran down the stairs and out into the starlit sky. Where was she, where was his mammy? She'd promised to be the brightest star, that she would always be with him. But she was gone, dead, and soon she would be put in the cold earth. John's control snapped, he fell to his knees on the damp grass of the lawn. The sobs shook his body and, throwing back his head, he howled into the night like a crazed animal.

CHAPTER SIX

Charlotte welcomed John Merriman back to the schoolyard without raising an eyebrow at his smart new clothes and fine polished boots. 'Condolences on your loss, John,' she said quietly. He bent his head without saying a word. 'Go into the classroom and take your seat.' She didn't want him to be stared at by the tactless but good-hearted women who had brought their own children to the school gates.

Charlotte had heard of the kindness shown to him by the school governor in the same way everyone else in the town had heard, through the usual gossip among women. She'd watched John's mother's burial from a distance, catching sight of Mr Harvard with his arm around John's slim young shoulders, and her heart had warmed to him for his compassion.

The group of mothers was still agog with all the gossip and Charlotte heard the voice of Green Mary, one of the noisier women of Swansea, above the others. The Irishwoman spoke loudly, not caring who heard her, and Charlotte was glad she'd sent John indoors.

'Bled to death she did, in the poor child's arms, Holy Mother bless her lost soul.'

Another woman spoke up. 'Just as well she's gone, though, her babba was taken from her by the good Lord, and herself getting weaker by the day.'

It seemed that all antagonism towards Mrs Merriman was gone now, faded out with her last breath.

'Poor little bugger tried to save his mother from the clutches of that vile coughing disease, spewing blood she was, and no one could do anything to help.'

Charlotte could bear no more. 'Mrs Peckham, bring the children into class if you will.'

Undaunted, Mrs Peckham continued talking even as she pushed her two young daughters in the direction of the classroom door. 'Mr Harvard found the boy crying his heart out, took John Merriman and the boy's mother into his home as if they were his own blood relatives. I suppose there's some good in him – not content by the money he gets from the copper, he owns that stinking nickel manufactory up in Clydach.'

That was something Charlotte hadn't known. He must be very rich to have a finger in so many pies. She went to her classroom and surveyed the children waiting for her.

'Get out your spelling books; I want you to learn that list of new words.' She looked at John. 'If you don't know them, John, because of your absence, I'll go over them with you.' She smiled. 'We can't have you falling behind the others, can we?'

Charlotte took her place at her desk and drew a pile of papers towards her. They needed to be marked and now, with the children memorizing the new set of words, was as good a time as any.

Later, she saw Luke in the tiny staff room.

'You're late for your break,' he said.

'I spent time going over the spellings with John,' Charlotte replied.

'Charlotte, you have your own life to lead,' he said. 'You have to mark books after school as it is. Don't you want any time for yourself, for us?'

'Of course I do, Luke, but when we're married we'll be together all the time and, for now, I can't discourage John, he needs all the help he can get if he's to realize his full potential. You know that as well as I do.'

'And he has Mr Harvard, who could pay for his education in a much better school than we have here.'

'He wouldn't do that.' Charlotte spoke with certainty.

'How do you know?'

'Justin Harvard is a wise man, he would understand that John needs all that's familiar to him, at least for now.'

'I suppose you're right.' Luke touched her arm and smiled. 'I like it when you talk about our marriage. Does it mean you are ready to set a date for the wedding?'

'All in good time, Luke.'

'But when is there a good time, Charlotte?'

She rested her hand on his arm. Taken by surprise, she didn't move when he leaned close and kissed her. Just then, the door opened. It was Justin Harvard.

Charlotte was flustered and then angry with herself for being so foolish. She was doing nothing wrong. Luke was her intended, she wore his ring on her finger, so why did it feel shameful to be caught kissing him?

'Sorry.' Justin stood in the door, his face

inscrutable. 'I didn't mean to intrude.'

Luke remained silent, but his shoulders tensed and he regarded Justin Harvard with ill-concealed displeasure. It was left to Charlotte to beckon Justin into the room, where he sat easily in an upright chair near the fireplace, his long legs stretched out before him.

'I have a proposition, Miss Mortimer,' he said, coming straight to the point. 'I'd like you to come and teach my two girls, and John Merriman of course, at my home.'

Charlotte looked at him with raised eyebrows. 'It might have escaped your notice, Mr Harvard, but I have a job here. These children need me.'

Justin drew a deep breath. 'You haven't heard then?'

'Heard what?' Luke spoke, his tone icy.

'The school is going to close. The owner of the Red Rock copperworks needs to find funds to rebuild the factories.'

Charlotte felt as if a huge cube of ice was melting and running through her bloodstream. She stared at Justin in horror. 'When is it going to close?'

'About six weeks from today, as far as I know.'

'But you're a governor. How can you sanction the closure of the school?' Charlotte heard the anguish in her voice, and so did Justin. He sat up straight and shook his head at her.

'I'm not the owner. I have a small share in the copper, and that's all. In any case, I can't tell a man who is floundering in a sea of financial problems what to do with his own property.'

'Why don't you take on the school then?' Luke's words fell like hard stones into the silence.

'I have enough business matters to deal with without taking on a few buildings that are badly in need of repair.'

'But the school is more than that,' Charlotte said forcefully. 'It offers hope to the children we teach.'

Justin shrugged. 'I haven't time for it,' he said, looking pointedly at Luke. 'In any case, I think it's a lost cause. I'm sure the owner is glad to have the school off his hands, it was running him into more debt.'

'We could see to the administration,' Charlotte said softly. 'Luke's good with figures and he can deal with people, too, and I'm a good teacher, if I say so myself.'

Justin held up his hand and stopped her flow of words. 'I know. That's why I've asked you to come to teach my children.'

'No!' Charlotte stood suddenly. 'I've no intention of giving up the school without a fight.'

'It's fruitless,' Justin said gently. 'The building is mortgaged, it will have to be sold and, anyway, who would pay your wages?'

Charlotte sat down again. He was right, of course he was right. 'We'd find a way,' she said stubbornly.

Justin got to his feet. 'Anyway, think about my offer, you could earn a decent living working for me, and you'd have a roof over your head.'

A roof over her head: Charlotte felt as if giant hands were compressing her lungs – of course, the schoolteacher's house would be sold off, without a school there'd be no need of it.

Angry, she waved her hand towards the door. 'Please go. While I still have a job here I have the authority to ask you to leave the property.'

He nodded and shook his head, as if bewildered by her attitude. He didn't seem to realize that if the school closed, a vital part of her life would be over. All she'd ever wanted was to offer a good education to the children of the district, to equip them for a life that was better than the one their parents led, to teach them there was more to the outside world than copperworks and coal mines.

Justin stood in the doorway for a moment. 'My offer is still open if you would like to take me up on it. Just think about it.'

'No thank you,' Charlotte said evenly, but he wasn't listening, he was walking swiftly away from the school towards the town, back to his life of luxury, with no more thought for the children who lived under the shadow of the forest of smoking chimneys.

She looked at Luke in despair. 'What are we going to do, Luke?'

He came to kneel before her and took her cold hands in his. 'We must be married,' he said. 'I can find another job and I will look after you, don't you worry, my darling.'

She looked hopelessly into his face. Even Luke didn't understand how much the school meant to her. 'Well, for the moment, we still have children to teach,' she said, 'so we might as well get on with it.'

Thomas Cooper, the owner of the Red Rock copperworks, was in his study resting in his wheelchair. His legs had been wounded in the fire. They burned like hell even now, but he knew that in time he would be able to walk again. Right now he was facing an unexpected and very pretty young school ma'am.

'Thank you for seeing me, Mr Cooper.' Her voice was light and lilting, with the singing tones of the Welsh.

'Please, Miss Mortimer.' He gestured towards the leather chair. 'I think you'll find it more comfortable than this contraption I'm in.'

He saw her quick glance at the wheelchair and, instead of the usual embarrassment his condition met with, she puckered her brows and stared at him earnestly. 'You could have the chair padded,' she suggested. 'A decent craftsman would do that for you with no trouble.'

He was startled. Her idea was so practical, so simple, he wondered why he'd never thought of it himself. 'There, see, a man always needs a woman's touch when it comes to comfort in the home.' He watched as she seated herself and noted with a tug at his heartstrings how tiny she was. Her feet, even in the neatly polished boots, didn't reach the floor.

He waited for her to begin. He had a good idea why she had come – it was the school, the one philanthropic contribution he had made to the children of Swansea. He and others like him had built manufactories that left a stink in the air and killed the foliage that had once made the hills green.

When he was young, he had had no guilty feelings concerning the role of the works in the town. He had paid good wages to his men and most had been eager to work for him. Now the buildings were gone, leaving blackened timbers and a huge patch of scorched earth where Red Rock had once stood. Perhaps this was just retribution, for now, without the works, he had nothing. He had grossly overspent, the new furnaces he'd installed at Red Rock had cost him a fortune, and there was no way now he could salvage the business.

'I want you to think again about selling the school. It's badly needed in Swansea, and it will serve the town well, producing educated young people and offering them hope of a better future.'

He looked at her eager face sadly. He recognized the zeal, her burning desire to help the children of the area. He had been like that once, young, wanting to grasp life by the neck and squeeze every drop of juice out of it. But that was a long time ago, he had had a thriving business then, the most successful copperworks in the town, until other men in far-off countries had found the way to smelt the shining copper out of crude ore.

'I'm truly sorry, Miss Mortimer,' he said, meaning every word. 'If there were any choice in the matter, I'd be happy to oblige, but I'm afraid it's all going into receivership, it's out of my hands now.'

He saw her swallow with difficulty. Her disappointment was almost tangible. 'I see. Well, thank you for your time.' She managed a smile. 'Good day, Mr Cooper.'

He wheeled his chair into the hall and watched her small figure walk away from him. She was a girl with spirit. Even now, in the face of the death of her dreams, her shoulders were square, her head held erect. He felt tears in his eyes as he turned the chair, wincing at the rub of the hard sides against his burned legs, and then he chuckled. Have the chair padded, she had said, with consummate sense.

'I might just do that, Miss Mortimer.' He spoke out loud even though he knew she could not hear him. 'I might just do that if I can find a few pennies to pay for the job.'

CHAPTER SEVEN

His daughters were restless today. Justin watched eight-year-old Rhian and her younger sister Morwen push and jostle each other for the most comfortable place on his knee. John Merriman stood a little way off, a look of envy on his young face. Justin felt a pang of sympathy for the boy: he was lost in a strange household in a world that was alien to him and he was finding it difficult to adjust to his new life. When he wasn't at school, he sat around the house not knowing quite what to do with his time.

'Look, girls,' Justin said easily. 'John is behaving himself, which is more than I can say about you two.'

'But John is older than us,' Rhian said with impeccable logic. 'And he's a boy, and in any case you're not his father, so he won't want to sit on your knee, will he?'

Justin, seeing the longing that briefly clouded John's eyes, knew that a show of affection was just what the boy needed but that he would not welcome it from him. John was old enough to feel it unmanly to have an embrace from another man. He gently pushed his daughters away. 'Go and find something to do,' he encouraged.

'But, Daddy, we've got no lessons today, remember?' Morwen had a slight lisp and, as she looked up at him, her elbows resting on his knees and her chin cupped in her hands, she looked so adorable that, on impulse, he bent and kissed her soft cheek.

'I know that only too well,' he said ruefully. 'John, did I tell you I asked Miss Mortimer to tutor my daughters and you, too, of course?' The boy's face lit up.

'When's she coming?'

'Ah, well, I don't know about that. I'm giving her time to think it over.' Justin smiled confidently. 'She'll come as soon as the school closes, I expect.'

'When is the school closing?' John stepped nearer to him, and Justin knew his answer was important to the boy.

'Within a few weeks, I think.'

'Why?' John's voice was clipped and his eyes narrowed as he looked at Justin. Justin held up his hand.

'Nothing to do with me, John. Mr Cooper

of Red Rock is short of money now that the works has burned down. He had the place mortgaged and, as he needs funds, he's obliged to sell the school and the little house that goes with it.'

John frowned. 'But Miss Mortimer lives in the house. What will she do? Where will she go?'

'As I explained, I have every hope that she will come to live here as your tutor and tutor for my girls,' Justin said.

John's head was lowered, his voice barely audible. 'Perhaps she'll marry Mr Luke,' he said, 'and never teach no more.'

Justin felt unsettled in a way he didn't understand. Why should he care if Miss Mortimer married or not? But care he did.

'I think Miss Mortimer will want to teach for a very long time yet.' There was an element of hope in his voice, and he paused for a moment, examining his feelings. She was attractive, a tiny, fragile girl, but there was an iron will behind the enchanting face. She was brave enough to fight for the school and he admired that. Miss Mortimer wore another man's ring, she was spoken for, and yet Justin had the feeling that marriage was the last thing on the schoolmistress's mind.

There was a knock on the door and one of the parlour maids popped her head into the room. 'Mr Harvard, there's a young lady to see you, a Miss Mortimer. Shall I show her in?'

His senses were suddenly alert. 'Thank you, Maddie, yes, show her in and take my children away from me. They're sure to want some milk and biscuits by now.'

He looked hopefully at the girls and, to his relief, they were both delighted with the idea of a treat in the kitchen with Cook and the maids fussing over them.

'Go along, John,' Justin said. 'I'll be sure to call you to say hello to Miss Mortimer before she leaves.'

'Perhaps she'll come to work for you, Mr Harvard. I hope so.'

John's eyes were alight and Justin nodded. 'I hope so too.'

Her bearing as she entered the room was almost regal, her back was stiff and her small mouth set in what could be called a full-lipped scowl. It didn't bode well for any negotiations he had in mind.

He rose and gestured with his hand. 'Please sit down, Miss Mortimer.'

She flounced on to a chair. 'I suppose you know I've been given notice to quit the schoolteacher's house.' Her chin tilted upwards as she dared him to deny it.

'I didn't know how soon it would happen, but it was on the cards. As I remember, I told you it was bound to happen.' His tone was edged with impatience, he'd been having a hell of a day with the girls playing up and the last thing he wanted was a scene over an event that was out of his hands.

She lifted her small hands out to him in an expression of disbelief, still glowering at him. 'I'm sure you could have prevented it,' she said, 'but then the school means nothing to you, does it?'

'On the contrary.' He got to his feet and stood before the fire, his hands thrust into his pockets. 'I think I was a most conscientious governor, but I am not the owner of the school or the house and I have no say in what Mr Cooper does with his property.' He paused. 'Oh, John has asked to see you. Would you like me to send for him?'

She nodded, seemingly at a loss for words. He rang the bell and asked the maid to fetch the boy into the sitting room.

John had a joyful look on his face. 'Miss Mortimer, I knew you'd come to see me. I spects you'll be my teacher then?'

Justin watched as she ruffled John's hair. 'Are you settling in well here, John?' Her voice was soft, gentle, and he could see how fond she was of the boy.

John nodded. 'Oh, yes, miss. Mr Justin bought me good clothes, real new ones from the shop in High Street. He's kind, he is, miss.'

Justin watched Charlotte's face with avid interest. She seemed to be battling with herself. After a while, she spoke without looking at him. Her face was flushed as she rushed the words out. 'I have come to take up your offer of a post.' She spoke truculently, as if she were doing him a favour.

'Well, thank you very kindly,' Justin said. For a moment he felt like telling her the post was no longer vacant, but that would be cutting off his own nose to spite his face. He remained silent for a moment, just long enough for an anxious frown to crease the soft skin of her forehead. 'Very well, Miss Mortimer. We will forgo the need for references in the circumstances.'

She appeared to be taken aback and he almost laughed. He stood there waiting for her to respond. She swallowed hard, as though she had a lump of ice in her throat. 'I take it there will be bed and board as well as a good salary,' she said, glancing at him with piercing blue eyes cold enough to freeze the sea round Mumbles Head.

'Of course. When would you like to start?'

'As soon as the school is closed. I could move my things in very quickly after that.'

'I'd be happy to provide you with one of my pony traps, when you need it.'

She swept to her feet and swished her skirts angrily around her dusty boots. 'No thanks, Mr Harvard. I can manage by myself.'

'Very well, be foolishly independent if that's your wish, but I hope you won't have heavy bags to carry.' He ran his eyes over her small frame and she blushed at his scrutiny of her.

'I'm stronger than I look.' She swirled her skirts again and headed for the door. He moved sharply to open it for her. She stopped and looked up at him, and her eyes were almost violet.

'Do you open the doors for your maids?' she challenged.

'Of course not!'

'Well, then, don't feel you have to treat me any better than your domestic staff. I'm just a paid employee, after all.'

'Right.' He stepped away from the door, a smile twitching up the corners of his lips. He could tell by her scowl that she knew he was amused by her.

'Goodbye for now, John.' Her tone softened, then she glanced Justin's way and without another word flounced across the hall and disappeared through the front door.

Justin was jubilant. He clapped his hand on John's shoulder. 'I'll tell the girls our happy news. Come on, John.' Justin ran down the stairs two at a time and called his daughters. The pair of them, eyes wide, looked up from their milk and biscuits.

'Girls, Miss Mortimer is coming to teach you. Are you pleased?' Both his daughters stared up at him with blank faces.

'What's so good about that, Daddy? We

were enjoying the holiday!'

'Well, John is pleased to have a fine teacher like Miss Mortimer, not like you pair of ungrateful little daughters.'

'Teacher's pet!' one of the girls mumbled, but Justin ignored it. As he made his way back up the stairs, his mood of jubilance vanished. Why was he so delighted to have Charlotte permanently under his roof? She wasn't free, she was betrothed and, in any case, a teacher wasn't a suitable wife for a man of his standing. But still, he felt a lift of pleasure at the thought of her packing her bags and putting herself under his roof and under his care.

Charlotte struggled to conceal her anger as Luke stood towering over her. 'I need a job and a place to live. Can't you understand that, Luke?'

'No, I cannot!' He stormed across the classroom, and she knew he was watching her. She stared at the possessions on her desk. They were the tools of her trade: a ruler, several ink-stained books and a half-eaten packet of sticky bulls' eyes.

'Did you have to work with *him?*'

'Where else would I get such an offer so quickly?' Charlotte regretted her words. At once she'd given Luke an opportunity to propose marriage to her again. And he took it.

'I've said we'll get married as soon as

possible.' He spoke impatiently, and she pursed her lips, biting back the furious words that flew to them.

'And in the meantime, should I live in a cowshed or under a hedge? Be sensible, Luke.'

'You could move into my house, and I'd stay at Ma O'Sullivan's place until we were properly married.'

She faced him, her hands clenched at her sides. 'Look, I've made my own way. I've had to with my family moving so far away.' She pushed her possessions into her bag, handling the books carefully. They were dog-eared enough now, but she loved her books – they were important to her.

'I always wanted to teach.' She softened her voice, trying to reason with him. 'That's why I stayed behind in Swansea while my loved ones sailed away to a new life in America.'

He turned on her. 'So I had no place in the equation?'

Charlotte bit her lip, she'd said the wrong thing again – she was always saying the wrong thing to Luke lately. The only way she would be right would be to marry him at once, as he begged her to. But she didn't want to be married, at least not yet.

'Of course I thought of you, Luke,' she said truthfully. 'You know how much I care for you.'

'But you are still going to live in that man's house?'

'I am going to *work* in that man's house, there is a difference, Luke, so don't make it sound as if I'm going to live in sin with him.'

His shoulders slumped. 'I suppose you're right,' he said at last.

Immediately, Charlotte warmed to him. 'Thank you for being so understanding,' she said softly.

'And we'll get married soon?'

She nodded. 'Of course.' And yet in her heart she felt frightened, unsure of her feelings for Luke, unsure of everything that had happened in her life. Perhaps she was wrong to stay in Swansea alone, perhaps she should have gone with her family and started afresh in a new country. Well, it was too late now, she would just have to make the best of things.

As she said goodbye to Luke at the ornate gates of Thornhill, Charlotte hesitated for a moment and then leant forward to kiss Luke chastely on the cheek.

'When will I see you?' he said, with such a doleful look in his eyes that she almost smiled. Almost but not quite. Luke would be mortified if he thought she was laughing at him.

'I'll have some free time,' she said, 'the Dark Ages have gone. I can hardly be locked in my room like a mad Mrs Rochester, can I?' She heard the gate swing open and turned to see a burly lodge-keeper waiting for her to step inside.

'Goodnight, Luke.' She felt breathless, as if she were about to stray into a place where she did not know the etiquette. She had been well brought up, but she knew nothing of living in splendour such as the massive towers of Thornhill offered.

'I'm called Pepper, madam. Let me take your bag.'

'That's all right, Mr Pepper, I can carry it myself, I'm a worker here just like you.'

She glanced back, meaning to wave, but Luke had vanished into the deep glade of trees that surrounded the estate.

'Are you, miss?' Pepper said agreeably. 'But I'll always carry a bag for a lovely little lady, if you'll pardon me saying so, ma'am.'

Pepper led her to the back of the house and pushed open the large, arched doors, the sort Charlotte had only seen on a church porch. 'There you are, miss. I'll take you to the kitchen and one of the girls can see to you after that.'

The kitchen was warm, with the appetizing smell of freshly baked bread filling the room. Charlotte realized how hungry she was.

Pepper put down her case and crept behind the cook, who was spooning jam into the waiting tart cases which sat warmly in front of her. She squealed and shook him away, but there was a smile on her face all the same.

She spared a glance at Charlotte, and the smile faded. 'You'd best go along to the hall.' She jerked with her mob-capped head and Charlotte muttered her thanks as she went through the door indicated. The cook ignored her and turned towards Pepper, offering him a jam tart.

The hallway was empty, and Charlotte stood there, not knowing what to do next. She stood there for a full half-hour and then, abandoning her bag, began to climb the grand stairway to an upper landing.

There she heard the sound of children's voices and made her way towards an open doorway. The two girls stared at her, silenced by her sudden appearance. John stepped forward and bowed his head for a moment and then chanced looking up at her.

'I'm sorry, miss. I know I should be in my own room doing my sums but...' He shrugged and Charlotte shook back a stray lock of hair that had flopped into her eyes.

'That's all right, John, I haven't started in my position as teacher yet.' She hesitated. 'But would you find a maid or someone to show me to my room?'

John ran full pelt down the stairs, eager to be of service, and after a while, a parlour-maid appeared, carrying Charlotte's bag.

'Up some more stairs, miss,' she said

breathlessly. She led the way upwards, and Justin's two girls stood watching. Charlotte was sure she heard the elder one snigger.

Her room was bare of all but the essentials: a narrow bed that creaked as the maid put Charlotte's bag on it, a clock, an ancient washstand complete with jug and basin and a gas light that must have been overlooked when the house was provided with electric lighting.

The maid was young and pretty. Her large breasts strained against the soft linen of her apron and her cap was set at a jaunty angle.

'I'm Polly,' she said in a matter-of-fact voice, 'and you must be Charlotte. Well, I shall call you Charlie – that's what the master's daughters are going to call you.'

'Oh, really?' Charlotte was indignant. 'And who decided that?'

Polly smirked. 'The master, he said you wanted to be treated the same as us servants.'

'Well, thank you ... Polly, you can leave me now. I can manage very well on my own.'

'So you'll be fetching water for washing yourself of a morning then?'

'That's what I always do, Polly. I didn't have servants when I lived in the school-teacher's house.'

Polly clucked in a noncommittal way and left the room. Charlotte sat down on the bed and put her head in her hands. So this was her life from now on, a bare, draughty room and unfriendly staff. She sighed as she kicked off her boots, but she was young, she was strong and well able to look after herself. As she lay down on the lumpy bed, she couldn't help wishing that she was in her cosy little house with her nice warm fire and a cup of hot milk to soothe her off to sleep.

CHAPTER EIGHT

Charlotte woke early the next morning and sat up in alarm, wondering where she was. The room was unfamiliar, the thin curtains let in too much light, and she blinked against it, her eyes feeling gritty and unrested.

She pushed back her tangled hair and, with a suddenness that was startling, the bells on top of the round-faced clock beside the bed went off loud enough to wake the whole household. Then she remembered. She was at Thornhill. The clockface showed it was five o'clock. Apparently, she was expected to get up at the same time as the servants.

She lingered under the thin wool blankets, as the air was bitterly cold so early in the morning. She huddled against the pillows for a few minutes, trying to collect her thoughts. Even if she got up, what would she do at this time of day? The children wouldn't be roused until the servants had built up the fires. Water would have to be warmed to be carried upstairs for washing, the stove would have to be breathed into life ready for Cook to prepare breakfast. Surely there was plenty of time for her to lie in her bed and try to come to terms with the changes in her life?

The servants' accommodation was at the back of the house and already she could hear the stableboys shouting directions to each other in the yard and the high-pitched whinnying of the animals, impatient to be fed. With a sigh she pushed back the bedclothes. Where was Justin now? Would he be out with the horses or still wrapped up in bed? She imagined him in bed, his face relaxed, his hair thick with a tendency to curl around his face. Would he wear a nightshirt in bed or nothing? She felt a smile tug at the corners of her lips at the thought, even as a blush deepened the colour of her pale morning face. The woolliness of sleep left her and now she was wide awake. Reluctantly, she slid out of bed and padded across the bare boards to where the washstand stood on thick, stolid legs strong enough to support the marble top and the ugly green tiles behind it.

There was no water in the jug. Charlotte remembered her conversation with the maid – she would have to fetch her water herself. She stood for a moment in indecision: should she dress and go unwashed to the kitchen or was it permissible to wear her patterned woollen dressing-gown? She shrugged and pulled on her gown. It was too cold to waste time wondering about such things.

She had no carpet slippers, so she went barefoot down the three flights of stairs, pulling her fingers through her thick, tangled hair, which had come free of its plait in the night.

The hallway was draughty, the door open to the cold air of the morning, and Charlotte hesitated. What if someone came in from outside? What if Justin saw her dishevelled hair, her dressing-gown? Well, either she went forward to get some warm water or she retreated to her room again and remained unwashed.

She crossed the hall and hurried along the passageway to the kitchens. The cook eyed her with disapproval. 'What the 'eck are you doing down here in your bedwear?' She put her cup down with a bang. The scent of the warm tea filled the room and Charlotte suddenly longed to be back home in the schoolteacher's house making toast and tea for herself in the peace of early morning before her busy day began.

Rattled by her thoughts, she felt anger rush through her – she was turning into a mindless, frightened rabbit, afraid of upsetting anyone and everyone. She was not here as some poor dependent governess out of an old gothic story, she was here to work. She saw a jug of steaming water near the fire and took it without a word to the cook. As she crossed through the hall, Justin came in from outside, his hair standing on end, blown by the rush of wind that was also plastering his shirt to his broad shoulders. She stared at him aghast for a long moment.

'Morning, Miss Mortimer.' He nodded and turned away, a tiny smile at the corner of his lips.

Cook bustled out of the kitchen, her face red with anger as she waved towards the jug of water Charlotte carried.

'Sorry, Mr Harvard,' Cook said. *'She's* taken your hot water.'

Justin's lips twisted into a full smile. 'How very uncharitable of you, Miss Mortimer. I wanted the water to wash a newborn foal.'

Charlotte stood looking into the steaming water, wondering what to do. She held the jug towards him, and he waved her hands away.

'No, please, I wouldn't be so ungentlemanly as to deprive you of your morning ablutions.'

She saw his eyes roving over her and she tried to push back the unruly curls, with little success. She ducked her head to him. 'I'm sorry for the inconvenience,' she muttered, and a drizzle of now cooling water trickled on to the flagstone floor, causing Cook to cluck her tongue in disapproval.

'Here, let me.' Justin took the jug from her numb hands and preceded her up the stairs. Charlotte felt embarrassed by Justin's apparent good humour, but at the same time she found she was enchanted by his smile, by the way he looked this morning, but mostly by the way his riding breeches clung to the curves of his body.

She blushed, ashamed of her thoughts. She was in danger of becoming a swooning Victorian lady, not a modern, independent product of the twentieth century.

Justin carried the water into her room, glancing for a moment at the tangled bed. 'Not a good night, Miss Mortimer? Restless were you?'

'I was.'

He put down the water and smiled at her. 'I'm sorry about the primitive conditions of my top-floor rooms,' he said. He turned to face her. 'I'm sorry, I've been teasing you. There's a room being made up for you on the main landing.'

Charlotte looked at him in surprise. 'What was the point in teasing me?'

Justin looked shamefaced. 'I'm sorry, Miss Mortimer, your need for independence awakened a devil of mischief in me.' He smiled widely and she caught her breath, he was so handsome, fresh-faced from the morning air, his eyes alight with laughter.

'I don't understand what you mean.' She stumbled over the words. 'I thought all the servants' rooms were on this floor.'

'No,' he said. 'This floor is unused and therefore a little behind the times. Downstairs you will have a comfortable room and a bathroom all to yourself.'

'And do all your servants live like that in your house?'

'Don't start all that "I know my proper place" lark again. You are a teacher, a good teacher, or I wouldn't want you to teach my children. You have a certain status at Thornhill, Miss Mortimer, whether you like it or not.'

'Oh, thank you,' Charlotte flared. 'You've made a proper fool of me, haven't you, Mr Harvard? I suppose all the servants are having a fine laugh. Well, I'm not laughing.' She strode to the door, waiting for him to leave, and with a wry smile, like a naughty boy caught in a prank, he went out.

She closed the door and stood there, hands clenched, wanting to kick and scream out her frustration like a little child, and then she began to laugh. He was right, she had been pompous, determined not to ask any favours of him. Her mood sobered – she'd better get ready to face the day.

Charlotte sat at her high desk in the schoolroom. Her teaching day was over and she was free to go for a walk, sit in her room and read, do anything that took her fancy. She was meant to be seeing Luke, but he had sent a message to say he would be in a meeting and would see her by the gates of Thornhill at six.

Charlotte marvelled at how quickly she had adjusted to life at the big house. It was peaceful in the empty room, which faced the front of the house, where green lawns swept into the distance to a copse of trees which provided a screen against the outside world. Evening clouds began to creep over the lawns and she could see the shadows falling on the grass through the tall windows.

Justin had made the room she sat in the very model of a modern schoolroom. Several rows of desks with slanting tops smelling of new-cut timber filled the body of the room, while she, the teacher, had her desk on an elevated dais from where she could see all the children. At the moment there were only the two Harvard girls and John Merriman. Soon, though, hopefully, other children would take their place at lessons. It was up to Justin Harvard to set the wheels in motion.

The door opened and Justin himself came in, looking as he always did, dishevelled but very masculine.

'I've had an idea, Miss Mortimer,' he said. 'Would you like to hear about it?'

'Does it concern the old school?'

He shook his head. 'The old school as we used to know it is finished, you must see that, Miss Mortimer.'

She nodded her head. 'Go on.'

'You know I want to set up a school here.'

She glanced round. 'But this room is too small to take more than a dozen pupils.'

'I do realize that.' He sounded impatient. 'I have an outhouse that would make an admirable schoolroom. It's big and roomy and, though it needs a coat of whitewash, there's nothing that can't be altered and improved.'

'How many would it hold?' Charlotte sat up straight, her interest quickened.

'At least twenty children, the brightest we can find, of course.'

An icicle of doubt crept along her spine. 'The brightest?'

'Of course. It's little use to teach children who have no interest in learning.'

'I disagree.' She pointed to Kilvey hill stripped of its greenery by the poison of the copper smoke. 'See the barren hill over there?'

He obligingly turned towards it. 'Yes, I'm familiar with Kilvey and its barren earth.' He turned back to look at her. 'Your point?'

'If you go up close to Kilvey, you'll see camomile flowers growing; they're bleached white but they are there, hidden by all the stunted grass and dried-up soil that is all you can see from here.'

'Ah!' he nodded. 'You're saying there are hidden talents in some of the children which need to be nurtured.'

She nodded. 'Don't you agree?'

'We have to be practical,' he said. 'We cannot accept all the children who need schooling, only the best and brightest.'

She saw he was not to be moved and nodded. Educating some of the children was better than educating none.

'Now, Miss Mortimer, I have a job for you.'

'Yes?' Her voice was cold. 'I would think my duty for the day is done and, believe it or not, I'm tired. Teaching is hard work.' He stood up straight and saluted her, and his mockery made the colour rise to her cheeks. 'What did you want of me anyway?'

'John asked for help. He seems to have problems with the way you teach English literature.' A ghost of a smile crossed his face. 'He thinks Jane Austen is "soppy", his word, not mine. He'd rather learn about Charles Dickens who, according to John, knows what real life is about.'

In spite of herself, Charlotte smiled. 'You always find a way of putting me in the wrong, Mr Harvard. Of course I'll have a chat with John. At least he's willing to read – that's a very good start.'

Justin smiled, and there was a wicked glint

in his eyes. 'I've asked for tea to be brought to you in the sitting room. You can share a cup with John, he won't think you're giving him a lecture then.'

He took her to the sitting room and left her there. Suddenly the colour had gone out of the day.

John looked embarrassed when he came in. He looked down and shuffled his feet.

'I'm sorry if I made trouble for you, Miss Mortimer.'

'Don't be silly, John, I'm only too glad you're asking for help with your reading.' She sat on the long, comfortable sofa and gestured for him to sit beside her. She was aware of the acrid smell of sweat. John was nervous, and she knew she must put him at ease or she'd never be able to help him.

'Don't worry, you didn't get me into any trouble. Mr Harvard simply asked me to have a chat with you about books.' She rested her hand for a moment on the rough wool of his jumper. 'You don't have to like the books I set you, all I need is your appraisal of them.' She smiled. 'And the fact that you don't particularly like the books of Miss Austen is no reflection of your ability to understand them or offer an opinion on them.' He didn't answer. 'You see, John, you need to read all sorts of books to widen your understanding of literature.' She waited patiently for him to speak. He frowned and knotted his hands together.

'The people in Miss Austen's books are all nice and clean and tidy and, see, none of the ladies do the washing and ironing or get dirty making the fire up or go to work.' He looked up at her, warming to his subject. 'All the books are about soppy girls going to posh dances and trying to get some rich man to marry them.'

'But that's just a description of the way some women lived in those far-off days, and though it's a different world to ours, we are entertained by reading about it. Do you see, John?'

He thought about it for a long time. 'I do see that, but Mr Dickens writes about the poor people in workhouses and sleeping in 'orrible smelly rooms, and thieves and things, even murderers.'

Charlotte smiled. 'Very good observation, John, and you are right, the world seen by Miss Austen is a very different one to that observed by Charles Dickens. They lived in different ages and circumstances, but each has value.' She paused. 'I'm very pleased with your progress, John.'

He looked up at her in surprise. 'Why, miss, when I've got the cheek to ask you questions about the books?'

'That's exactly what pleases me, John.'

'What, miss?'

'You're thinking for yourself, making judgements, trying to understand different sorts of lives from ours. I have great hopes of you, John, I'm sure you'll do very well when you choose a career.'

His expression warmed. 'I want to be a writer, miss, like Mr Dickens, show people what it 'as been like to be poor in Swansea.'

Charlotte smiled. 'My sister Letty is a writer.'

'Would she talk to me, miss, tell me 'ow I can be a writer?'

'Letty lives a long way away, John, but remember this, every book you read teaches you something, how to use your imagination, your powers of understanding, the meaning of words. One thing I learned from Letty was to write what you feel in your heart.'

She glanced at her watch and bit her lip; it was almost dinner-time and she'd completely forgotten her arrangement to meet Luke. She excused herself quickly and hurried out down the long drive to where Luke would be waiting, but he wasn't there, the roadway was empty, and Charlotte felt a heavy burden of guilt as she turned back up the drive towards the house.

CHAPTER NINE

'I'm sorry, Luke.' It was cold in Victoria Park but Charlotte was wrapped up in her good wool and had a thick scarf around her head and didn't feel the chill of the morning, only the chill of Luke's impatience with her.

'I waited an hour for you.' He sounded dejected. 'A whole hour, when I could have been busy with my studies.' Luke was reading for a higher degree and Charlotte was very much aware of how important it was to him.

'I just had to talk to John,' she said, 'and I've said I'm sorry. It won't happen again, Luke, I promise you that.'

'I don't like the way you're becoming involved in Justin Harvard's life. Since you went to live with him, the man has taken you over, body and soul.'

Charlotte resisted the sharp retort that rose to her lips. 'Aren't you exaggerating just a little, Luke? You are the only man I'm interested in.' She pushed her arm through his, and at once he turned to look down at her. His expression softened.

'You wicked little witch,' he said, 'how do

you always get around me?' He led her out of the park and across the road and stood with her for a moment watching the sea lave the shore, driven by the fierce wind. Eddies of sand drifted like ghostly shadows across the wide beach. The smell of salt and sea was exhilarating, and Charlotte hugged Luke's arm to her side.

'Perhaps I am getting caught up in my work too much,' she said, 'and yet I'm so keen to educate the Harvard girls, and John, of course, especially John.' She paused. 'I haven't told you about Mr Harvard's plans yet, have I?'

'Which plans?'

'He's going to turn one of the outhouses into a schoolroom, encourage the children of the area to attend.'

'I thought you had a schoolroom already,' Luke said sharply. Charlotte looked up at him. There was a strange expression on his face which she couldn't quite read.

'What's wrong?'

'I've heard about these plans,' Luke said. 'The only children to attend the school will have fathers who can pay and pay well.'

'That can't be right.' Charlotte spoke defensively. 'We're going to move from the classroom in the house to accommodate more children. Mr Harvard wants only the brightest children to benefit from the school. That's not such a bad thing, is it?' She didn't

114

mention her own reservations about the scheme.

'Aye, but isn't it fortunate that the "brightest" children will be those of works' managers and the like?'

'Mr Harvard hasn't mentioned anything of the sort to me.'

Luke shook his head. 'And are you and Mr Harvard on such good terms that he discusses his business with you?'

'Of course not, but he led me to believe...' Her voice trailed away. What *had* Justin told her? Not very much, it seemed. 'Oh, let's forget him,' she said. 'Why spoil our time together by talking about *him?*' Charlotte was silent for a moment. She saw now that Justin's plans served only his interests, increased his already overflowing coffers. But he wouldn't get away with it – her instinct all along had been to reinstate the school as it had been before the fire at the works, a school where she was in sole charge. How she would afford to secure a building fit for use as a school she wasn't quite certain. It needed a great deal of thought.

'Anyway,' Luke said, 'there's not much we can do about it.'

'As I said, let's forget him.' Charlotte sounded calm, but inside she burned with the injustice of Justin's decision. She'd believed he had the interests of the children at heart, but now she realized it was all about money and profit.

'Let's talk about something else.'

'Quite right.' Luke smiled, really smiled, for the first time that morning. 'I think I'll treat you to a hot pot of tea in the beach tearooms. Now, aren't I the most generous fiancé you've ever had?'

'That's because you're the *only* fiancé I've ever had.' It was their little joke, and they laughed together. Charlotte felt her tensions leave her. She was with the man she loved, it was her day off, and all she wanted to do was enjoy her outing with Luke by her side.

'Hello, John.' A small hand caressed his arm, and John knew at once who was standing close beside him in the dark back scullery, unused now because of the smart new kitchen Justin Harvard had had installed.

John steadied himself, trying to ignore the effect her soft little hand had on his senses. As casually as he could, he turned his head to look at her.

'Mornin', Lizzie, shouldn't you be peeling vegetables or something?' He swallowed, hoping his Adam's apple wasn't noticeably bobbing up and down. He felt beads of sweat on his forehead, his armpits were suddenly damp.

'Ha'penny for your thoughts,' she giggled. 'I can't afford a penny, see.'

John had been staring out of the window

into the darkness of the garden. This was the only place he could feel free from Mr Harvard's two girls. They plagued him unmercifully, wanting him to play Snap and then cheating like the spoilt brats they were. But soon they would have to go to bed and in the meantime he could hide here, below stairs, and be alone.

'Not worth it.' His voice was gruff – at least he'd avoided the shame of speaking in the dreaded squeaky voice that sometimes came out of his mouth.

'Do you like me, John?' Lizzie was looking up at him, her eyes wide and innocent. They protruded a little, but her body was lush and full – even with her starched apron on, her breasts stood out boldly. His eyes roved over her curves before he swiftly looked away.

'Why shouldn't I like you, Lizzie?'

'Well, I'm just a drudge, a poor scullery-maid who gets all the 'orrible jobs, and you–' her hand caressed his arm again '–you are the master's favourite boy. I've heard him say to Cook you're like the son he never had.'

'That's just silly,' John said, unnerved by the thought. 'Mr Harvard is being kind to me, he's sorry for me because I got no one else to look after me. A lot of bosses like to do that sort of thing. I suppose they call it charity.'

He didn't like the word and, he thought

suddenly, he didn't like the implications behind it.

'I wish I could have some of that charity for myself.' Lizzie moved closer and John felt her breasts pressing against him. His body began to betray him, he moved away and lowered his hands to cover his flies, but she knew what effect she was having on him and it pleased her.

'Lizzie, you're playing with fire.' John spoke in a breathy voice and tried to push her away. 'You should be careful or one day someone will take advantage of you.'

'I don't fancy just anyone, mind,' Lizzie said crossly. 'I don't let any old footman play fast and loose with me, and you should know that by now, John. I'm a good girl, I am.'

He softened. 'I know that, Lizzie.' She was very close to him, he could taste her breath; it was sweet, honeyed. His body was still responding to her nearness, he felt an overwhelming desire to throw her down on her back and take her. He licked his lips, his mouth was suddenly dry. 'Oh, Lizzie. You little temptress.' He put his arms around her and, innocently, she lifted her face for his kiss. When their lips met, John was shaken by the way she thrust her tongue into his mouth.

'Will you come to my room with me?' She held him away from her and her eyes were half-closed.

He let his hand slip over her breasts as

though it was an accident, and he felt the small nipple beneath her clothes harden at his touch.

'I'd like to come to you, Lizzie, but when?' His body was throbbing with his need for her. He could feel his blood pounding through his veins.

'We could go up now,' she said.

'But what about your work?'

'I'll tell Cook I've got a bad belly, I'll tell her it's the curse come on me and she'll let me go and lie down in my room.' She touched his hand and smiled, and he saw the desire in her eyes. With a burst of excitement mingled with fear, he knew she was willing for more than just kissing.

'You go upstairs to my room,' Lizzie said. 'Make sure no one sees you. I'll be up as soon as I can get away.'

John left her then and crept up the back stairs, praying that neither Mr Harvard nor his daughters would see him.

In Lizzie's room, he sat on the bed breathing in its soft floral scent. There were two beds in the room, and John was anxious for a moment, worrying that they would be disturbed, and then he remembered that one of the maids had left a few weeks ago. For the moment, Lizzie had the room all to herself.

While he was waiting, he picked up a book, a book about the Bible, its pages filled with coloured pictures. The devil was depicted on one page, complete with horns and a long tail and eyes blazing red. The text was large and easy to read and John realized with a pang of pity that Lizzie was making an attempt to learn her letters.

Perhaps she had aspirations, as he did. For a moment he lingered on the word 'aspirations', enjoying his knowledge of it, knowing that if it weren't for Miss Mortimer's teaching, he wouldn't be such a good scholar himself.

By the time Lizzie came into the room, he was stretched out on the bed, his hands behind his head, feigning sleep, though his body was so tense, his muscles seemed to hurt with the strain of it. Lizzie turned the key in the door and came to lie beside him. He turned to her and was surprised to see an expression of something almost like fear in her eyes.

'Tell me, Lizzie,' he said gently, 'have you ever lain with a man before?'

'Don't be bloody soft!' Her voice was edged with anger. 'I'm only doing it with you, John, because I love you.'

'Do you?' The thought of being loved came as a surprise. 'Do you really love me, Lizzie?'

'Aye, I do that, but that don't mean I'm not scared half to death.'

He rolled on top of her and pressed his hard body up against hers. He knew he should take his clothes off and hers, but he didn't really know where to start.

Lizzie lay inert, leaving John to take the initiative. He unbuttoned his flies and pushed down his trousers, feeling a little ridiculous. Still Lizzie didn't move. He slipped his hand up her skirt and touched the soft flesh of her thighs, and he felt her shudder.

Desire for her filled him so much he was a little rough as his fingers searched for her unknown and intimate places.

'It's not going to hurt, is it, John?'

'I don't know, Lizzie, I hope not, but I'll go slow, and don't you worry, I'll take care of everything.' She shook her head, not knowing what he meant. He didn't rightly know himself but he'd heard other men say it, men in the street where he had lived with his mam, and he felt grown-up assuring her of something neither of them understood.

He opened the buttons of her blouse and through the soft, thin cotton of her camisole he could see her nipples small and hard and, instinctively, he pushed the cotton aside and let his mouth close warm and soft against her breast.

Lizzie tensed beneath him and her breathing became ragged. Was this a sign that she liked what he was doing? He fervently hoped so.

Slowly, he drew down her bloomers and bent to kiss the sparse sprinkling of hair that adorned her secret place.

'Oh, John!' His name came from her lips like a soft caress and, with a flare of pride, he knew he was doing the right things to please her. And John wanted to please her. He knew enough about the rough panting and heaving that happened in the poor streets where he once lived. There the walls were thin and sometimes he heard the sound of a woman crying piteously. Loving shouldn't be bad or hurtful, he knew that much. People were not animals, they had sense and feeling, and love between them should be a thing of beauty.

He caressed Lizzie and heard her moan. Did that mean she was ready for him? He forced himself to speak, confidently and gently. 'Are you ready, Lizzie?'

She moaned again and he eased himself on top of her, his hardness close to her belly. It seemed as if Lizzie was acting on instinct too, as she opened her legs, making way for him to enter her.

He pressed into her soft moistness and, after gently probing, found a resistance to his hardness – this must be the virginity he'd heard the boys talk about in the streets. There the act called love was laughed and jeered at. 'Force your way in' was the mantra of those who had possessed a girl, but John cared too much about Lizzie to risk hurting her.

Tentatively, he probed deeper. Lizzie

gasped with pain but clung on to his shoulders for dear life, almost as though she were drowning in a deep river. He paused in his thrusting and stroked her face and her neck.

'It's all right, Lizzie, the hurting will soon be over and then we can enjoy our love, I promise you.'

He felt her relax under him and he gave a hard push and was past the barrier. A sense of exhilaration filled him as, after one sharp cry, Lizzie began to moan softly. He held himself back, not wanting to cheat the girl of her pleasure. She writhed against him, pressed upwards as if to encompass him entirely. And then he could wait no longer. With one mighty thrust he felt a million sensations course through him. It was as though a thousand stars had gone off in his head and travelled through his body, and he gasped and fell relaxed on Lizzie's soft little body.

Neither of them had heard the door open. It was only when the flickering light of a candle was held over them that Lizzie cried out in terror. She pushed John away from her, and he fell beside her and looked up into the face of Mr Harvard's elder daughter. Rhian was holding a key in her hand and smiling, her face demonized by the flickering light of the candle.

'Rhian.' John's voice was hoarse. 'What the hell are you doing here?'

'I saw what you did, you filthy pig!' she

said, her voice sharpened with disgust. 'You poked that *thing* into poor Lizzie and made her cry. I'm going to tell my father what you are really like – a common boy from the filthy streets of Swansea not fit to live in his house.'

'No, miss,' Lizzie said. 'It's not what you think. Me and John are in love, see, and folks in love do that all the time.'

'No, they don't. You are a rotten liar!'

Lizzie straightened her clothes. 'They do, honest, that's how folk get babies, mind.' Then Lizzie made a fateful mistake. 'I expect your father did that to your mother.' She hesitated. 'And now he's got that other lady who lives in the big house by the sea, his mistress, the posh people call it, but she's no better than a whore. But don't worry, all the grown-ups do it. I suppose even Miss Mortimer and Mr Lester do it.'

Rhian flew at Lizzie and pulled her hair. Lizzie cried out and smacked the girl's hand away. Rhian began screaming, running out on to the landing and calling at the top of her voice for her father. John put his head in his hands, knowing that some dreadful fate awaited him. He'd done wrong and now he was going to pay for it.

Charlotte looked up at Justin as he sat reading his paper. He filled the room, as he always did, with his presence. Charlotte, along with the rest of the household, had heard Rhian's scream. Now the girl was pounding down the stairs telling anyone who would listen about Lizzie's lies about her dear father and some woman called a 'whore'.

Charlotte blanched when she heard her own name mentioned. She looked aghast at Justin. He left the room, his face white and angry, and was gone for some time. Charlotte sat, confused by the strange anger that was rising within her at the thought of Justin with a mistress, a 'whore'.

When Justin returned she looked up at him and he told her what had happened. 'I've given the boy the sound whipping he deserves,' he said in answer to her unspoken question. He sat down heavily in his chair and looked at Charlotte.

'You're going to get rid of him?' she asked flatly.

'I have no choice. We'll have to be grateful that Lizzie is making no complaint of rape against the boy.'

'But surely she consented to what happened?'

'That's no excuse. Lizzie is still a child, she's vulnerable. What if that young fool leaves her with a child to look after?'

Charlotte agreed reluctantly. She supposed Justin was right – having John in the same house as Lizzie was courting trouble. 'Isn't there some other way we can deal with this, send John off to a school somewhere, a boarding school, you could easily afford that, couldn't you, Mr Harvard?' She took a deep breath. 'Or you could finance a new school near the site of the old building. Couldn't you do that much out of the goodness of your heart?' Justin stared at her closely.

'Even if I could afford to buy the land and build a school, I can't believe you'd allow a boy like John into your class. He'd be there alongside the other young girls. How could I trust him to behave like a gentleman after this?'

Charlotte was silent. Justin spoke sense, she knew that, and yet suddenly her anger got the better of her good sense.

'You're so smug!' she said. 'It seems everyone in town knows you have a mistress, even the lowliest scullerymaid. What of the scandal if you got her with child? What about the reputation of your mistress then?'

His eyes became hostile. 'I am a grown man,' he said in a hard voice, 'old enough to arrange my affairs with discretion.' He crossed the room, took her in his arms and shook her. 'I need a woman in my life, I don't have the heart to live like a monk and, after all, I have no wife to betray, have I?'

She pushed against him. 'And you, a single man, who carelessly keeps a mistress, think yourself a pillar of society.' She pulled from his grasp. 'You are not fit to run a school, and I won't be a party to it. Find another teacher to fulfil your whims, Mr Harvard, because first thing in the morning, I'm leaving this house for good.'

Charlotte pushed him away and hurried up the stairs to her room. Flinging herself on the bed, she began to cry. Justin was no knight in shining armour after all, he was as base and common as any man lying drunk in a Swansea gutter, and she hated him.

CHAPTER TEN

In the morning, Charlotte regretted her hasty words of the night before. She packed her bag slowly, hoping for something to happen which would allow her to change her mind. And something did, in the form of Justin's elder daughter complaining that her head was aching. Justin called Charlotte as she came down the stairs.

'Miss Mortimer, I'm sorry to detain you, but it's Rhian. She's looking really pale and her skin is so hot to touch.'

'You should get a doctor then,' Charlotte said calmly.

'Just give me your opinion and then, if you wish, I'll fetch the trap for you and take you wherever you want to go.' He followed her to his daughter's room. 'Though I'd much prefer it if you stayed. The children need you, they've had so much change and upset in their young lives it would be hard for them to see you go.' He looked directly at her as they reached the door of the bedroom. 'It would be difficult for me too.'

Charlotte saw at once that Rhian was really sick. Her face was flushed with fever and she shivered restlessly, moving under the warm bedding Justin had wrapped around her. Charlotte put the back of her hand to Rhian's forehead.

'You're right. She has a very high temperature, and she has far too many blankets around her.'

'But my daughter is shivering – surely she needs the heat of the fire and the warmth of the bedding to keep her warm.'

'She is far too warm already,' Charlotte answered flatly. She opened the bedroom window. 'I think you had better send for the doctor, Mr Harvard. In the meantime, have one of the maids bring a flannel and some cool water so I can bathe Rhian's face and body. We must hope I can bring her temperature down.'

As Charlotte sponged Rhian's poor, hot flesh, she heard a misery-filled cry, and Morwen ran into the bedroom. She stood close to Charlotte and looked down at her sister. 'Is she going to die, Charlotte? Cook just told me Rhian would be lucky to live through the day.'

'Rhian is not going to die,' Charlotte said firmly. 'Not if I've got anything to say about it.'

Morwen buried her face in Charlotte's skirts and began to cry even harder. 'John has to go away because he made Daddy cross. Are you going to leave us too? Have we been naughty like John and Lizzie?' She gave a great gulping sob and Charlotte brushed back the child's soft curls.

'You've done nothing wrong and I promise I won't leave – not just now anyway.'

'Thank God for that!' The strong masculine voice startled Charlotte, and she turned to see Justin standing in the doorway with a man carrying a bulging leather bag – the doctor, Charlotte surmised.

The two men crossed to the bed. 'Dr Brand,' the older man said, bending over Rhian. 'She's got a fever.' Charlotte clucked her tongue in exasperation.

'We'd worked that out for ourselves, Doctor,' she said. 'What can we do about it?'

The doctor shook his head and listened to Rhian's chest, then he gently felt the glands in her neck. 'I can't see any signs of a rash, so it isn't measles.' He nodded to Charlotte. 'I expect you'd deduced that for yourself also,' he said edgily.

Charlotte nodded. 'I've been around

children long enough to know what measles looks like.'

Dr Brand continued his examination, opening Rhian's mouth and looking inside, holding her tongue down with a spatula. He straightened. 'Well, then, Mrs Harvard, what do you think ails the child?'

Charlotte looked at him in confusion. 'I'm not... I mean...' Her voice trailed away. It was Justin who explained.

'Miss Mortimer is a teacher, Doctor, and my girls have taken a great liking to her.'

'Well, that explains her shortness of tone. Teachers are invariably bossy – if you'll excuse me saying so, Miss Mortimer.'

Charlotte remained silent, knowing there was some justification for his words. The doctor finished his examination and put away his instruments.

'Well, Miss Mortimer?' Doctor Brand was waiting for her to offer her diagnosis.

'I'd say it was a very bad chill, Dr Brand, accompanied by a sore throat and a high fever.'

He nodded. 'Close enough. A cough might develop, though, hampering the use of her lungs, and that would delay the child's recovery, so watch her carefully, don't allow her up from bed for at least a week. Give her hot soups throughout the day and at night a little brandy in hot water.' A faint smile crossed his face. 'And because childish tastes are not like those of adults, add a little sugar to the mixture.'

Justin thanked the doctor and, as the sound of the men's footsteps faded, Morwen cuddled close to Charlotte.

'Is Rhian going to get better, Miss Mortimer?' Her eyes, huge and anxious, looked into Charlotte's face.

'Of course she is.'

Morwen hugged Charlotte, clinging to her legs like a limpet. Justin came back into the room and smiled for the first time that morning.

'I think Miss Mortimer will be busy looking after Rhian for the next week or so,' he said, 'but I'll still expect you to do your lessons, Morwen, do you understand?'

Morwen nodded eagerly. 'I'll be a very good girl, and then Miss Mortimer will stay with us, won't she?' She looked to her father to make everything right. Her faith in him was touching, and Charlotte felt her eyes brim with tears. She realized then that she had formed ties with the Harvard household, ties that would not easily be broken.

'I thought you were going to leave Mr Harvard's employ.' Luke was standing on the sandy beach looking out at the sea. Part of his mind admired the curve of the bay, the strong lines of the Mumbles lighthouse and the white water running over the rocks, but the other part of him was worrying about Charlotte. He turned to look at her. She had taken off her feathered hat, and it whipped to and fro in the sea wind as if it were a live bird.

'I know you can't leave the family in the lurch at such a time. As you say, the elder girl is still sickly and both children have come to depend on you. I do understand the position you are in, Charlotte.' He smiled. 'And, after all, if you do stay with the Harvards you will still be teaching some of the Swansea children to read and write.'

He saw her shake her head. 'I badly want to start up the old school again,' she said softly. 'I want all the children of Swansea to benefit from it, not just the well-off, well-connected children. Mr Harvard has made a lovely little classroom for us, but the children of the very poor are not allowed near Thornhill. In any case, it's too grand, too intimidating and too far away from where the poor live to be of real use.'

Luke saw the set of her lips and wondered just how far she would go to realize her ambition. Sometimes her dedication to her chosen path unsettled him.

He stood close to her and put his arm around her small waist. She was like a china doll: beautiful, ethereal even – but she had a will of iron.

'Why don't you marry me, Charlotte? You could still teach, couldn't you?' He laid his cheek on the softness of her hair and love for her overwhelmed him. The thought of having her in his arms, possessing her, teaching her the secrets of being a woman, warmed his blood. 'I wouldn't expect you to give up your dreams.'

Her reply was edged with impatience. 'It's not a dream,' she said, 'it will be reality, you just wait and see.' She hesitated. 'Look, Luke, I'd better get back.'

'Why?' His heart sank. 'Don't you want to be with me any more, Charlotte?'

'Of course I want to be with you, I've spent most of the day with you, but you must realize I have new responsibilities, the girls are not just my pupils now, they've become much closer than that.'

'And what about John?' Luke's voice was deep with the hurt he was feeling. 'Have you forgotten about him?'

Her face flushed and Luke knew he'd made her angry. 'Why do you think I want the old school back?'

Luke felt he'd said enough. 'Come along, then, I'll walk you back home.' Home – that's how he thought of Thornhill now – as Charlotte's home. But more worryingly, so did she.

Dinner was over in the Harvard household. The girls were tired, Rhian still pale from her enforced stay indoors and Morwen, her eyes closing sleepily, was ready for bed. Charlotte saw the girls to their bedrooms. Morwen and Rhian had imprinted their own tastes and interests on them. Morwen had dolls set around the place, on the deep window ledges and the rattan chairs. On the walls were dark and beautiful pictures of fairies and a huge picture of moonlight over a frosted landscape of hills and dales. Morwen loved to write and she'd attempted some poems. Young as she was, they expressed vivid truths. Her love of writing reminded Charlotte of her sister Letty. Perhaps one day Morwen would become a writer too.

Rhian's room was different. It held a sensible table for writing and a bookcase filled with practical books on etiquette and household hints. Already, Rhian had begun to put together a collection of recipes, tied with a black ribbon and covered with some thick, discarded wallpaper. Rhian would one day make a fine wife and mistress of her own household.

Justin was waiting for her when she returned to the sitting room. He handed her a beautiful glass, the contents gleaming bronze and gold. 'Brandy?' Without waiting for a reply, he put the glass into her hands.

'Charlotte, sit down, I want to talk to you.' It was more like a command than a request and Charlotte found herself obeying him.

She felt that what he was going to say was important. Perhaps it was about the school, a new one to be built to replace the old, a school where poor children could find a way to escape their circumstances, people like John, bright, intelligent, but with no one to shape his future for him.

'You seem to be getting along with my girls very well,' he began. 'I want to thank you for what you did when Rhian was so sick. I'm very much aware that she still needs care. Both my girls have come to rely on you for comfort and affection.'

Charlotte waited impatiently for him to go on. She realized she was sitting on the edge of her seat, expectant, though she didn't know why. His next words were a shock.

'I would like to marry you.' His statement fell into the silence, and Charlotte sat back in her chair, almost spilling the brandy into her lap. She took a sip, and the strong taste of the liquor ran like fire down her throat.

'But I don't love you,' she said, and immediately knew how foolish she sounded. 'In any case, there's the matter of my fiancé.' She stared at him. 'And why on earth would you want to marry me?'

'I want a mother for my children,' he said. There it was: no mention of affection for her, no sentiment at all, just a flat proposal.

'If that's all you want, you could marry one of many ladies in Swansea, any one of them willing and eager to marry you.'

'You've noticed?' His words were spoken with a hint of dry humour. 'But those ladies have dreams of marrying a rich man, a man with a good future before him, what they call a good prospect.'

'And so what would be different about me?'

Justin rose from his chair and stared into the fire, swirling the liquid round and round in his glass as if looking for inspiration. 'I loved my wife very much,' he said at last. 'I will never be able to replace her, I know that. But my daughters have needs, they want someone to love them, not a woman who will scarcely notice their existence. I have observed affection between you and the girls – more than affection: they have come to love you.'

Charlotte put down her glass, staring as though mesmerized at the glint of light on the brandy inside it. She looked up at him at last.

'And what is in it for me?' she said icily. 'Why should I give up my freedom, be chained to your house and your children? And why should I put aside the man I'm betrothed to?'

'I notice your fiancé comes last on your list of priorities.' He returned to his seat. 'This marriage would be an agreement between us,' he said. 'I know how strong your desire to build a new school near the river is, to bring to the children of the lower orders a sound foundation on which to build their lives. You could have all that, Charlotte, and more, I promise you.'

Charlotte thought of Luke, a good, solid man, a man who loved her. How could she let him down so badly? She felt a shock tingle in her fingertips: she was actually considering this, this business proposition. How could she be so fickle? And yet a new school, a place where she could bring so much to the uneducated children of what Justin thought of as the 'lower orders'? To raise up these very children was her aim in life, to make a difference to their prospects.

'Of course you would have your own room.' Justin's soft, seductive voice broke into her thoughts. 'I would not expect any conjugal rights.' He made a wry face. 'As you so succinctly pointed out some time ago, I have my lady friend. I would not ask for nor need anything of that sort from you.'

His words were flat like sea-washed pebbles and, for some reason she didn't understand, they angered her. She stood up. 'No,' she said, 'it is impossible.'

'Nothing is impossible. Just think about it – your own purpose-built school with anything you feel you need. No financial problems, nothing to bother about except teaching the children.' He paused for a moment. 'And it would do my girls good to see how the other children progress, especially John Merriman, of course.'

John – now there was a thought. She had a great affection for the boy, had kept in touch with him and, to give Justin credit, he had treated John fairly. As for little Lizzie, even when it became clear she was with child, he had managed to find a household to take her in as kitchenmaid.

'Just think about it for a few days,' Justin said. 'I won't press you on the matter – but think of the poor of Swansea and how you could help them. Now, you may retire, if you wish. I have to go out.'

'Of course,' Charlotte said edgily. 'It wouldn't do to keep your lady friend waiting, would it?' Now why had she said that? It indicated that she cared about the affair, and she most certainly did not.

He half smiled. 'Goodnight to you, Miss Mortimer. I'll doubtless see you in the morning.'

Feeling dismissed, she left the room and made her way up the stairs. A good fire was burning in the ornate grate and, closing the door to her room, Charlotte stood before it gratefully, feeling rather chilled.

'It's utter madness!' she said in a whisper, watching the flames dance and lick up the chimney. 'Not worth my consideration.'

She kicked off her boots and slumped on to the bed, staring up at the ceiling, wondering what a marriage without love, without even a trace of affection, would be like.

She'd never let herself think about the intimacies of marriage. Luke was like a much-loved friend, she'd never thought about lying with him, allowing him to touch her, own her, possess her. He'd never stirred those feelings within her, she reflected, but then, she felt, marriage would somehow miraculously change all that.

Of course, she'd experienced the remarriage of her dear father, Jolly, the man the townspeople of Swansea loved and respected, had seen the love that had flowered between him and Ella. She'd thought of all that in relation to herself and Luke but she'd never considered the act married couples shared; she had no carnal desire for Luke. Did that mean she didn't really love him?

Suddenly weary, Charlotte began to prepare for bed. She needed to sleep, to clear her mind of everything troubling. Perhaps in the morning, everything would be sorted out.

She stared around the room. It was like home to her now, a comfortable, familiar place where she could relax at the end of each day. And it could be hers for ever if she accepted Justin's proposition. Heavily, she sighed, her thoughts became hazy and, thankfully, she welcomed the sleepiness that swept over her and gave herself to its comforting hold.

CHAPTER ELEVEN

In the days that followed Justin's proposal of marriage, Charlotte was swayed one way and then another. She thought of the school, of the good she could do the poor of the town. John Merriman could continue his education – with help, he could rise high, perhaps even attend university. The thought touched the heart of her ambition, the hunger to make a difference to the lives of the children who lived beneath the blight of the copperworks.

Her conscience pricked her as she thought of Luke, good, kind Luke, who loved her. But then the regret swiftly passed and her thoughts turned to Justin Harvard, seeing not the man but the funds she needed to realize her dream.

She saw very little of Justin. He was true to his word, giving her time to weigh up the pros and cons of her situation. In a way, little of her lifestyle would change; she would be married but still her own woman. It would be in some ways an enviable situation – wife, albeit in name only, of one of the most influential men in Swansea.

It was afternoon, and Charlotte was in her

room. The children had gone out with their father, leaving Charlotte to get on with her chores. She was sitting at the writing desk. She had finished her letters to her far-away family. She folded the letter to Ella, her stepmother, and sealed it. Soon it would wing its way across the Atlantic Ocean. As for now, she should be out in the garden breathing in the fresh spring breeze that swayed the soft curtains wafting in the scents of the new buds.

She looked down at her last page of good, cream writing paper and her own neat hand and wondered at the words she had written to Letty, her dear sister.

My dearest sister Letty

I must tell you some exciting news. I've received a proposal of marriage from my employer, Justin Harvard. He is a fine, honest man, rich and yet with a social conscience, who promises me a school of my own for any children I would choose to teach. But I would like your advice – it would be a loveless marriage, and I would have to disappoint Luke, who is a good man, and live only for my career. Please let me know your thoughts.

Your loving sister
Charlotte

It would take a long time for the letter to

reach Letty, longer still before Charlotte would have any reply, too late to receive caution or encouragement. She knew that she would have to make her own decisions. But writing the letter brought home to Charlotte just what she would be giving up – a proper marriage and children of her own. But then, did she want children of her own? The way she felt now, she would prefer to be 'mother' to Rhian and Morwen and a classroom full of students.

Charlotte crushed up the neatly written page and threw it into the waste-paper basket. A walk might help to clear her mind. She stepped on to the large landing outside her bedroom. A fine walnut table stood against the wall at the far side bearing an Etruscan vase filled with the first tentative blooms of spring. Their perfume mingled with the scent of bees' wax. The winter was well and truly over and spring would be a good time to build a new school.

Charlotte stood on the first stair, noting the silence of the downstairs rooms. Without Justin and the girls, the house seemed empty. She felt alone, even though she knew that in the kitchen Cook and the maids would be busy preparing a high tea of bread, butter and jam and a variety of cakes for when the little family returned home.

Charlotte realized in those silent moments that, if she married Luke, she would have to leave this life behind her. She had become part of the household now, used to taking care of the girls, used even to sitting with Justin on the nights he stayed at home, she reading her books on the history of schools, of teaching methods, and he reading the newspapers. Already they had become like an old married couple, used to each other's presence, making no demands of each other, comfortable as an old pair of well-worn house slippers, uncluttered by passion.

It was cool in the garden, and Charlotte settled herself on the bench that lay deep within the maze. It was a private place, a lovely, peaceful place. Here Charlotte could think. She took out her writing pad and, pencil in hand, began a list of pluses and minuses under the heading 'Marriage' followed by the names of both men.

Under Justin's name she'd written the school as the main plus. Then came self-interest, contentment, comfort and, lastly, no emotional ties between them except for the children.

The list under Luke's name was virtually identical, but with the addition of a great affection. Was that really all there was between them?

After a while, she lay down the pencil and paper – she was getting nowhere. It was with a feeling of relief that she heard the rumble of wheels on the long drive that curved from the green hills outside the grounds towards the graceful arched doorway of Thornhill.

Charlotte heard the happy chatter and laughter of the children. They had obviously enjoyed the day out and now they were home they were looking for her. She felt the lift of pride and strong affection, even love, which drew her to them.

She heard her name being called. She sat still, a smile curving her mouth. Soon the girls would realize where she was hiding and come to find her. The thought gave her a rush of happiness that brought tears of warm emotion to her eyes.

It took only a few minutes to see the smiling face of Morwen peering around a hedge, laughing with triumph as she caught sight of Charlotte.

'Charlotte!' Morwen, always the more demonstrative of the children, wound warm arms around her neck.

'You should have come with us.' Rhian showed less enthusiasm than her younger sister and sat decorously beside Charlotte. 'We saw a great many people, most of them very boring.' Rhian liked to act as if she were much older than her years. 'Your Mr Luke Lester was at the town hall. He gave an address on the state of the poor housing on the east bank of the river, and do you know what he said?'

Charlotte had stiffened on hearing Luke's

name. 'Go on,' she said.

'He said that some poor people are still drinking water from the river. Can you believe such ignorance?'

Charlotte nodded. 'Yes, I can believe it. Some people are not educated, you see, they don't realize that many sicknesses come from bad water.'

The older folk of the town might be past educating, but their children and grandchildren were not. Someone needed to inform the older people of the dangers of poor hygiene, and it seemed that Luke was doing his best. They had grown up with the belief that river water was drinkable. Even though proper sewerage and water supplies had come to Swansea more than half a century earlier, the townspeople would still drink and urinate in the river water without realizing the potential damage to their health.

The young would know better, if Charlotte had her way.

That was the moment she knew that she would take up Justin's offer and marry him; it was a sacrifice she was prepared to make so long as it helped future generations of Swansea folk to enjoy a better life. If she felt a little bit holier than thou, she pushed the thought aside. She would speak to Luke at the earliest opportunity. It was not a task she relished, but she had to tell him.

After his speech at the town hall, Luke felt he had let the audience down in some way. Despite his gifts at oratory, he had somehow failed, and this had been underlined by the shuffling of the people sitting in the hall. Some, nearer the back, had taken the easy way out and escaped through the large doors into a splash of sunlight.

Later, he took a walk to the docklands end of the long, curving Swansea bay. There was a ship sailing in on the incoming tide, and he stepped out on to one of the wooden struts around the dock. There, he felt as if he could almost touch the ship. He sat with his legs dangling over the deep water of the dock. A buoy bobbed and swayed in the wash of the tide.

Charlotte would have been able to reach the people of Swansea more than he ever would. She would have delivered her message with humour and passion. He had seen her, in her enthusiasm for teaching, become flushed and pretty and, most of all, powerful. He ached with love for her; he'd missed her since she'd become so involved with Justin Harvard's family. But now, he was about to meet her in the lovely gardens of Victoria Park, just a short walk away.

She was there before him, sitting with her ankles primly crossed, staring as though fascinated at the fountain throwing diamond drops of water from the mouth of a stone fish into the wide bowl beneath.

'Good evening, Miss Mortimer,' he said, a hint of laughter in his voice. He was so pleased to see her that he wanted to clasp her in his arms, to kiss her, so she would share the passion he felt. But she wouldn't welcome such an outward show of emotion.

As he sat beside her, she reached for his hand, and he felt thrilled by the feeling of her small fingers twining in his.

'I have to speak to you, Luke.' Her voice was sombre. 'I have something important to say.'

He felt a thrill of elation rush through him. She was ready, at last, to name the day. Her next words came like a deluge of icy water thrown in his face.

'I can't marry you.'

'But ... what on earth do you mean, Charlotte? We're engaged to be married, you're wearing my ring.'

'I know and I'm sorry.' She was pale. Even her lips had lost their soft, glossy look as she pressed them together.

'If he has dared to lay a finger on you...' There was no need to mention the man's name. Hate rose in Luke like bile. 'Has he dishonoured you in any way? If so, I'll kill him with my bare hands.'

'No, of course not!' Charlotte was impatient with him, and Luke made an effort to curb his anger.

'Then what has happened to change your mind? I thought you were mine. I love you, Charlotte, I would lay down my life for you.' He felt like a callow youth. His voice shook and his dignity had vanished.

'I'm sorry. Marriage to you, dear though you are, just isn't the right path for me, or for you, if you're truthful.' She looked at him with limpid eyes. 'We have affection between us like brother and sister but I feel no passion for you in my heart, Luke.'

He could see she meant it. 'But you have not yet experienced passion,' he protested. 'That comes with the union a man makes with a woman in the bridal bed.'

'You may be right, Luke.' Charlotte was almost whispering. 'But I'm not ready for it, for marriage or for passion. I'm so very sorry.'

'And if I gave you time to think it over? So much has happened to put thoughts of love out of your mind – we lost the school, you lost your home – but we can bring it back, everything.'

'I know, and I've thought it all out, but the change in me is...' She hesitated. 'I searched my mind and realized that when the school went, so did our relationship. What we had was a mutual ambition to help the children of Swansea.' She rubbed her eyes. 'It was a worthy wish but not enough to make a marriage between us work. That's all we did have, Luke, if we're honest, a desire, no, more than that, a need to educate the children of the poor.'

'That's not what *I* feel, Charlotte. The need to help, of course, but my heart burns for love of you – *you*, not the damned school.'

'You can argue, we can quarrel, but I'd rather not.' He saw her face was white and set. Whatever she had once felt for him, she was like a stranger now. He stood up. He felt his shoulders tug into a straight line, his head was high, he would not stay and beg her on hands and knees to marry him. He had his pride, after all.

'Very well, Charlotte, if that is your decision I will have to accept it.' He paused for a moment, looking down at her bowed body. The line of her face was pure, like that of a Greek goddess, her hair glinted in the late sun and the urge to kiss her was almost unbearable. 'Goodbye, Charlotte.' He felt the words choke in his throat and turned away from her abruptly so she wouldn't see his tears.

'Luke, I'm so sorry.' The anguish in her voice almost halted him. He hesitated for a moment. 'I'm sorry,' she repeated, 'but I know we've made the right decision.'

Only when he was out of her sight, walking among the parkland trees did he give full vent to his tears. He leaned against the trunk of a tree, his face rubbing against the hard, uneven bark. 'Oh, Charlotte, my love,' he whispered. 'I'll be desolate without you.' But no one heard, and the words were carried away on the soft spring breeze to be lost for ever.

CHAPTER TWELVE

Charlotte was surprised and a little disappointed that, over the next few weeks, Justin did not mention his proposal of marriage to her. He had noticed the absence of her betrothal ring – she saw him glance at her naked finger and, for a brief moment, she thought she saw a glint of triumph in his eyes – but for now, he kept out of her way, busy with his own affairs.

That night there was to be a dinner party at Thornhill. The maids were busily dusting and Cook was in her domain making a grand feast. And, so far, Justin had given her no indication that he wanted her to be there. Stubbornly, she had no intention of asking. More often than not, she was excluded from such evenings; being only tutor to his children, she had no place at his dining table, not when he had guests.

To her surprise, Justin stopped Charlotte in the hall just as she was going up to her room to while away the afternoon with a new book.

'I'd like you to dine with us tonight,' he said brusquely. 'Wear something nice but not too showy, would you?'

She was dismayed: she had nothing appropriate.

'Oh, Justin, Mr Harvard,' she called, and he turned to face her.

'Is there a problem?'

'Well, yes – I'm not sure I've anything suitable to wear.'

He sighed as if he had the weight of the world on his shoulders. He took her arm and propelled her upstairs to the master bedroom. There, he flung open the doors of the huge, well-polished wardrobe.

'These belonged to my wife. See if there's anything among them. There's some jewellery, too, in the box there on the dressing-table. I'll expect you to be with me to receive my guests at six-thirty.'

He turned and left her standing in the bedroom as though he had no more interest in her.

Charlotte glanced around her. The signs of his masculinity were stamped on the room – there were no frilly bedclothes, no knick-knacks on the dressing-table beside the jewellery box. The only evidence to show he had shared the room with his wife was a small painting in a silver frame of a young woman with unfashionable flowing hair and a flimsy dress, revealing against the sunlight. His wife had been beautiful.

Charlotte turned her attention to the wardrobe. She could see at once that the dresses, hanging down like flat, dead bodies, would be too large for her. She took one out, a simple, well-cut gown of dark blue; with a belt and a few pins she could make it do for the evening, she decided. From the little box she took out a necklace of sapphires and a large sapphire ring. She slipped it on to her finger, but it was far too big for her and she quickly replaced it. For a moment she felt guilty and sad, and she closed the box with a snap. She had no right to wear a ring, not now she was no longer engaged to Luke.

Later, standing in front of the mirror in her own bedroom, she saw at once that the deep-blue gown suited her. The bodice, with the help of some safety pins, fitted her tolerably well, and the skirt rustled around her slim ankles, the shot silk changing colour in the brightness of the electrical lighting.

Her hair, always unruly, was thick and curly and unfashionably long. She'd attempted to cut it once into the short bob that was in vogue but her hair would just not stay flat and at last she'd given up, let it grow. Now she piled it on the top of her head in a rough chignon.

Her eyes gleamed with violet flecks against the glow of the sapphire necklace, and her cheeks were pink. For the first time, she wondered how she must look to Justin Harvard. Did he think her beautiful? She wasn't sure. Still, he would be the means to help her achieve her dream of a new school. Surely it wasn't wrong to use a man to gain what she wanted so badly? Hadn't women done just that from Cleopatra to Elizabeth I? Her reflections didn't make her feel any better. With a lift of her chin, she left the room. She had made her choices and now she would have to abide by them.

Luke had found a new position at the grammar school perched on the hill above the town. Situated as it was on the other side of the hill, turning away from the stink and fumes of the copperworks, Fair Pastures was spared the worst of the hovering yellow cloud that hung perpetually over the workers' cottages on the eastern side of the river.

It was a good school, the rooms were bright and airy and the windows looked out over the stretch of sea in the distance. The staff of teachers was enthusiastic about informing bright pupils, the children of affluent parents, and Luke's brief was to teach classics of Greek and Roman literature, a job that was neither as demanding nor as satisfying as teaching the ignorant children of the poor their sums and their letters.

Luke had managed to get John Merriman a place at the school by claiming that he was the boy's guardian and, most evenings, back at his house, Luke spent an hour with John, bringing him up to the standard of education enjoyed by the other children.

At evenings and weekends, John was working with a saddler, a friend of Luke's who had a shop in Gomer Place, near the docks, and at nights John slept on a mat in the back of the saddler's premises. Luke was satisfied that he was doing his best for the boy. Just as well, Luke thought: Charlotte seemed to have forgotten all about John, brushing the boy out of her mind as she had brushed Luke away.

Now, standing in the staff room, looking through the window at the tiny waves of the ocean timidly creeping up to the shore of golden sand, Luke allowed himself to think of Charlotte. He missed her so much that the feeling physically hurt him. Her rejection of him was like a heavy weight in his gut; life had little meaning for him now. He knew she would despise him for giving up the struggle to educate the poor and taking a comfortable post in Fair Pastures grammar school, but he needed to work, and teaching was the only job he knew.

He felt anger then. Charlotte had taken the easy way out herself: she was working privately, teaching in the comfortable surroundings of Justin Harvard's beautiful home. She had called it a means to an end, the end being enough money to set up a new school in the town, a school that once again would be there for the poor. But that was an impossible dream. Even if she had stayed faithful to him and they had put their salaries together, he and she would never have had enough money to build and run a school.

Sighing, Luke picked up his copy of the *Aeneid,* and a flash of excitement ran through him. The youngsters in his class were enjoying Virgil's adventure story, particularly the romance between Aeneas and Dido, Queen of Carthage. He had to edit out any unseemly description of the affair as he went along, but at least he'd caught the imagination of the pupils, and that, to Luke, was a taste of triumph.

He left the staff room and then paused for a moment, breathing in the now familiar smells of the school; of ink and the musty smell of books, of damp clothing when it rained and the sweet scent of flowers from the gardens when it was sunny.

He allowed himself one more painful thought about Charlotte – her sweet arms around his neck, the softness of her lips touching his – and then, with a pain that was almost beyond bearing, he walked briskly along the corridor to his classroom.

The evening was proving a success, though Charlotte was aware that the ladies there were curious about her presence at the dinner table of the rich and influential widower Justin Harvard.

Charlotte had hoped to be inconspicuous, but when Justin seated her at his right hand, it was clear he meant her to be his hostess. Beside her, Martin Southwark, industrialist and perhaps the only bachelor at the dinner party, leaned in close to her, and she could smell the scent of hair oil. It reminded Charlotte of the entertainers who had performed at the Palace Theatre, once owned by her late father.

She felt a drag of nostalgia. She missed her family so much, and yet she'd known at once she was destined not to sail with them to the new land across the sea. Swansea was where her destiny lay, but not even in her wildest dreams had she imagined herself seated in the dining room of a rich man with the glitter of silver cutlery and crystal glasses around her.

She became aware that Martin Southwark was whispering in her ear. 'You are a very beautiful woman, my dear. I expected a woman from the working classes of Swansea to look like a drudge,' he continued, unaware of Charlotte's growing annoyance. 'I expected an elderly woman to be engaged to teach Justin's children, and someone who looked more like a servant than a guest at Justin's table. And–' he paused and lifted the sapphire necklace, his fingers lingering against her skin '–wearing such baubles, perhaps you are more than a teacher to my dear friend Justin.' He paused, his eyes staring insolently at her breasts.

Charlotte quashed the desire to slap the man's face. Instead, she moved as far away from him as she could, forcing him to relinquish the necklace. Ignore him, she told herself, he was an ignorant pig who, if the gossips were correct, had built up his fortune by dubious means, ruining a few honest businessmen on the way.

The coffee was being served and with a deft movement of her hand, Charlotte tipped his cup so that a small amount of very hot coffee landed in his lap. He gave a shout of pain and outrage, and Charlotte was quick to apologize.

'I'm so sorry Mr ... sorry, your name escapes me but, here, let me help you.' She pushed her napkin into his groin so that the heat in his well-cut trousers was pressed against his delicate parts.

He squirmed away from her and stared at her with half-closed, accusing eyes. 'I think you did that on purpose, you low-born bitch,' he whispered in her ear.

Charlotte put her hand to her mouth and spoke in a loud voice. 'I'm sorry, but did I hear you right, did you just call me a bitch?'

He went pale, and then a rich red flushed into his face. 'I'm sure you misheard me, madam,' he said. 'There is no way that I would refer to any lady in such terms.'

After a moment, Charlotte nodded. 'Your apology accepted.'

Justin looked suspiciously at both of them, and his eyes narrowed as they rested on Martin Southwark's face. Martin managed a smile in return to Justin's gaze.

'I do apologize, but I assure you the woman – er – lady misheard.'

Charlotte nodded. 'Of course I must have misheard, you are quite right, Mr ... er ... um, no gentleman would call a lady a bitch.'

The little scene had silenced the other guests but, suddenly, they all started to speak again and the silence filled with the tinkle of spoons on saucers. After a moment, Martin Southwark accepted a newly filled coffee cup from the servant. He deliberately turned away from Charlotte, his shoulders hunched, virtually blocking her view of the other guests. None of this escaped Justin's notice and what had happened had clearly made him angry, whether it was with Martin Southwark or with her,

Charlotte didn't know.

After coffee, the guests drifted away from the table. Justin indicated that the brandy and cigars should be served. Charlotte watched him, marvelling at how the effect of his presence subdued the chatter of his guests. He rose to his feet, and the silence was immediate.

'I have an announcement to make,' he said easily. He looked at Charlotte and smiled. 'I have asked the lady at my side, Miss Charlotte Mortimer, daughter of the late Mr "Jolly" Mortimer, if she will be my wife. I thought this would be a good time to get an answer. I can only hope it will be in the affirmative.'

The eyes of the guests were turned towards her, and Charlotte felt the hot colour sweep into her face. This was the last thing she had expected, a public announcement of their plan to marry.

Justin took her hand and drew her towards him. She stood at his side, very aware of the height of him, tinglingly aware of his hand holding hers.

He took a small box from his pocket and flipped it open, and the brightness of the large diamond flashed in Charlotte's eyes.

She felt a stab of panic, she wanted to run away and hide. She longed for her little house and her safe love for Luke and the humdrum way her life once was.

'And, now, my dear, if you mean to accept my proposal, may I?' Justin lifted her hand to his lips and then slipped the ring on her finger, looking down at her as though he were an ardent lover, not a man making a cold bargain with a woman he scarcely knew.

He bent towards her. 'Charlotte, will you show the ladies to the drawing room? We men will join you for the piano recital I have planned to celebrate the occasion.'

Charlotte stood for a moment, staring at the big diamond glimmering on her hand and comparing it to the tiny emerald and diamond ring Luke had given her. The diamond had probably cost enough money to build and maintain a fine school for a good number of years, and the thought brought her no joy.

As she moved to pass, Martin Southwark leaned forward to whisper in her ear. 'I didn't know your cunning little plan was to hook a fish with more money than sense. He must be out of his mind to take on a cheap little scrubber from the slums of Swansea.'

Charlotte beamed at him, and he blinked rapidly in surprise. 'Thank you for your warm congratulations, Mr ... er ... em ... well, thank you.'

He concealed his chagrin well but his eyes glittered with malice and Charlotte hurried to the door knowing she had made an enemy for life.

CHAPTER THIRTEEN

'I'll expect you to wear a white gown, of course.' Justin looked at Charlotte's pale face and momentarily felt a rush of pity, then he steeled himself. He couldn't afford to think of her feelings: he had to concern himself with his future security and that of his daughters. He knew Charlotte was proud and independent, but some devil inside him pushed him into questioning her.

'Were you and Luke Lester ... intimate?'

He saw the blush stain her cheeks and then her eyes met his, blazing with anger and something he couldn't quite read.

'How dare you!' She stood up, and he saw her fiddle with the large diamond on her finger as if to twist it off. 'My past has nothing to do with you, I didn't ask for this marriage and I still don't understand why you want me to be your wife, but we can forget the whole ludicrous scheme, if that's what you want.'

'No.' Justin thought of the codicil in his father's will: the whole of his not inconsiderable fortune would come to Justin on condition he was well and truly married by the time he reached his thirtieth birthday.

No one, least of all Justin's late father, had anticipated that Justin would be a widower by the time he was twenty-five.

Justin's father had not lived to see his son's first marriage, nor had he known of the birth of his two granddaughters. And Justin, at twenty-nine, had been instructed by his solicitor, old Maurice Wagman, to obey the letter of the will, just to avoid complications – not to mention the gaggle of would-be heirs to the Harvard fortune if Justin didn't meet the requirements of the will to the letter.

'I know your business is in need of a shot in the arm,' Maurice Wagman had said. He was the only one who knew of the financial difficulties that beset the nickel works and perhaps the only man who would dare raise the subject so openly. He had been a family friend for many years.

Justin moved to the window and stared at the luscious gardens rolling away from him. He would never give up his house, his lands, his business, whatever it cost him.

He turned to glance at Charlotte, comparing her in his mind to his late wife. Lucinda had been fair-haired, delicate, ethereal; she had worshipped him and needed him. Charlotte was so different, with her mop of unruly dark hair, thick and curly. As for her character, she would never need any man other than to provide the money to ensure the success of her dream. No, he needn't feel sorry for her: she was getting what she wanted from the marriage, just as he was.

Justin knew he would never fall in love again: his wife, his darling Lucinda, had been his heart and soul, his very life. For a time after her death he had believed he wanted to die too. But he was pulled out of his despair by the needs of his girls, his lovely daughters. It was because of them and their evident love of Charlotte Mortimer that he had chosen the young schoolmistress as his bride.

Now he looked at her quizzically. 'I expect you'll want to get on with your plans for a new school as soon as possible,' he said. 'I know that's the only reason you agreed to this marriage, and I think it will be a bargain that will suit both of us.' He was on the point of telling her about the true reason he needed to marry, but held his tongue – care for his daughters, she would understand; the need for money, she might not.

She nodded. 'Don't worry, I know this is little more than a business arrangement between us, and I'll wear a white dress if that's what you want.'

He smiled dryly. 'We must observe the proprieties, keep up appearances – that sort of thing – if only for the sake of the girls.'

She sat down. 'What else have you planned?'

'Not much. I don't think a honeymoon will be necessary, in the circumstances. I will plead pressure of business keeping me at home. In any case, I wouldn't like both of us to be away from the girls, they are at a vulnerable age and–' He shrugged. 'I think you know what I mean.'

'I do,' she said, feelingly, and he half smiled. 'You and I thrown together for days on end would be hell for both of us.'

'Right then.' He rubbed his hands together as if washing them clean of the whole business of the marriage. 'That's enough talking now, you'd best go give the girls their lessons and, by the way, Charlotte–' he saw her pause in the doorway '–tell Rhian and Morwen about the wedding and try to make them believe it's the romantic idyll they will want it to be.'

Charlotte stood outside the sitting-room door trying to control the shivering that had suddenly seized her. Did Justin have to be so blunt, so cold in his denial of any face-saving mutual regard they might have for each other? He had spelled out the situation in a brutal way and it had taken the heart out of her. All right, they didn't love each other, but that was understood – he would get a permanent teacher and substitute mother for the girls while she would get her school – but couldn't they at least be friends? She smiled wryly. They would have what the old gothic romantics would call 'a marriage of convenience', but did that exclude enjoying a harmonious relationship?

In the schoolroom, Charlotte frowned to see Rhian perched on the top of her desk, her knees up to her chest, her hands wrapped around her legs. Morwen stood beside her sister, eyes wide as she gazed entranced at Charlotte. Rhian smiled like a conspirator.

'Lessons are late today and I think I know why,' she said. Charlotte sat down at her own desk and tapped the ruler against her hand.

'And what do you know?'

Rhian shrugged. 'Only that you've got something important to tell us.'

'Yes, I have.' Charlotte tried to infuse her voice with some enthusiasm; she needed the girls to believe the marriage was a happy one, engendered by love. 'I hope you'll be pleased.' She looked down at her fingers, took off the huge diamond and held it out to Rhian, who nodded and passed it quickly to her younger sister.

'Grandmother's ring. Mummy had a brand-new one when she married Daddy, but I don't think he would want to give you that.'

Charlotte felt Rhian was putting her well and truly in her place: she was second choice and Rhian was making sure she was aware of that.

'Told you, little squirt,' Rhian said disdainfully to Morwen. 'Daddy's proposed to Charlotte and she's accepted. They're going to be married, isn't that right?'

Charlotte nodded. 'I hope you will both be glad for us. I'm sure we're all going to be very happy together.'

Morwen gave the ring back to Charlotte and hugged her, clinging to her skirt and pressing her head against Charlotte's waist. 'You won't leave us, not like our mummy or the other teachers Daddy got for us did?'

'No, of course I won't go away and leave you. I'll never do that.'

'Daddy's only marrying her so she'll stay with us. Cook said something about money, then she spotted me listening and didn't say any more,' Rhian said in a matter-of-fact voice.

Charlotte was startled – so the servants knew the marriage was a sham and that Justin had bought a bride with the promise of money to build a school. A feeling of shame brought angry colour to her cheeks. How dare he discuss their plans within the hearing of Cook and the other members of the staff?

'But you do love Daddy, don't you?' Morwen asked pitifully. 'You love us as well, don't you?'

'Of course I love you.' Charlotte was

relieved to be let off the hook. 'I love both of you as much as if you were my own little girls.' They were the only family she would ever have.

She felt a momentary twinge of doubt. Was she doing the right thing, giving up all that most women hold dear, the love of a good man and the bearing of his children? Then she thought about the school. Without a decent education, there was nothing but poverty and drudgery ahead of the children who grew up in the slum areas of the town.

'Come along, girls.' Now Charlotte had rationalized her plans, she felt almost happy. She would soon achieve her ambition: she would have a fine new school and the challenge of eager young minds, she alone would be able to mould the raw clay, fashion her pupils into confident, knowledgeable citizens of Swansea. For now, that was all she wanted.

The church was crowded. Charlotte, in white, the girls in palest pink flanking her, entered the arch of the doorway and heard the beautiful strains of organ music reaching out to her like welcoming arms.

The interior of the church was splashed with spring sunshine, pale and luminous, falling across the altar like a blessing. Justin was standing in the aisle, tall and handsome and proud, and Charlotte wondered if he ever thought of offering up a prayer to heaven. Somehow, she doubted it.

And then she was at his side. She glanced up at him, but he was staring straight ahead, as though concentrating on the stained-glass window facing him and the jewel-bright light falling like a rainbow into the gloom of the church.

The vicar began the service with scant enthusiasm. It was as if he knew this marriage was far from the holy wedlock he was familiar with. Charlotte mumbled her responses, doubts assailing her even now. She was giving up her freedom, selling herself into a marriage that had no love in it.

She became aware of Morwen clutching at the back of her skirts, and her face softened. Yes, she would have love, at least for Justin's children.

Justin took her hand, and she was surprised at the warmth of his grip. He slipped the wedding band on to her finger, and she stared down at it glinting in the sunlight. And then the organ music swelled and Justin was leading her to the chancel, where they were to sign the book that made them legally man and wife.

Outside, the sun had strengthened, the glow of the roadway ahead shimmered before her eyes and Charlotte realized she was shedding foolish tears. A crowd gathered round the couple and at a short distance stood Luke, his face pale in the light, his shoulders slumped. She wanted to run to him, to plead with him to forgive her treachery, but Justin's hand was on her arm, guiding her towards the gaily decorated horse and carriage that was waiting to take them to a wedding feast at the Mackworth Hotel in the Stryd Fawr.

The dining room of the hotel was large and gracious. Iridescent lights flashed from the overhead chandeliers, pristine damask cloths covered the tables and spring flowers scented the air, the brightness of the blooms competing with the sun slanting in through the windows.

The guests at the wedding were Justin's friends, and some of the beautifully dressed ladies stared at Charlotte with open curiosity.

'How long have you known our dear Mr Harvard?' A voice spoke at her elbow and Charlotte became aware of the heavy perfume which drifted around the plump figure of the woman at her side.

'A fair time.' Charlotte spoke guardedly. 'Justin was governor of the school where I taught.'

'Oh, it's all so romantic ... and so sudden.' The woman's gaze ran over Charlotte's slim figure suspiciously. 'I'm Mrs Davina Gore Brown, a woman of note in the area, of course. And I did harbour the hope that it would be my daughter Mr Harvard chose for his bride.' Her pale blue eyes narrowed. 'And to think that such an elegant man would marry a schoolteacher. You are very lucky, do you know that?'

'If you'll excuse me–' Charlotte's tone was icy '–I see my husband is beckoning me to join him at the table.'

Justin took her hand and slipped it through his arm, not in any display of affection, she knew that, but appearances had to emphasize the fiction that this marriage was born out of love.

'Mrs Davina Gore Brown has made you look all pale and defensive.' There was a humorous lift to his eyebrows. 'Don't let your guard down with her. She's a bad loser, as you have no doubt learned. She thought her daughter would have a catch if she married me, as did half the good mothers of Swansea.' He said it flatly, without boasting. 'Sit down now and smile as my groomsman makes a little speech about us. Pretend you're a happy bride.'

Charlotte hardly listened to the speeches. She fixed her gaze on Justin in what she hoped was an adoring, bride-like way and turned away only when Morwen tapped her arm.

'You look like a fairy from the story books,' she said. 'So pretty, so happy, and I'm happy too, because you're going to be my new mother.' Charlotte felt warmed by the child's happiness.

She hardly tasted any of the food put in front of her. She picked at the quail and duck pâté, and when a hot meal of beef and horseradish sauce was served on a white china platter, she accepted only a little of the meat and helped herself to a few potatoes and vegetables, hoping no one would notice her lack of appetite.

She breathed a sigh of relief when at last the many courses of the meal and the speeches were over. She sat patiently, waiting for Justin to make a move to take her home. But crowds of guests surrounded them both and Charlotte's face felt stiff with the effort of smiling.

At last, Justin shouldered his way through the press of people and helped her into the gaily decorated carriage. Charlotte sat up straight, glancing now and then at the relaxed figure of her new husband, not believing any of this was really happening. Rhian and Morwen were allowed to ride with them and sat opposite her, the hems of their pink gowns like fallen petals around their feet.

Rhian waved to the crowd of guests, lifting her hand as though she were a queen, and as always, Morwen copied her, her small face beaming with enough happiness for all of them.

Charlotte gave a sigh of relief as the carriage finally turned in through the large gates of Thornhill. By then Morwen was half asleep, and Charlotte, still in her wedding gown, took the girls upstairs and helped them get ready for bed. Rhian disdained her help and climbed sleepily into her bed.

When they were tucked in among the quilts, Justin came to kiss them goodnight. 'You must kiss the bride, too,' Morwen said. 'You should have kissed her in the church, but you forgot.' Justin looked at Charlotte for a long moment before taking her in his arms and kissing her chastely on the cheek.

'Not like that, Daddy!' Rhian said, and there was a hint of spite in her voice. 'Kiss her properly. You are married now, remember?' Justin held Charlotte close and kissed her full on the lips. His mouth lingered on hers, and Charlotte had a sudden foolish desire to cling to him but then, abruptly, he released her.

Morwen giggled and clapped her hands. 'There we are. You're really married now, good and proper.'

Charlotte tried to regain her composure. 'Morwen!' She brushed down her skirts with hands that shook. 'I expect you to be grammatically correct when you speak, otherwise you're letting me down.'

Morwen put her hands over her mouth and giggled again. 'John Merriman always speaks like that,' she said.

Charlotte took a deep breath. 'You have no reason to copy John Merriman.' She turned to leave the room, her priorities in place again. No sentiment was to be allowed into this bargain she had made with Justin Harvard: he was nothing but the gateway to a new school and a new dawn in the education of the poor.

CHAPTER FOURTEEN

The building of the school was in full progress, the foundations dug near the old school. Charlotte had persuaded Justin that his outhouse would not be suitable. She stood a little away from the gangs of workmen and watched with a stab of triumph as the building began to take shape; she knew by now how big the sacrifice she'd made was. She had lost her freedom, for a start: as Justin Harvard's wife, she was expected to attend social functions with him and make a show of being a happy newly-wed. There was no chance of having children of her own either – but she would have a class full of them once she was teaching again, and here in front of her was the hard evidence that her sacrifice had not been in vain.

'Good morning, Mrs Harvard.' A voice

close to her ear made her turn away from the building work.

'Oh, Luke.' She felt flustered, not knowing how to act with the man she had once promised to marry. 'I hope you're keeping well.'

'As well as can be expected for a man who has been publicly humiliated.' His voice was hard, made more so by the way he spoke through clenched teeth. She stepped back from him. She had never seen Luke in this mood before and she felt a little afraid. He seemed to be breathing out hatred and malice, and his eyes glittered even though they were narrowed against the sunlight. She noticed for the first time that Luke's hair came into a widow's peak on his high, intelligent forehead. He was so clever, she respected him so much, and now she'd shamed him.

'I'm sorry, Luke, truly sorry, but you know how much the school means to me, don't you?'

'Oh, yes, I do know. You want it so badly, you'll prostitute yourself to get it.' He paused and turned away from her, and his profile stood out in relief against the brightness of the sky. He had a strong profile: a good nose, a square jaw. You would think him a good-looking man if it weren't for the way his mouth was clamped together like a sprung trap. Perhaps she'd had a lucky escape not marrying him. He turned and met her eyes, and for an instant he looked his old, gentle self.

'That man who bought you, he'll have no peace so long as he's married to you.'

'What do you mean? You've changed, Luke, so much.'

'And it's you who has changed me.' He gripped her arm, and she could feel the pressure of his forefinger and thumb bruising her flesh. His head jutted forward as though he were going to kiss her and, instinctively, she tried to pull away from him.

'Take your hands off my wife. Now!' Justin was astride a grey stallion. He flicked a long whip that seemed an extension of his hand dangerously near Luke's face. Charlotte had not heard him coming.

Luke gave her arm another painful squeeze and then dropped his hand to his side. 'Good morning, Mr Harvard.' Luke's voice was low. 'Make the most of your wife. You might not have her long.'

Justin dismounted. 'Is that a threat?' Lights of bronze and gold reflected off his hair.

Luke laughed. 'I just meant to say that, once the school is built, you will play second fiddle to it, take my word. Charlotte is driven by this urge to educate the children of the poor at whatever cost to herself or anyone close to her.' He grimaced, the smile gone from his eyes. 'I'm a prime example of that, as you well know.'

Justin took Charlotte's arm in a proprietary gesture and, without uttering another word to Luke, drew her towards the school. 'That man is a bully!' Justin said. 'I don't understand what you saw in him, Charlotte.'

She trembled. 'Neither do I.' She glanced back over her shoulder and saw Luke still standing where she had left him.

'If he ever threatens you, be sure to let me know,' Justin said.

Charlotte didn't look at him, she wouldn't let him see how shaken she was by the way Luke had spat venom at her. That was a side of Luke she had never seen before and didn't want to see ever again.

The foreman on the site of the building, Ben Taylor, tipped the brim of his cap to them as they drew nearer. 'Building work is going well, sir,' he said, wiping a rag across his forehead. 'Weather's on our side, see?' He smiled at Charlotte. 'Would you like to step into your new schoolroom, Mrs Harvard?'

Smiling back, she stepped over the marker that indicated the lie of the building; it comprised two big rooms, a dinner hall and a small corridor at the side with a staff room and a WC. Ben Taylor pointed a hand covered in red brick dust.

'That there is going to be two more lavvies, if you'll pardon me saying so, missis.' He nodded thoughtfully. 'There'll

176

be lavvies by yer for the boys and lavvies the other side for the girls, and hooks to hold coats and things.'

Charlotte knew what he meant by 'things'. Some children had never owned a coat, and if the weather was cold or wet, they covered themselves with washed potato sacks. Swansea had not come far in the last fifty years.

Charlotte couldn't resist a glance over her shoulder but, to her relief, Luke had disappeared and, if she had ever known him at all, he would be regretting the vile words he'd uttered. Justin left her for a moment to inspect the timber allocated for the construction of the roof.

She took the plans for the building from Ben and looked round at the skeleton of her school. Her spirits lifted. Soon, very soon, she would be seated behind her high desk teaching the children to read and write. Justin returned to her side. His voice was light when he spoke.

'Anyone would think you were staring at the Holy Grail.'

Charlotte clasped her hands together. 'In a way I am. This is the beginning of my life's ambition.'

'Which is?' Justin arched a dark eyebrow.

'You know that already. My ambition has always been to have my own school.' The words spilled from Charlotte's lips. She was so excited she could hardly contain herself.

'And now I have achieved it. Thanks to you,' she added as an afterthought.

Charlotte saw him staring at her as though seeing her for the first time. He took her arm and threaded it through his own as he led her back to where his horse was being held by one of the young apprentices employed on the site.

'You will ride with me.' He hoisted himself easily into the saddle. The magnificent animal he had chosen from the stables was well-built, a fine, huge stallion.

He held out his hand and lifted her on to the horse and she fitted into the saddle in front of him. Charlotte felt a flash of desire as his arms closed around her. He flicked the reins and the animal moved smoothly into a canter.

'Lean back against me if it will make you feel safer. After all, we *are* married.' He sounded amused as he clucked at the stallion. She saw immediately what he meant: she was forced against his broad chest.

The wind tugged at her hair, flaring her skirts out around her. She saw a wall looming up on them. It was solid stone and she held her breath as Justin urged the horse into the jump. Charlotte laughed aloud in delight. The wind was tossing her hair across her eyes, so she didn't see the figure of Luke standing on a low rise of rock, tears raining down his cheeks.

Luke watched the flying figures disappear into the distance and angrily dashed away the moisture from his eyes. In that moment he didn't know if he loved or hated Charlotte. How could she do this to him?

Justin Harvard looked like a man very well pleased with himself. At night she would be lying with him, close in a warm bed. How could any man resist the charms of a beautiful woman like Charlotte? The bitter gall of jealousy, like venom in his blood, was poisoning all he'd hoped and dreamed of. 'Forget her!' he said out loud, but he knew that wasn't going to be easy.

'I'm taking you to the home of one of my colleagues tonight.' Justin was standing at the door of her bedroom and Charlotte, about to go inside, was startled by his sudden appearance. 'I want you to wear some of the diamond jewellery I've left on your dressing-table.' His tone was perfunctory, his eyes as they looked down at her hooded. He was so handsome, in a dark, brooding way, slim at the hips and broad at the shoulder. Suddenly Charlotte remembered the way she'd been thrilled by his closeness as they rode the magnificent horse, and she was angry with herself. 'I don't take orders,' she said. 'Even from you.'

Justin shrugged. 'Please yourself.' He left

179

her then, and Charlotte was curious to see the diamond jewellery he referred to.

As she entered the bedroom, the gleam of colour attracted her eyes to the dressing-table. Justin had not thought to put the expensive items in a case but had left them in a shimmering heap on the table.

Full of wonder, she picked up a diamond necklace. The stones were perfectly matched and a huge ruby hung from the blazing white of the diamonds like a teardrop of red wine. There was a matching bracelet and pair of earrings. Gently, she put them back on to the table.

The gems had probably belonged to Justin's late wife and somehow she felt as though she were intruding on a private world, a world in which she had no part. Instead, she clipped on a simple silver locket her father had once bought for her birthday. How she missed him, how she hated thinking of his death and the poverty they had all faced once he was gone.

Tears misted her eyes and her image in the mirror became blurred. Her family had been a close, loving one, she'd shared her childhood with her four sisters and her baby brother. A pain caught her – Father had not lived long enough to see his son grow up. But it was no good raking over the past: her future was here and now, and she would have to make the best of it.

Later, when she joined Justin in the sitting room, she found him pacing to and fro impatiently. 'You'll wear a hole in the carpet if you keep that up,' she said, not looking at him.

'Very droll.' He stood before her and held her arms to her sides. 'Your gown will do well enough, it's a good colour for you – the blue brings out the colour of your eyes.'

Her brows lifted and she stared at him. 'Kind of you to say so.'

'But your décolletage... Why didn't you want to wear the jewellery I left for you?'

'Because it wasn't bought for me.' She touched the slender silver chain and smoothed her fingers over the locket. 'This, on the other hand, was a present from my father. It was given with love.' Now why on earth had she said that? The last thing she required from Justin was love. 'Not that I expect anything from you–' her voice was hard to cover her embarrassment '–it's not required of you even to like me.'

'I'm quite aware of that, Charlotte.' The roughness of his voice matched her own. 'Hurry now, get a shawl or something, the air might be chilly by the time we return from our dinner engagement.'

The ride through the darkened night was a silent one, Charlotte sitting in the carriage, her husband by her side. They were careful not to touch and, if the rolling of the carriage threw Charlotte against Justin, she moved away quickly, disturbed at the sense of unexpected happiness just brushing against him gave her.

Major Johnson and his delicate wife stood in the wood-panelled hall of the impressive Beaufort Manor waiting to greet their guests. The party was to be a small one, and Charlotte surveyed the other four people present with a suspicious eye, wondering how they would respond to a mere schoolteacher.

As the two couples were introduced to her, Charlotte caught a spiteful look in the eyes of a Miss Larkman, who was accompanied by her brother, Professor David Larkman. The two other guests were an aged professor and his wife.

The small group chatted and laughed over a glass of pre-supper sherry, but Charlotte remained silent, aware that she was being ignored by the ladies. Only the hostess bothered to speak to her at all. Miss Larkman watched her carefully, her narrowed eyes filled with spite, and her mouth stretched in an unconvincing smile when her gaze drifted in Charlotte's direction. She'd had her eye on Justin, that much was clear.

The food served at the Johnson table was hot and rich and, though she ate only a little, Charlotte appreciated that an enormous amount of care had gone into compiling the menu.

The men present, including David Larkman, were eager to engage Charlotte in conversation and, though the women stayed aloof, they watched her every move, trying to catch her unawares if she fumbled with any of the array of shining silver cutlery.

Charlotte was mildly irritated by this: she had been properly brought up by a father who, although far below the status of these people, had been an educated man. Manager of a local factory and then proprietor of the Palace Theatre, a fine building standing out against the twin hills of Townhill and Kilvey, Jolly Mortimer had been a respected member of the Swansea community and as such he should be remembered.

As Major Johnson kept faith with the old tradition of the ladies withdrawing, allowing the men to smoke cigars in peace, Charlotte found herself alone among the ladies. The hostess made an effort to talk to her, but the conversation was stilted, and Charlotte, resentful of the grudging politeness being offered only out of respect for Justin Harvard, fell silent and drew a little apart from the other ladies.

To her surprise, Muriel Larkman approached her, eyes fixed like fish eyes, cold and dead. 'I do pity you, my dear,' she said. Muriel was almost attractive, with soft, fine hair, and though her figure was not shapely, she dressed with a certain panache which concealed her imperfections.

'Why should you pity me?' Charlotte was in no mood to humour anyone. Already she was sorry she hadn't listened to Justin and worn the blazing jewels, they would at least have competed with the plethora of diamonds and precious stones the other ladies had chosen to wear. Muriel's eyes rested meaningfully on the modest silver locket at Charlotte's neck.

'Well, you can't hope to keep his interest, can you? I mean, once the novelty of having a lower-class woman as a wife wears off... See how poorly he treats you.' She looked again at the locket.

Charlotte was taken aback by the direct rudeness and duplicity of the other woman. As soon as the men entered the room, Muriel became soft and sweet, turning to Justin and laying her hand on his arm in a familiar way.

'Your wife is charming, Justin, so shy and retiring, so very modest.' Charlotte was astounded by the change in Muriel's expression. 'So sweet, so young, she has a lot to learn but, I'm sure, being an intelligent lady, she will adapt in time to a higher stratum of society.'

For a moment Charlotte thought Justin would be taken in by the honeyed words and miss the snobbish insult. He smiled and gently removed Muriel's arm. 'My wife is every inch a lady,' he said softly.

'Of course she is,' Muriel said stoutly, her tone implying that she was with Justin all the way when it came to defending Charlotte. She hesitated, then looked up at him with wide eyes. 'I'm sure she'll be a loyal and grateful wife, happy with your charm and good looks – and not inconsiderable fortune, of course.'

Charlotte forced herself to be calm. Retaliating against the dreadful woman's spiteful barbs would only give them some credence.

'You are too kind, Miss Larkman,' she said sweetly, 'much too kind. After all, you know nothing about me, and here you are offering the hand of friendship.'

Charlotte moved purposefully away, leaving Justin's side. He was still talking to the awful woman, whose cold eyes were following her across the room. She smiled at David Larkman. He blinked, and then his face became animated.

'I say, it was pure luck that Justin found you first,' he said warmly. 'The old dog always did have the luck of the devil when it came to the ladies.' He stopped abruptly, wondering if he had spoken out of turn, but Charlotte smiled her sweetest smile at him and she could see that he was genuinely attracted to her.

185

She glanced back at Justin and Muriel. Both of them had sour looks on their faces as they watched her talk animatedly to David as though she were unaware of their joint displeasure.

She was grateful when, at last, the long and uncomfortable evening was over. As Charlotte said polite goodbyes to the Johnsons, she was pleasantly surprised when her hostess kissed her cheek with sincere friendliness. 'Goodnight, dear. Come again, won't you?'

Sitting at her side in the coach, Justin spoke only briefly. 'Muriel means well, you know,' he said. 'She's a little tactless, but she means no harm.'

Charlotte didn't answer. She had read Muriel correctly, and she was definitely one of the enemy.

CHAPTER FIFTEEN

It was late summer and, at last, the school was ready for classes to begin. Justin had chosen the Mayor of Swansea himself to cut the ribbon and a small crowd had gathered. The shabbily dressed women from the local area chatted in a group, arms folded or clinging to babies in shawls. A few old men, grandfathers of the children, stood in a knot, caps pulled down but faces shining with the hope of a better life for the youngsters.

The children themselves were less eager. The younger children wanted to play on the swingboats or the chained seats they called jerkers, the older ones looked moodily away, unaware that the school was offering them freedom.

John Merriman was different. He held his head high, his thick hair tousled untidily in clumps. Charlotte guessed his blond hair had not seen the benefit of a comb for some days. But, unlike the other youngsters, he was beaming with happiness; he had left the grammar school and was pleased that he would once again have Mrs Harvard as a teacher. It was only when the mayor magnanimously announced there would be several hours every day when the children would be excused work to pursue their education that the wan faces of the older children brightened into smiles. If this thing called 'education' brought them time away from the grinding work of the copper industry – hours spent carrying coal for the furnaces, cutting green saplings to be thrust into the boiling golden metal to free the gases, the unremitting heat of the sheds, which burned faces and lungs, impregnating the skin with tiny particles of copper – the children were all for it.

Charlotte read them well, and made a grim, silent promise to herself: 'I will make you work till you drop. Your free time will be paid for in hours of book work.' But today, in the sunshine, the children could simply enjoy themselves, be happy, and then, one day, with her help, some of them would forge a new and better life for themselves.

Justin watched Charlotte's face: it was alight with the zeal of a reformer; she scarcely looked his way, so engrossed was she in her dreams of a new world for the children of Swansea. But then that was the bargain they had made: he would have his respectable wife on his arm, a wife who would buy him a fortune and his just inheritance, and she would have her school. Both of them would reap the benefit of a strange but hopefully workable relationship.

Watching her now, Justin was aware that she was a truly beautiful woman, unawakened to physical love, a virgin on the threshold of her life. He felt a bitter taste in his mouth. Had he cheated her? Didn't she have the right to be a proper wife to a man who loved her? A man like Luke Lester? He sighed. Well, she had chosen her path and together they would tread it, he with his fortune and she – well, she would fulfil her dreams.

He took the tour of the school with Charlotte, who by now knew every corner, every niche of the building, as well as the playground where the children would take their exercise and enjoy their leisure time – very necessary, according to Charlotte, for their mental as well as physical health.

He smiled at the gasps of admiration from the women as they stood outside the door of the lavvie, as Ben called it. The long bench of seats and the shining porcelain basins gleamed with cleanliness. It was a great improvement on the lavatories at the bottom of the gardens shared by all and sundry, the doors of which, more often than not, were hanging from the hinges, a drunken father having kicked his way in after drinking as many pints of beer as he could hold.

Justin was relieved when he, as school owner, had made his short speech of welcome and was able to slip away, to indulge himself with the new mistress he'd acquired, having grown tired of the last one, who had become too clinging and demanding.

Elizabeth was pleased to see him – she was always pleased to see him, even if, as now, she had not yet indulged in her morning toilet. Her hair was almost corn-coloured, her skin porcelain, her eyes pale blue and fringed with light golden lashes, she was curved in all the right places, her breasts showing now through the thin cotton of her night attire. Perhaps she had been expecting him to call; she hadn't yet dressed.

He stepped into the house he'd rented for her and noticed the pink tips pointing towards him. She was roused merely at the nearness of him. It always amazed Justin.

He kissed her rosy mouth, still sweet with the taste of the champagne she had taken for breakfast. She was an expensive addition to his life but she was worth every penny. She adored him and that charmed him. She put her arms around him and drew him close, and he lifted her and carried her to the bedroom.

The bed was still unmade, the pillows scattered anyhow. Elizabeth grimaced. 'I rose late,' she said. 'Flo hasn't had time to work in here yet.'

He kicked the door shut with his foot and put Elizabeth gently against the pillows. She reached white arms towards him, beseeching just like a child. He removed his clothes and lay beside her, kissing her softly and, then, with more passion. She struggled with her nightgown, and there she lay at last in all her pale beauty. She was a born wanton, but it was he who brought the passion out in her. He might have felt guilt, but he knew she would have lost her maidenhead soon enough – a man was vital to her life, she wanted loving so badly, and at any time of the day or night.

Sometimes he asked himself why he didn't feel committed to her, but he knew the answer well: if he had to be away from her for any length of time, she would take another lover; she was like a greedy child, she needed constant attention to her bodily needs. Impoverished as she was when he met her, with no father or brother to take care of her, she would have fallen into a role natural to her, a role she would have fulfilled easily, that of a courtesan of the highest order. Her tricks to inflame a man were born with her, she did not have to force herself to please him, her instincts led her to acts that a respectable married lady would scorn.

His dear dead wife, much as he had loved her, had been too shy, too ladylike, to show pleasure when he made love to her. And Charlotte. Sometimes when he looked at her, he admitted to himself, he really did want her fragile, innocent body. But, now, he was in the skilful hands of his mistress. She teased him with her lips, her tongue and the warmth of her mouth until he was roused to the heights of blind, nameless passion.

At last, he rolled away from her and, as a gentleman always should, he held her in his arms long after passion was spent. A picture of Charlotte came into his mind, her eager face, her bright eyes, the blush on her cheeks not brought there by passion, or certainly not the carnal kind. Her passion was

191

reserved for a building, a dream, and as he lay drowsing in the afterglow of lovemaking, he wondered if his wife's passion for lovemaking would ever be roused.

The first day at school went well. The children, ranging in age from seven to fifteen, sat before her, proud at their individual desks, lifting lids, peering fascinated at books, savouring each moment of freedom from the dark, stifling works. Only John Merriman, who at fifteen was the oldest boy at the school, sat up straight, hungry for knowledge.

Charlotte smiled at him encouragingly. 'John, will you read the first words of your new book? Stand up and face the class, John, so that we can all hear you.'

He read haltingly, even though the book had been written for children, but Charlotte saw he was proud he could make sense of the jumble of words.

She signalled to him to stop. 'Thank you, John, you may sit down.' She turned to the blackboard and wrote the alphabet, speaking each letter out loud. She was aware that the children would be baffled at first by the strange look of the letters. All any of them saw of writing was their father putting his mark on a rentbook or when they ran up a tab at the local food store.

After a time, whatever interest there had

been in the new letters waned and the pupils began to shift and murmur among themselves, their attention gone. Charlotte had expected this and called the class to order.

'That's enough work for today. Now I'm going to read you a story.' She heard one boy sniff

'Me mam can do that at home by the fire,' he said in a low voice, 'without even having a book.'

Charlotte asked the boy to stand. 'It's all right,' she assured him, as the hot colour ran into his face, 'I'm not going to chastise you. What's your name?'

'Joseph, Mrs Harvard.' He stumbled over the words, mortified to be picked out from the safety of the crowded classroom.

'Well, it's very good that your mother tells you stories, Joseph. She must be a very wise woman indeed.' Joseph preened visibly to hear the teacher praise his mother. His shoulders relaxed a little. 'But wouldn't it be good if *you* could read to your mother, read real words, words on bills and rentbooks?'

Joseph nodded in silent agreement, and Charlotte continued. 'Just think of it – your mother could give you a list of things she wanted from the market, for example, and you could write it all down for her and take the list to the stallholders. And one day soon when you learn your figure work, you can make sure no one is cheating your mother by overcharging.'

'Bloody 'ell,' Joseph exclaimed. 'Mam is always saying the money-lender is gypping us, I could watch 'im and make sure 'e's bein' honest wiv us.'

If Charlotte felt shocked and saddened by Joseph's innocent comments, she didn't show it. Most families resorted at one time or another to the money-lender, never realizing they were paying back more than double the sum they had borrowed.

'Tell us a story then, miss. Please,' Joseph said eagerly.

Charlotte knew she had won the first round of her battle. She'd inspired in the children the desire to learn; they had quickly seen the advantages of being able to read and write. But now they were tired, so she read to them, and their rapt attention was the perfect ending to her day.

On her way home, Charlotte paused for a moment as she stepped out into the road: 'home' – was that how she felt about Thornhill? The idea made her tremble. Had she made a prison for herself, a prison of silks and lace? She might never be able to roam free now, taking her teaching to children in other countries – perhaps even to America, where her family now lived. She shook off her depressing mood and cheered herself with the knowledge that tomorrow her school would resound with the voices of children who would come eagerly through the gates that led to their future.

CHAPTER SIXTEEN

Charlotte stared into Luke's face, aware of the coldness between them. He sat on the edge of his seat in the staff room of the new school, which Justin had named after her: The Charlotte Harvard School. She'd protested that the school should be named after Red Rock, in memory of the works, now burned to the ground, but Justin had been adamant.

'What's the point in saddling the school with an unlucky name like Red Rock?' Justin had smiled at her then. 'I want it to be named after you, Charlotte. You are my wife and, as such, have a standing in our fair town.'

Now, Charlotte was aware that Luke was still waiting for her to speak. His face was set in hard lines that pushed his jaw forward, high and almost belligerent behind the stiff collar of his shirt.

'I'll come to the point.' She coughed and waited, hoping for a smile, but his forehead furrowed into lines, making him seem older than his thirty-two years. 'I want you to come and teach at the school,' she said. 'I don't know anyone better qualified to teach the children than you.'

He was silent for so long she thought he was going to turn her down flat. She sat quite still, her hands clenched so tightly together in her lap that her knuckles gleamed white.

'Why would I want to work side by side with you, *Mrs Harvard?*' His tone was cold; his eyes rested on a line somewhere above her head. There was a long silence, during which Charlotte hoped he would speak again. When he remained silent, she took a deep breath, trying to still the anger rising up inside her.

'The terms I'm offering you are generous, and look at it this way, Luke, why should our split affect your future as a teacher?'

He mulled it over and at last met her eyes. 'All right, I'll take your thirty pieces of silver. The children deserve a good teacher.'

Charlotte prevented herself from speaking the angry words that rose to her lips and forced a small smile. 'Good, I'll expect you to start tomorrow, if that is convenient.'

As Luke left the room, she heaved a sigh of relief. She'd expected the interview with Luke to be difficult and it had lived up to her expectations, but now it was over.

She stood at the window and watched

Luke walk away. Tears came to her eyes. She didn't want to be his enemy. She hoped and prayed that he would unbend in time and forgive her for breaking the engagement. It was a forlorn hope and, deep inside, Charlotte knew it.

Justin sat at the desk in his study and looked at his wife, a little angry that she had invaded his sanctuary.

'Well? Do you think it's a good idea to employ Luke or not?'

He pondered her question and wondered how to answer. Should he be tactful, accept that the school was her domain?

'Well?' Charlotte raised her chin and, her hands on her hips, waited for him to speak.

'All you need now is a rolling pin and you'd look just like a labourer's wife awaiting her beloved's return from the public bar so she can give him a good beating.' He hoped to sound humorous, but the words came out like hard stones.

Self-consciously, Charlotte dropped her hands to her sides. 'I don't see anything remotely funny about this situation.'

Justin shrugged. 'Come to think of it, neither do I. All right, so you've hired Luke Lester to teach the children how to add and subtract. That won't tax his brain too much, will it, so I suppose you may as well let him have the post of teacher. Just so long as the man doesn't have any ambitions in other directions.'

There was more than a touch of sarcasm in his voice and he saw Charlotte's mouth become tight and her eyes flash fire. After a moment, she spoke.

'There is a great deal more to educating children than understanding arithmetic, you know.' Her voice was stern and Justin smiled again.

'Now you look like the archetypal teacher.'

She sighed heavily. 'Look, I'll be spending your money, so at least tell me if you agree to have Luke on my staff or not.'

'Well, I wouldn't call two teachers staff as such but, all right, he seems the best man for the job.' He hesitated. 'And, after all, he does come cheap.'

'And that was a cheap and nasty remark,' Charlotte said. 'Look at it this way: all the more ambitious teachers run like scalded cats from Swansea into the bigger world where the salary is good and the teachers are shown the respect they deserve.'

'All right. I'm growing tired of the subject, so you just get on with running the school, Charlotte, and leave me to see to the real business of making a living.'

She didn't reply but she was flushed with anger. She'd never looked more attractive. His eyes slid over the pert shape of her breasts, her small, nipped-in waist and narrow virginal hips. Charlotte was just a young untried girl but, by God, she had guts and determination. He offered her a word of caution.

'Just make sure you act as my wife in every respect. I don't want to be a laughing stock in my hometown, do I?'

He saw the rich colour in her face deepen, scalding her skin. 'I don't know what you are implying.' Her voice fairly crackled with suppressed anger.

'Yes, you do,' he replied. 'You know exactly what I mean.'

'If you are insinuating I'd behave improperly with Luke, then you are insulting me in the worst possible way.'

He relaxed and smiled. 'I apologize,' he said at once. 'That was uncalled for, and I apologize unreservedly.'

She sighed again, heavily, and her eyes were hidden from him by her long, thick lashes. She really was a beautiful young woman, albeit one from a poor background. She was nothing without the school and yet he couldn't help feeling a sense of pride that she was his wife. Well, he hoped they had both made a good bargain.

All at once, he was utterly tired of the whole matter of the school, of Luke Lester, of what the gossips would say about his wife working side by side with a man to whom she had been betrothed.

'Do what you will.' He turned back to his papers, effectively dismissing her. He expected her to creep away, but she stood there, rigid as a carved statue, and impatiently he looked up at her. 'What now?' He was growing exasperated.

'There is one other matter I must speak to you about.'

'Can't it wait? I've had a very long day.'

'No, it can't wait! It's about your elder daughter.' She was as impatient as he was now and, with a sigh, he put down his pen and turned to face her.

'She's started asking questions.'

'What sort of questions?'

'About...' She bent her head, refusing to meet his eyes '...About us, about babies. She has an idea about how they are conceived – she's doubtless listened to gossip in the kitchen – and she's been asking when you are going to come to my bedroom so that we will produce a child. What am I to say to her?'

'Just tell her that I have enough children, that she and her sister are all I want. Is a little tact beyond you, Charlotte?'

'You forget!' Her anger was swift. 'I know little more than Rhian about the business of childbearing.'

He smiled then. 'Poor Charlotte. Am I to instruct you in the ways of women?'

'I'm sorry.' Her voice was low and, even though her head was bent and her hair swinging thick and free over her face, he could tell that she was blushing. 'I'm not the right one to talk to Rhian. Can't you get your friend Muriel to do it?'

'You talk to Muriel if you wish. She has plenty of nieces and nephews, she'll help you.'

'I can't!' He saw that Charlotte was scandalized. 'I can't ask Muriel, she'd soon be gossiping about us. Are you blind, Justin?'

He sighed again. His wife would have taken this sort of thing in her stride. He didn't see the unfairness of his comparison until Charlotte spoke again.

'I know I'm a disappointment to you, Justin, but I'll never know how to talk to the girls about love and marriage and motherhood, will I? All I know is how to teach them to read good literature, to instruct them in the proper way an unmarried lady conducts herself.' She glanced down at the gold band on her finger and shook her head. 'This ring is meaningless, isn't it? I'm not a wife, not in the real sense of the word.'

He saw her glance at him quickly, her cheeks rosy, her eyes sparkling with – was it anger or tears? He couldn't tell.

'That was our bargain,' he said sternly. 'I didn't want another wife and you didn't want a husband. All you wanted from me was the wherewithal to build a new school. You have that now, Charlotte. Deal with domestic

201

problems as you see fit. Now, I have work to do. Close the door as you leave.'

He didn't know why he was in such a bad mood – was it the fact that Lester and Charlotte would be working side by side at the damned school? He looked down at the papers in front of him and in a fit of anger pushed them away.

He was suddenly restless. He kept seeing Charlotte's puzzled, innocent face, her slimness, her girlish figure, her diminutive hands and tiny feet, and he smiled ruefully. She was nothing more than a girl, she didn't know what passion was, she was admirably suited to the vicarious pleasure of being surrounded by children with none of her own to trouble her.

He rose to his feet. Suddenly the room crowded in on him, he needed to be free, to lie in a woman's arms, the arms of a *real* woman who knew what passion was and received and gave it without a thought. Tonight he would lie in the arms of his mistress and, when he woke in the morning, he would have forgotten all about Charlotte and her damned questions.

Charlotte faced the mixed class of children. The boys outnumbered the girls two to one. It was easy to see that the other children looked to John Merriman, as the eldest, to be their leader. He stood before her now, his serious eyes searching her face, begging for understanding.

'Tell me, John, what's the problem?' She sat at her desk, hands folded in her lap, her skirts neatly covering her legs. 'Don't be afraid to speak up, I'm always ready to listen.'

'It's the work you want us to take home, Mrs Harvard.'

'Go on, I'm listening.'

'It's so hard for us, see?'

'What do you mean? Are the questions I've set too difficult?'

'It's not that, Mrs Harvard, it's the fathers, mind, some of them think going to school is daft, especially Teddy O'Sullivan's father. Last night he snatched the book away from Teddy and threw it in the fire.'

Charlotte heard the strangled gasp coming from the young boy seated in the front seat. She looked down compassionately at Teddy and saw he was struggling with his tears.

'Don't worry, Teddy,' she said at once, 'I can give you a new book.'

Teddy gulped. 'No good doin' that, Mrs Harvard, me dad will burn it again, and any other book I take 'ome with me.'

Charlotte looked down at her hands, wondering how to handle this unexpected problem. 'I will come to talk to your father,' she said. 'Don't worry, Teddy, I'm sure we can sort this out.'

The boy looked doubtful but, just then, the bell rang, calling the children to another lesson in the other classroom. The usual noises – the grinding of chair legs against the wooden floor as the children scrambled to their feet, the sound of desktops being banged down and the slapping of feet as the children pushed their way to the door – washed around Charlotte.

After her class had gone she sat at her desk and rested her head in her hands. What could she do about obstructive parents? She felt a touch on her arm and looked up to see Rhian smiling mischievously at her.

'It's sums next, Charlotte.'

'I know that,' Charlotte said. 'Now hurry along or you'll be late. You mustn't keep Mr Lester waiting, it's not polite.'

'I'm going to ask him things,' Rhian said, and her dark eyes sparkled.

'What do you mean "things"?' Charlotte felt a twitch of unease.

'Well, I thought he might know about babies and all that sort of thing.'

'No!' Charlotte said quickly. 'You can't do that, talk to a man about personal things, it's just not ladylike.'

'He won't mind,' Rhian said. 'One of the boys asked him what made babies grow under a gooseberry bush and Mr Lester just laughed and said he'd know soon enough when he was more grown-up. Well, I'm quite grown-up, so he will tell me.'

Before Charlotte could protest further, Rhian was skipping towards the door, her plaits bobbing up and down on the crisp white straps of her pinafore dress.

All of a sudden, Charlotte felt weary. She didn't know how to deal with Rhian, who was always full of mischief. A little smile twisted her lips and she rose to pack away her books. Luke's lesson was the last one before the bell sounded for home time.

True to her promise, after she had finished at the school for the day, Charlotte made her way to Teddy O'Sullivan's house. Once that difficult task was done, she could look forward to taking the ferry boat across the river towards the plush green slopes on the west of the town where Thornhill stood in its magnificent splendour. Justin's two girls would have been picked up by now in the pony and trap driven by one of Justin's footmen.

Charlotte always made her own way home. Justin had more than once voiced his displeasure about the arrangement, but it was part of Charlotte's job to collect and correct the spelling papers the children left on her desk and in this she would not be rushed.

Now, as she stood outside the row of tiny cottages rented to the men from the copperworks, she felt her heart begin to pound. She didn't relish the meeting with Teddy's father: his reputation was that of a bully and a drunkard.

The door was opened by a thin, dowdy-looking woman who kept glancing behind her as though fearful of a beating. 'Please, missis, go away.' The woman spoke in a whisper.

'Are you Teddy's mother?' Charlotte asked, ignoring the woman's begging tone. The woman swallowed hard but before she could speak she was pushed roughly to one side.

'What the bleedin' 'ell do you want?' Mr O'Sullivan's face was mottled, his eyes bulged and his red-veined nose had been punched out of shape by the many blows it had sustained in numerous fights.

'I'd just like to talk to you about Teddy's schooling.' Charlotte's voice quavered. She could see at once that she would get nowhere with the belligerent bully facing her. 'But if this is a bad time, I can come back another day.'

'You can sod off. Get away from my door, you uppity little madam.' He poked his face close to hers. 'Just because you married that high and mighty Justin bleedin' Harvard, don't think it makes you a lady.'

Charlotte backed away, but O'Sullivan caught her arm and twisted it. 'Let's 'ave a look at you, a proper look.' He dragged her into the dank passageway. 'Aye, Miss High and Mighty, let's see the dog for the bone.' He pulled at her skirts and Charlotte froze in horror.

'Let the woman go, for God's sake!' Mrs O'Sullivan begged. 'You'll cause nothing but trouble if you pick on Justin Harvard's wife.'

The man ignored her and dragged Charlotte into the kitchen, which smelled of rat droppings and stale food.

She caught sight of Teddy's stricken face as he rushed past her and darted outside, bawling loudly. Twisting around, seeking help, Charlotte caught sight of John Merriman. 'Fetch help, John,' she said, and then rough hands were clamped on her mouth.

'Don't harm her, for God's sake,' Mrs O'Sullivan pleaded, catching her husband's meaty arm. He gave her a backhanded swipe and she fell to the stone floor, her eyes flooding with tears.

Charlotte was forced into a chair. She heard Mr O'Sullivan's boot connect to his wife's spine as she curled herself into a ball. 'Fetch some rope, you snivelling bitch.'

Charlotte's arms were twisted behind her and then she was being tied to the wooden chair, the rope cutting into her wrists and ankles.

'Please let her go!'

'Shut your trap,' the man snarled. 'I'll 'ave my bit of fun with 'er, and then I'll sell 'er back to 'er 'usband – if 'e still wants 'er.'

'You're drunk, Tommy, can't you see this will bring bad trouble down on our heads? Let her go now before it's too late.'

He turned and slapped his wife and punched her until she fell to the floor again, bleeding and half-conscious.

'Bloody women,' he said. He dragged at Charlotte's blouse, and the cotton tore away under the strength of his fingers.

Charlotte glanced down. Her petticoat was still intact, covering her breasts, but Tommy O'Sullivan would not let a flimsy bit of silk stand in his way. He tore the petticoat from her and beamed as her small, firm breasts were uncovered. Charlotte gasped. No man had ever seen her like this. It horrified her that Tommy O'Sullivan really did mean to have his way with her, when he was ready.

He sat at the table and slopped up the cooling gravy on a pie, running a thick piece of bread between his grubby fingers and filling his gaping mouth to capacity. Charlotte averted her gaze, and she heard the man laugh.

'Just wait, you, yer goin' to see a lot more that might surprise you, Madam School-teacher.' He touched the buttons on his flies in a vulgar gesture and suddenly Charlotte felt sick with horror and fear.

When the man had slopped up the rest of

his meal, he pushed the plate away. His wife was lying moaning on the floor and he kicked her aside carelessly. 'Now for my fun.'

He had reached out to lift Charlotte's skirts when there was an almighty bang and the door was pushed in, off its hinges. Justin burst into the room, a bull whip in his hand.

Charlotte saw him glance at her nakedness and cringed away in shame from the terrible anger in his eyes.

'Woman!' he said to the beaten figure of Mrs O'Sullivan. 'Get a shawl to cover my wife.' He turned to the man, who gaped at him like a beached fish. 'You, outside.'

'I didn't mean no 'arm.' O'Sullivan, like all bullies, was a coward. 'It was only right, see, that I show this woman that no one tells O'Sullivan what to do with his brats.'

The whip swirled neatly in the small kitchen and curled like a snake around Tommy O'Sullivan's shoulders and chest. The man breathed in sharply as though he had been dipped in cold water, and then he was howling in pain like a dog. He ran outside and Justin followed him.

Charlotte felt the ropes loosen about her wrists and ankles and a smelly shawl was draped over her bare breasts.

'Go stop your man,' Mrs O'Sullivan begged, 'or he'll kill my Tommy for sure.' Charlotte staggered outside. O'Sullivan was trying to twist away from the whip, which was winding round his thick torso, stinging him repeatedly and taking the skin from his body.

Justin continued whipping the man until he fell quiet and was lying on the rough road outside the cottage. Still, and with a nightmare feeling of horror, Charlotte realized he was no longer breathing.

'Justin!' she cried. Justin shook the sweat out of his eyes, and Charlotte saw the sanity of calm come into his face as he looked down at the ragged bundle at his feet. The man's face was raw and cut like a piece of beef, his body striped with blood, the pieces of his shirt in ribbons around his bloody torso. Slowly, Justin lowered the whip.

'John,' he said softly to the boy who was looking at him in awe, 'run and fetch a policeman and tell someone to get a doctor.'

Charlotte sagged weakly against the wall of the cottage, unable to believe what had happened in the hour or so since she'd knocked on the cottage door and confronted Teddy's father.

Turning her eyes away from the inert figure on the ground, she knew, without a shadow of doubt, that O'Sullivan had paid a high price for his drunken and violent attack. He had paid with his life.

CHAPTER SEVENTEEN

The murder of the Irishman was a seven-day wonder and most of the townsfolk were of the opinion that Mr O'Sullivan had got his just deserts, while Justin Harvard was a gentleman whose wife had been roughly treated and well within his rights.

The courts were dragging the case out, knowing it would fade from the memory of most people in a remarkably short time. No one wanted to see a good-living man with a family to care for shut away for doing what every red-blooded man would have done in the same situation.

The gruesome slaughter of a whole family in the shabby area around the docks came to the judiciary's aid. The death of O'Sullivan had to be dealt with quickly then, as the new case demanded everyone's attention. The verdict was accidental death of a drunken no-good, a fellow who had fallen awkwardly and broken his neck.

Teddy O'Sullivan changed after that; from having been an introvert boy, he became a keen student, outspoken and made popular by the publicity in the newspapers. He was freed by the death of his father, and Mrs

O'Sullivan had been heard to say it was an ill wind that brought nobody any good.

Charlotte relived the nightmare many times in her head. She was horrified when she thought of what would have happened if Justin hadn't arrived in time to save her. She was still hot with shame when she thought of her nakedness, her breasts on show to anyone who cared to look. She lost confidence in herself and, even though she was determined her teaching would not suffer, she knew it did.

Luke, from her first day back at school, had avoided her. When she did see him, he looked the other way, and she knew that, to him, she was soiled goods. Not only was she married to a thug but she had behaved in a most unseemly way by confronting O'Sullivan in the first place. Luke doubtless thought he was fortunate to be rid of her and the problems she seemed to bring with her.

Justin, as always, was polite, and his manner when they entertained guests to dinner remained impeccable, beyond reproach, but something had changed between them – he had seen her nakedness, her body was no longer sacrosanct, untouched, and sometimes she saw him look broodingly at her, as though she were a stranger. Only Rhian and Morwen behaved as though nothing had happened, but she knew that the girls would have heard the flood of gossip among the servants in the kitchen.

They all sat now around the dinner table, silent, the two girls half-asleep. It was long after their usual bedtime, but Charlotte knew their father wanted to speak to them. She waited, eyes downcast, wondering what Justin was about to say and fearing it would affect her in some way. When the meal was over and brandy was served to him, Justin waved the servants away.

He looked at his two girls and, though he made sure his features hid his true feelings, he felt like a traitor. 'I've found you both a place in a very good ladies' college down in the West Country,' he said firmly. 'You are a little young to attend yet but, until you reach a suitable age, one of the finest teachers in the whole of Somerset will coach you both.'

Immediately, Morwen began to grizzle. 'I don't want to go away, Daddy, I want to stay here and have Charlotte teaching me.' She glanced at her older sister. 'Rhian can go, she's older than me.'

'You are both going.' His tone brooked no argument. 'Now, go on upstairs, and the maid will see you into your beds.'

'I want Charlotte to tuck me in and tell me a story–' Morwen spoke truculently '–like she always does.' Rhian was strangely quiet.

'I'll come up later, Morwen,' Charlotte said softly, 'but, for now, be a good girl and do as your father says.'

Charlotte followed Justin from the dining room into the sitting room, at a distance, her footsteps dragging. She felt empty, washed of her last shred of dignity, heartbroken that Justin was sending the girls away.

'Please sit down, Charlotte.' Justin's voice was impersonal, and he avoided her eyes. He hesitated, choosing his words carefully. 'I mean no disrespect to you, Charlotte, by sending my daughters away to college.' He paused. 'I know you are a fine teacher, a dedicated teacher, and the pupils at the school will be grateful to you in years to come.'

'So I'm good enough to teach the children of the workers, but not your two girls.'

Her voice was flat and, with a pang of feeling he didn't understand, he saw she was too downhearted even for bitterness.

'The gossip,' he began, 'surrounding both of us, myself as much as you – I'm worried it will affect my daughters.'

'I understand.' Charlotte, her head bent, looked abstractedly at her whitened knuckles, and Justin realized she was exerting all her control, determined not to resort to tears. She risked a glance at him. He turned his head, still unable to meet her eyes.

'I'm sorry if that hurts you, Charlotte, but I have to think of the girls. They are so innocent, and I don't want them worried by wild gossip.'

'All right, I understand,' Charlotte said, 'but there's no need to send the girls away. I'll move out first thing in the morning.'

'No!' Justin's voice cracked like a whip and, startled, she looked up at him. 'What sort of reputation would I have as a man and a husband if I allowed you to leave the protection of my home?'

'So you care about your reputation. What about mine?'

'What's done cannot be undone,' he said, turning away from her. 'Now, go up to the children, tell them a story, do what you like – but they will go away as soon as I can arrange transport for them.'

'Please, Justin, you said yourself the two of them are fond of me, they need me as a substitute mother, so why are you denying them my company?'

He poured himself another brandy, picked up the crystal glass and studied the amber liquid in it as though it were of the greatest importance to him. 'I've told you my plans and, as my wife, you will do your duty and obey them. You'll only cause Rhian and Morwen more grief if you become hysterical.'

Charlotte nodded. He could see by the colour that rose to her cheeks that some of her spirit had returned. 'If you've said all you want to say, I'll go and tuck the girls into bed and pretend that nothing is wrong. I'll go further, I'll try to convince them that they are heading for a bright future, that a place in the college is an honour, as of course it is–' She made a last protest: 'But do they have to go away so soon?'

'Goodnight, Charlotte.' Justin's voice was clipped, an edge of anger to it, and Charlotte rose.

'I can see my little protest has done nothing to change your mind.'

He knew she was struggling to hold her head high but he saw the heavy tears run from her eyes and splash on the bodice of her gown. He sighed with relief as the door closed behind her. He felt uncomfortable in her presence now, he couldn't forget the sight of her, bound and humiliated, her small virginal breasts bare to anyone. He felt as violated as she must have felt, he was sorry for her and yet absurdly furious that she had allowed herself to get in such a dreadful situation. Did she think she was invincible, that the town rabble's behaviour would alter just to accommodate her?

He took a sip from his glass and sat down in his chair, trying to relax but unable to get the hurt look in her eyes out of his mind. He had seen her tears in spite of her efforts to hide them. He had seen the downward, beaten slope of her shoulders and he knew he had hurt her badly. And yet the devil of it was that having seen her even more helpless, her breasts exposed, had brought him a hunger he didn't understand, a hunger to possess her.

Impatiently, he brushed the feelings aside. He had a pretty, willing mistress to share his passion with – and yet he had not gone to her since his attack on O'Sullivan. That was something he must remedy, and at once.

He left the house and took his horse from the stable. It was growing late; the moon was a tiny curve of light against the sky. Soon he would drown himself in the bed of a warm woman, a woman who gave him comfort and who demanded nothing from him – not even his love.

The two girls were standing ready on the platform, waiting for the train that would take them away from everything that was familiar to them. Charlotte held their hands and acted as though they were simply going away for a jolly holiday. Morwen clung to her side, hiding her face in the folds of Charlotte's skirts, trying not to cry. Rhian was determined not to show that she was upset, but every now and then her small mouth trembled. Charlotte squeezed her hand. 'You are a young lady now, Rhian, and you will enjoy the company of girls of your own age.'

'I've something I should tell you,' Rhian said softly, avoiding Charlotte's eyes. 'It's about Mr Lester.'

'Not now, Rhian. Look, the train is pulling

into the station – see the burst of steam? Can you feel the judder of the wheels on the tracks? Oh, how I wish I was coming with you – it will all be so exciting.' Charlotte swallowed her own tears as the monster train shuddered to a halt.

'But, Charlotte,' Rhian protested, 'I wanted to tell you something I said to Mr Lester. It was spiteful of me, and I feel very bad about it now.'

'Don't worry about it.' Charlotte dismissed Rhian's attempt to shed the feelings of guilt she was obviously harbouring. 'I don't suppose it matters now.' She adjusted Morwen's hat and braced herself for the parting that was to come. She loved the girls as if they were her own flesh and blood, they had filled the space in her heart left by the family she'd lost when the magnificent ship *Carpathia* had sailed away.

'Where's my father?' Rhian demanded, changing the subject rapidly. 'He said he would be here to see us off.'

'And he will.' Even as Charlotte spoke, she heard the sound of firm footsteps behind her. Justin brushed past her and swept his two daughters into his arms. Charlotte was thankful he had arrived – he was just in time: the doors of the train were being slammed shut.

With Justin was the woman he had hired to take his girls on the journey. She was thin and straight as a rod and, although Charlotte had only met Miss Carver once before, she instinctively liked and trusted the woman.

She'd told Justin it was her place as stepmother to the girls to travel with them. He had hesitated, and she knew then he was ashamed of her. He had no intention of blighting his daughters' futures by allowing a woman who was a humble teacher, and a shamed one to boot, to present his girls to the school authorities.

'I need you here as my hostess. We have fences to mend,' he'd argued and, though she'd known it was an excuse, she'd given in. But now, as she saw Morwen's tear-filled eyes, her heart felt as if it were breaking.

The girls' faces were framed in the small carriage window, Miss Carver behind them, and with a last squeeze of Morwen's hand, Charlotte stepped away from the train, which was straining like a beast about to burst free of its confines.

Justin at her side, she watched the huge beast get up a head of billowing steam and jerk away from the platform. Charlotte waved until the train passed out of sight behind the big curves of Kilvey and Townhill.

Justin took her arm and she looked up at him through a haze of tears. 'How could you do it, Justin?' Her voice shook with emotion. 'How could you be so cruel as to send them to live among strangers? When I was a girl, the family all stayed together, my stepmother and my father were always with us children.'

'Things are managed differently these days.' Justin tugged her arm, hustling her away from the platform and into the busy Stryd Fawr, the high street that cut a direct line through the town, leading from the railway station to the busy docklands. She found herself seated in the small trap, watching as Justin took the reins of the gentle old mare. Charlotte felt an emptiness within her. She looked around. There were a few eyes staring at her as though she were a curiosity. The stigma remained with her; they thought she was a scarlet woman, a murderess; she'd caused the death of a man.

The trap pulled forward and Charlotte fell back against its hard edge. Justin didn't seem to notice; he drove on, staring ahead of him, and Charlotte felt once again that he had no respect for her, no affection, not even a modicum of understanding. Briefly, Charlotte wondered what Rhian had said to Luke Lester – something spiteful, she'd insisted. Well, it didn't matter now, nothing mattered except that Charlotte was an outcast and a burden to her reluctant husband.

CHAPTER EIGHTEEN

Charlotte was sitting alone in the small room off the corridor, her head in her hands. She was tired and dispirited. She wanted her family, her sisters, who would comfort her and tell her she was making the right decision, but they were far away, across the wide Atlantic. Outside in the playground, she could hear the sounds of the children at play and her heart quickened with gladness: at least they were happy, freed for a time from hard toil in the manufactories that spread like a fungus along the banks of the river Tawe. A few of the older boys were employed at the nickel works a few miles away, in the village of Clydach, and they had a long walk up into the valley before they even began to work in the poisoned atmosphere of the works.

The school bell rang loudly, announcing the end of the short play-time. Charlotte peered through the high window and saw Luke marshalling the children for the last lessons. She sighed with relief. In less than an hour, she would be able to lock up the school and go home. She was so tired, these days, so lacking in enthusiasm, even at home – if she could call it that – she was lost, the girls gone,

Justin out all hours of the day and night. But now, she must concentrate on teaching. She had prepared a lesson on foreign lands.

John Merriman sat in the classroom that afternoon, trying to concentrate on what Mrs Harvard was saying. She seemed very partial to the continent of America, telling her pupils of the people who first inhabited it. Red Indians, some people called them, but John knew the proper name for them was American Indians. Mrs Harvard turned the book she was holding to show the picture of the indigenous population. The men were almost naked, huge feathers tucked into their long, dark hair. Behind them were strangely made tents which rose to a peak at the top.

'They won't come over here, will they, miss?' Lizzie looked at John when she spoke, begging him silently to notice her. He kept his eyes on the picture in the book and cursed the fate that had brought Lizzie to the school. She was part of his past.

It had been Mrs Harvard's express wish that Lizzie be allowed into the school. She didn't blame Lizzie or John for the unfortunate affair, which had ended in disaster, at least for Lizzie. She'd been ostracized by the whole class from the day she first stepped into the room, her chin on her chest, her hair stiffly set into neat, tight plaits that seemed to pull the skin back from her face, making her eyes protrude and seem more like frog's eyes than ever. How could he have done such things with her, things which had led to an unwanted baby and disgrace for Lizzie?

'John Merriman, are you listening to what I'm saying?'

'Sorry, Mrs Harvard.' He bent his head, his cheeks colouring with embarrassment, and tried to concentrate on his books. The colour in his cheeks was not entirely due to the reprimand from his teacher, his flies were bulging, pushing against the buttons of his trousers, and he hoped no one else would notice the protuberance below his belt. He glanced at Lizzie and, when she smiled, he turned quickly away, seeing a vision of her naked on the bed, her legs apart to make his entrance easy.

It was all her fault, making him hungry for things that were wicked, things he shouldn't have until he was a married man.

'John! If I have to talk to you again, you will leave the classroom. Other pupils want to learn, even if you don't.'

'Sorry, Mrs Harvard.' He sounded meek, and was congratulating himself on hiding his troublesome feelings. Involuntarily, he glanced at Lizzie. She had a little smile on her face and winked at him. He gave her an angry look before making an attempt to give his mind to the lesson.

When school was finished for the day, Mrs

Harvard stopped him. 'John, what on earth was the matter with you today?'

'I don't know, Mrs Harvard.' He hung his head, ashamed that his eyes were on a level with hers: he was tall now, a man – what was he doing studying lessons when he should be out working, going to the pub of an evening, being a man instead of a schoolchild?

'Well, buck up, John. I didn't win this school easily, and it would hurt me if you were to fail to progress because of inattention at lessons.'

'I'll try harder, I promise.'

'All right, John, you may go.'

He ran like a hare across the grassy bank beyond the school. At last, breathless, he fell into a saucer-shaped gap in the grass and covered his face with his hands. His thoughts were in turmoil. If it was wrong to have these feelings for girls, why had God given them to him?

A soft shape cuddled up against the curve of his spine. A small hand reached around him and found the buttons of his trousers. He groaned and turned, knowing by the assured touch and her scent who was lying alongside him.

'My God, Lizzie, what are you doing? Didn't we fall into enough trouble last time we did that?'

'Ah, but I know how to stop it making babies now.' Lizzie breathed against his cheek. 'Oh, John, I do love you, and I want you, and I know you want me too. I could tell in class today that you were ready to burst if you didn't have me.'

She wriggled until she was under him, her hands busy again, and though he tried to push her away, the fierce fire burning in his loins made his hands tremble. She felt his hardness and smiled, and all at once she looked like the most beautiful creature on earth, her hair tousled, her cheeks pink and her tongue licking around her lips.

Lizzie was pleased with herself. She'd made John hers again and, though it had been a struggle to make him lose his seed on the ground, she knew it had not gone inside her and so she would be sure not to have another baby.

Lizzie shivered, remembering. She felt again the weight of the child inside her, the awful swelling of her belly and then the agony as she had fought to bring the poor unwanted child into the world. Worse still had been the scorn poured down on her by everyone, from the midwife who'd attended her to the lowliest scullery maid, and now by the other pupils in her class at school. Well, it wouldn't happen again. She had made sure of that.

Now, in the room she shared with Flossie, the other kitchenmaid in the Buckland household, she tucked herself into her comfortable bed and closed her eyes, seeing John's agonized face as he battled with his lust for her. He had given in and she exulted in her power over him. He was hers again. He might not admit it to anyone else, but she knew John, she loved him, he was her man whether he knew it or not, and one day he would love her and marry her and they would live happily ever after.

John washed vigorously in the cold stream that ran alongside the track called Gorse Road. The water appeared black, silvered in the places touched by the moonlight. He tried to wash away his shame – what a fool he'd been giving in to his need, taking the gift Lizzie had offered him so freely. A terrible thought struck him: what if she gave herself to any man, what if he caught one of the sicknesses he'd heard about from the stableboys when he'd been working in Harvard's paddock, sicknesses that could drive a man mad?

Well, he would never do it again. Lizzie could make eyes at him all she wanted, but he wouldn't give her the opportunity to catch him unawares, to drag him into her like a spider trapping a fly.

It was a cold night and he was shivering. He rubbed at his body, drying himself with his undergarments. Later, he sat in his room and tried to read his books; he would be a scholar, a teacher perhaps, like Luke Lester.

He wondered if Mr Lester was plagued by troublesome feelings, by the urge to take a woman. It seemed unlikely – his teacher was always calm, he concentrated on his work.

And yet, Mr Lester had once been betrothed to Mrs Harvard so he must have wanted marriage, a good lady wife who would give him children, a woman as educated as himself so that, together at night, they could talk, communicate.

He rolled the word around his tongue, it was a good word; he'd heard it from Mr Lester, who had explained its meaning. John sighed and put his books away. He felt drowsy, he needed to sleep, and yet sleep evaded him. Again and again he cursed himself for falling so foolishly into Lizzie's arms. Well, it would never happen again, he would wait for the woman he truly loved.

The school day finally over, Charlotte closed the windows and turned out the excellent electric lights Justin had had installed. She lifted the keys hanging from a chain at her waist in preparation for locking up.

Luke was waiting at the door, a heap of exercise books under his arm. He studied her in a way that made Charlotte feel uncomfortable. His gaze rested a little too long on her breasts, travelled insolently over her hips and rested on the lower part of her stomach. Charlotte was uncomfortable; it was almost as though Luke could see her body through her clothes. She shuddered, remembering her treatment at the hands of O'Sullivan. It almost felt as if Luke had been there and witnessed her shame.

'It's rude to stare,' she said coldly.

'Well, you are hardly the shrinking virgin now, are you?' His words hit at her, hard and cruel, and she pulled back with the shock of it.

'Apart from the fact that you sold yourself to get a school, you've been looked on in all your nakedness by that rough character O'Sullivan. He probably had his hands all over you.' He came closer to her. 'And to think I treated you with respect. I never touched you, not in all the time we were betrothed.' He paused, and his hands reached out for her breasts. Charlotte didn't stop to think. Her hand flew up of its own volition and she felt her palm crack against his face.

Luke stepped back from her, his eyes blazing. 'You brazen woman! You have no virtue. You're like one of the whores walking the streets along the dockside.' There was a gleam of menace in his eyes. 'One day, madam, one day, I'll have from you what I should have had long ago.'

Charlotte turned sharply on her heel. Was Luke threatening her? She felt weary, as though the world rested on her shoulders.

Was this going to be her life, to be spurned and shamed because of the pact she'd made with one man and the violence of another? She sighed. She was too weary to care any more. Perhaps she should shake the dust from her feet, leave Swansea and follow her family out to America.

A wave of homesickness swept over her. She longed for her sisters, and her little brother, who would be growing up now in the strange new world they'd adopted. Her stepmother would have understood how Charlotte felt. Ella was good and patient and had worked hard to bring up the family after the death of Charlotte's father. But that was Charlotte's past, this was the present and, however painful it was, she'd have to live with it.

Once she was home in the empty house, Charlotte ate a little of the food Cook had prepared for her and then, utterly down-hearted and weary, thinking only of the comfort of a warm pair of arms around her, she went up to bed.

Unbidden, an image of Justin came to her: he was smiling and holding out his arms to her, kissing her, telling her he loved her. Tears started in her eyes, and her whole body longed for comfort from the man she had married, the man she had fallen in love with against her will. It was time she recognized how much in love she was and how much she missed the close evenings they'd shared before O'Sullivan had come between them.

Justin rose from the bed of yet another new mistress. None of them made him happy now, none could take the place of his wife, the wife he had lusted after ever since he'd seen her virginal body. He went to the window. The sun was breaking through the early morning greyness. Even as he watched, the trees and shrubs in the garden sprang into life under its light.

Clara – he was sure that wasn't her real name – stirred sleepily and, bending over to kiss her goodbye, he knew he wouldn't come to her again. She was comfortable, like a pet animal, loving enough and well able to please a man – she'd had much practice at it, of that he was sure – but now she failed to please him. When he lay beside her in bed it wasn't her face he saw but, ridiculously, that of his wife.

He could see her now in his mind's eye, small and defenceless, bound to a chair, her breasts almost childlike in their nakedness. He saw again the shame in her eyes and her horror at his savage beating of O'Sullivan and he knew there was a wedge between them that nothing would move.

Justin handed his outdoor clothes to the

maid and nodded a greeting. 'Thank you, Maddie, most kind.' He never treated his servants as inferior beings, he respected them and, in return, they gave him the utmost loyalty. 'Where is Mrs Harvard?'

Maddie looked troubled. 'She's been in her room since she came 'ome from school, sir, I heard her, crying she was, very upset and pale. Cookie took her some tea but she 'aven't eaten a thing.'

'Thank you, Maddie. Ask Cook to hold dinner back half an hour, would you?'

Upstairs, Justin halted outside the door of his wife's bedroom. All was silent. He turned the door knob, and his eyes went straight to the bed where Charlotte was lying, her arms stretched out as if she were waiting to welcome him. It was a silly, idle thought and, stepping into the room, he saw that she was asleep. Her hair had come undone and spread around her on the pillow like a soft, dark cloud. Her face was pale, there were smudges under her eyes, and pity filled his heart.

'Charlotte,' he said softly. She opened her eyes and, for a moment, they were unfocused. They were beautiful eyes, slanting, almost almond-shaped, seductive and fringed with thick dark lashes. She sat up quickly.

'Justin, what are you doing in here?'

He almost smiled – it was his home, he could enter any room he wished to and, yet, he accepted he was intruding.

'I'm sorry.' He moved away from the bed and from the stupid feeling that he should take her in his arms and comfort her. 'Maddie seemed to think you weren't feeling well.'

'I'm tired.' Her voice was flat, lacking emotion, and he saw she was physically drained.

'Bad day at school?'

She nodded and her hair fell across her face. As she moved it aside, he saw her sweet, full lips trembling.

Unable to stop himself, he put his arms around her and, for an instant, her head lay on his shoulders. There was a sweet scent from her hair as it brushed his cheek, and a feeling rose in him that he didn't understand. Was it pity, or was it love and tenderness?

She drew away. 'Don't.' Her voice was thick with tears. 'Don't be kind to me, I don't think I could bear it.'

At once he released her. 'Would you like to talk?' he offered. 'There's no reason we can't be civil to each other, is there?'

She pushed herself to her feet and faced him, and he saw her vulnerability. She was very young and very unhappy. He felt angry with himself. He didn't want feelings to come into the marriage, he didn't want to be married at all; all he wanted was a token wife so that he could claim his inheritance. Now, his plan seemed sordid, mercenary. Charlotte deserved better than a loveless marriage.

He had planned to offer her a divorce once the money had come through from his inheritance. The marriage could be annulled, there had been no consummation, but how could he do that to her now? Her reputation was bad enough simply because she'd been attacked by a drunken man, a divorce would make her even more of an outcast.

He sank into the wicker seat near the window and stared at her. 'I've been so unfair to you, Charlotte,' he said gently. 'I can only say how truly sorry I am.'

'It was my decision to marry. You didn't force me into it.' She almost whispered the words. Her head was bent and he couldn't see her expression. After a moment, she looked up and tossed back her hair and there was a determined look on her face. 'I *will* make a success of the school.' Her small jaw was thrust forward and in her eyes was the expression of an almost holy light.

'I have no doubt you will.' Justin rose and made his way to the door – this Charlotte, with the fanaticism of the chosen one, the woman who would alter the lives of the poor, was one he could cope with. He left her, his mood altered. She had what she wanted, her wretched school, and he, well, he would inherit his father's estate and hand it on to his two daughters. That wasn't so bad, was it?

The weak sunlight streaming in through the

window drew Charlotte out of her sleep. She sat up groggily, realizing it was morning. She thought about the previous night, about Justin's unexpected kindness, and her heart sank with despair. He would never love her, he'd never claimed he would love her, they had made a bargain and that's all it was.

'I'm glad that he doesn't often show me kindness.' Charlotte spoke the words out loud as she brushed her hair and tied it back, twisting a comb in its thickness to hold it away from her face. His businesslike attitude distanced him from her, he was a stranger, the man she had married for the sake of a dream, and now she must put all her energies into realizing that dream. How easy it would be to give up, to run to the bosom of her family, but that idea had been a momentary weakness and she must put it behind her.

When she went downstairs she found a letter placed at the side of her breakfast plate. She saw the beautiful script of her stepmother and smiled at the coincidence of hearing from her family so soon after thinking of them.

She was the first down. It was the weekend and Justin's girls were coming home that day, a welcome break from their fine school. Charlotte would be so happy to see them. Her own school was closed for the weekend and, for once, she was glad she wasn't teaching. She had so much to think about.

She opened her letter and read it avidly. Everything was fine with the family and Ella was expecting another child. Once again, Charlotte thought about being with them all, enjoying the fine climate in their part of America; she thought about being loved and needed, being part of a family again.

'Good morning.' Justin's voice was impersonal. He swung into the room and didn't look at her. It was as though the friendliness of the previous night had never been. She was so very aware of him, of the masculine strength he radiated. She risked a glance at him but he was busy with his breakfast and didn't meet her eyes.

'I've had a letter from America,' she said quietly. 'They are all so pleased I made a good marriage. If only they knew the truth, how hurt they would be.'

'That you sold your soul for a school, you mean?' His tone was curt, and anger and pain burned in her anew like a fire.

'Is that what you think of me?' In spite of herself, her voice trembled. 'But then, what could I expect from a cold fish like you?'

He didn't reply but set about his meal, his appetite undiminished, while she pushed away her plate, too upset to eat. 'You couldn't make an honest marriage with some high-society lady, someone you could love. You want your freedom so you can visit your mistress without a sharp tongue scolding you.

You've sold your soul as well, if you ask me.'

'I no longer have a mistress.' The words sprang from his lips and, at once, he seemed to regret them.

He picked up his newspaper and hid himself behind it.

She was startled into silence. She wanted to ask why he'd given the woman up, but her tongue refused to move. In any case, it was none of her business. She glanced at the clock.

'I'll need to be away in about half an hour to meet the girls at the station,' she said, moving on to a safer topic. 'It will be good to see them again.'

'I'll come to the station with you,' he said abruptly, without looking round his newspaper. He would want the girls to think the marriage was a happy one, a real one.

Charlotte rose to her feet. 'I'll go and get ready.' She moved to the door and his voice followed her.

'I'll meet you in the hall in twenty minutes,' he said brusquely, and once again she felt dismissed, like a servant.

It was a fine day. The pale sun of the morning had warmed to a mellow sunlight. The air was fresher here at Thornhill, set into the hillside away from the killing smoke of the works along the river. Soon, Justin was driving the trap through the busy streets of

Swansea towards the railway station.

The train was early. It drew in to the platform like a long fire-breathing monster, sinuously following the lines of the Great Western steam-engine track. A strong breeze blew under the ornate roof of the station and drove discarded newspapers along the platform. Charlotte was a little afraid of the steam and the noise and hung back until she saw the two girls jump joyfully on to the platform.

She hugged them both and marvelled at the way Rhian had grown taller in such a short time.

'Charlotte, I love you so much!' Morwen clung to her, burying her head in the warmth of Charlotte's neck, trying to hide her joyful tears.

Charlotte kissed her hair and tipped up her face. 'My dear, sweet Morwen, I'm so happy to see you.'

The drive home was filled with excited gossip about the college and about the teachers who took time off to teach the girls privately until they were old enough to attend classes with the other girls. Charlotte felt Morwen's hand clasp her own and a sharp pain of happiness clutched at her heart.

When they arrived home and stepped into the sunlit hall, the smell of roasting meat drifted towards them. It was lunch-time, and the girls quickly deposited their cases near the stairs and hurried into the dining room. Both Rhian and Morwen ate ravenously, enjoying the meal, which Cook had made especially for them. There was rich brown gravy with the beef and a sticky jam pudding after it.

Justin excused himself as soon as lunch was over. 'Someone has to work to keep this family afloat,' he joked, and Rhian laughed derisively.

'I don't think it's work you have on your mind,' she said. 'I expect you will go to your club and smoke and drink with other men like you.'

'What do you mean, "like me"?' Justin paused and faced his daughter.

'Well, you're a married man and yet you still act like a bachelor,' said Rhian in a grown-up voice that held a touch of hostility. 'Why, you don't even sleep in the same bed as Charlotte. I find that a little strange.'

'It's not strange,' Charlotte said abruptly. 'Even the members of the royal family have separate rooms.'

'Well, in that case, how did the late Queen Victoria have so many children?'

Justin looked startled. 'Well, of course I sleep with Charlotte,' he said quickly, caught off guard. For a moment Charlotte didn't know whether to laugh at him or be sorry for him. 'It's just that sometimes I'm restless, and then I go into my old room so that I won't disturb her.'

'Well, we'll just see tonight, won't we?' There was a sharpness to Rhian's tone, an inflection that Charlotte couldn't quite understand.

Justin looked confused, and Charlotte spoke up. 'Of course you will, you silly girl, why else would we get married if we didn't...' she hesitated '...care about each other?'

'I can think of some very good reasons.'

'That's enough, Rhian!' Justin said sharply. 'Remember your manners, and don't talk about adult matters that don't concern you.'

Charlotte watched him go and wondered, deep in her heart, why Rhian was being antagonistic to her father and, more to the point, what he would do about the challenge she had flung down in anger? Well, that was something only he could deal with and, for this afternoon, she meant to sit with the two girls, listen to their gossip and simply enjoy their company.

CHAPTER NINETEEN

Luke sat in his study in the house that stood on the lower slopes of Kilvey hill. The room was the epitome of masculinity, and one wall was covered in shelves to hold his many

239

books. But Luke wasn't seeing his room, he was thinking of Charlotte and how she had cast him aside. The very house he now owned had been bought with the tastes and comfort of the woman who was to have been his wife in mind. What a fool he'd been to tie himself to a building that would be expensive to finance. He'd believed that his and Charlotte's combined salaries would give them a comfortable lifestyle. Again, he cursed himself for a fool. Money was tight now, even though he'd taken in lodgers. Eventually, he might have to sell the house, go back to being a lodger in someone else's house.

With a sigh, he pulled his thoughts back to the present. His desk was piled high with papers to be marked, the scribblings of the schoolchildren new to written English. Some of the pupils spoke Welsh as their first language but, strangely, these children adapted well to written and spoken English.

English was such a beautiful language, Luke mused, the language of poets past and poets to come. Although his first love was the teaching of numbers rather than letters, he put his heart and soul into all his work and, at the moment, English dominated his mind.

He came to the small composition written by John Merriman, and his pulse quickened. The boy was an undoubted scholar, with a fine brain. Some of his sentences were grammatically incorrect, he seemed unsure of the varied meanings of the words 'to', 'two' and 'too', but a good stint at Luke's special lessons, aimed at the brightest pupils of the school, would soon correct that.

As if on cue, the door downstairs was pushed open and John's voice, deep now it had broken, and eager, called up the stairs. 'It's me, Mr Lester, can I come up?'

'Come.' The routine was an established one and Luke didn't even bother to rise from his chair. He gave the boy extra lessons in the evening, and although the school was closed today, John had wanted to carry on. He came into the room.

'Sit,' Luke instructed, waving his hand towards the upright chair at his side. John shifted uneasily, seeing his own writing and the red penmarks of the corrections Luke had made. Luke smiled, wanting to put the boy at ease.

'This is very good, John, very good indeed. I like your description of the works, how it burned and how the flames jumped like a startled animal to set the surrounding buildings alight.'

John shuffled his feet and looked uncomfortable and Luke knew why. His heart had warmed to the boy's writing, it had restraint, modesty; he had not written of his courage in returning with Justin to pull Charlotte to safety. Even now, he was embarrassed by the thought of someone else reading his account of the fire.

'However, you are having difficulties with your grammar,' Luke continued. He saw John's eyes cloud with disappointment. 'That's only to be expected, and we'll soon correct it.' John nodded, relieved, and Luke smiled, feeling he'd got through to the boy. John's earnest determination to improve himself was laudable and, in all fairness, showed that Charlotte's dream of bringing enlightenment to the children of the Swansea poor was worthwhile.

For over an hour, Luke worked with John, and it was time well spent. The boy sighed in satisfaction and sat back in his chair, and Luke watched him, pleased he had such a fertile mind to work with.

'If you continue to apply yourself, you could go far.' Luke stood up, dropping his pen, and a splash of ink fell on John's composition. 'I'm sorry.' Luke blotted the ink as best he could. John picked up the paper and looked at it in awe.

'You are such a good teacher, Mr Lester,' he said. 'Thank you for taking so much trouble with me. Sometimes I feel stupid but you make me feel I can get better at my lessons.' He followed Luke to the door and stood in the hallway for a moment, his eyes shining like beacons in the semi-darkness.

Luke rested his hand on John's shoulder. 'It gives me pleasure to teach you. Keep up the good work. Do as much writing and studying as you can.'

'I will, sir.' John left him and ran along the narrow street with the joyous ease of the very young.

Soon he would be a man, he would need to find himself a decent position. It was only down to Harvard's generosity that John was able to attend lessons at all. Without the patronage of Charlotte's husband, he would be forced to work at the mouth of the furnace or down the dark holes of one of the many mines in the area. The boy might even have been placed in the Harvard nickel works in the Clydach valley, walking miles every day. The knowledge that his deliverance from all that was due to Justin Harvard left a bitter taste in Luke's mouth.

He returned to his books, pushing aside the unwelcome thought of Charlotte in that man's bed, and concentrated on his marking.

A little later, Mrs Smithers, the woman who cleaned his house, called him for the evening meal. This was a treat, as Mrs Smithers cooked only for dinner, the rest of the day Luke and his lodgers had to fend for themselves. The smell of lamb rose tantalizingly into the study, and Luke realized how hungry he was. He spent a moment wondering what sort of food the pupils of the little school would be eating, probably potato stew or bread and cheese – and those were the lucky ones: most children got by with dried bacon rinds and stale crusts, sometimes pockmarked with mould.

His lodgers were already seated. Luke knew all three of them; they were, like him, poorly paid, but were struggling to save enough money to buy a property of their own. Dewi Thomas was a clerk to a local solicitor, Billy Jeffreys was a warehouse man and Twm Blackwood owned a small shoeshop in the Stryd Fawr. The three were older than Luke by a few years and Luke wondered if his fate, like theirs, was to live out his life without a wife.

He ate his meal. The food was good – he wasn't doing so badly for himself and, as for a wife, he wouldn't find one sitting by the fire every night reading or playing chess with Dewi Thomas, isolated in his own little world. He must push himself to go out of an evening, join the teachers from other schools at their favourite haunt near the beach.

The Colossus was a hostelry fronting the road alongside the curve of the bay. The building was old and elegant and frequented only by those able to pay the price of a good drink of whisky in the comfort of a watering hole that was more like a hotel than a public house. None of the men from the works patronized the Colossus, it was too elegant and too expensive. Only professional men were to be seen sunk in the huge, comfortable chairs and sofas that gave the place its name.

If he made friends with his fellows, he might be invited to attend dinners and dances and find himself part of Swansea's social scene. Tomorrow, he told himself, he would put aside his work and go out and seek the company of educated men, men of his own age. He became aware that Mrs Smithers was addressing him.

'Mr Lester, you're far away, so you are, you haven't even started on your *cawl*. You like lamb stew, what's ailing you?'

'It's nothing, Mrs Smithers, I'm just tired.'

'Well, if you *will* teach those heathen children who don't even know their Bible, then you bring it all on your good self.'

Luke's mouth twitched. He resisted the urge to tell Mrs Smithers to mind her manners and instead bent his head and began to eat the excellent stew.

As night fell, Charlotte began to worry about the sleeping arrangements. Would Justin come to her room or would she be expected to go to his? The girls were already asleep, tired after the excitement of the long train journey. Perhaps there wouldn't be a problem after all, perhaps she could retire to her own bed and Justin to his.

She ate little of the late snack of milk and biscuits Cook had set out for her on a little side table in the drawing room. Apprehension filled her as Justin entered the room and sat near her, sitting forward in his chair, hands on his knees, eyes refusing to meet hers.

'About tonight...' she began, but Justin held up his hand for silence. 'The girls are asleep,' she put in hastily.

'Rhian is not a fool,' he said flatly. 'She will make sure that she sees us going up to bed. You are too easily taken in, Charlotte.'

'What are we to do then?'

'Play a role, as many parents do, pretend our marriage is solid, unshakeable. I don't want to disillusion my daughters so early in their young lives.' He paused. 'Just tell me when you are ready to go up.' He picked up the newspaper that had been neatly folded beside his chair and sat back. The discussion was apparently over.

Charlotte hung her head, her cheeks red as she fought the tears welling in her eyes. Suddenly there was a great emptiness in her heart. She wanted to be loved as her long-dead father had loved her, unconditionally, unstintingly. She had expected that to come from a husband.

When she was with Luke Lester, her hand through his arm, his respectable fiancée, she thought for a while she had just that, unconditional love. Now he hated her, she saw it in every glance; he thought her cheap, a gold-digger without shame.

At last, tiredness claiming her, she got to her feet. 'I'll have to go up, now,' she said softly. She stood, hands folded neatly before her, feeling like a child about to be punished for some wrongdoing.

Several tense moments passed with agonizing slowness, and then Justin put down his paper and swung to his feet. He looked almost jovial.

'Come along then, wife.' His voice was laden with sarcasm. 'Let's go to bed. My room, I think?'

She nodded her head, bent her face, turned away from him. He took her hand as he led her up the stairs, and her fingers curled in his, his touch causing her a great tenderness she did her best to deny.

Justin had been right in his assessment of his daughter. Rhian peered round the door of her bedroom and watched them with narrowed eyes.

'Back to bed, young lady,' Justin said, releasing Charlotte's hand and instead slipping his arm around her slim waist and pulling her against him. 'You should have been asleep a long time ago.'

Rhian had a stubborn look on her face and remained in the doorway. Her white nightgown, now too short for her, revealed her narrow, still childish feet. It was for her sake, or so Charlotte told herself, that she reached up and caught Justin's chin in her hand and put her lips against his. Their lips clung for a long moment, and then Justin drew away and opened his bedroom door.

'After you, my dearest.' For once there was no mocking sarcasm in his voice and, swallowing hard, Charlotte went into the bedroom, her feelings in such turmoil and her heart pounding so hard she thought he must hear it.

'Undress and get into bed.' Justin's tone had altered. 'I don't trust that minx not to follow us.'

To Charlotte's surprise, her nightgown had been laid out on the bed, and she slipped into it quickly, hiding her body from Justin. She need not have worried. He had turned away from her and was undoing his clothing.

She climbed into bed and, though she tried to turn away from him, she felt compelled to watch until he stood naked and magnificent beside the bed. His shoulders were broad, well-muscled, his belly flat. Her cheeks flamed with embarrassment as she saw his arousal, standing proud from within the curling hair.

He shrugged. 'Don't be fooled, Charlotte,' he said, as he pulled back the quilt. 'A man would be aroused to see any woman undressed and waiting in his bed.'

'I'm not waiting,' she said quickly.

'Come along, Charlotte, your father owned

the Palace Theatre – you must have seen actors standing about naked and readily excited at the sight of the half-naked actresses, who we all know are trollops anyway.'

'They are not!' Charlotte was stung by the accusation. 'Don't believe all you hear about theatre people, because it's not true.'

Justin slid into bed beside her and put his arm around her, drawing her close. For a moment, Charlotte tried to pull away, and then she saw the door open a crack.

'Come in, Rhian,' Justin called, 'we know you are there.' He put his mouth close to Charlotte's ear. 'Now, if you learned anything from the theatre, just act the part of a doting wife. I know it will come hard to you because you despise my motives just as I despise yours.'

Charlotte had no time to ponder his words before Rhian came into the room and ran to the bed.

'I'm glad, Father,' she said, kissing his cheek, 'I'm glad the gossip isn't true, that you and Charlotte do love each other, that you do sleep in the same bed.'

Justin moved away from Charlotte and held both his daughter's hands in his. 'Gossip is for those who do not know the true facts,' he said, 'so never believe it.' He kissed her cheek. 'Now be a good daughter and go to bed and, for heaven's sake, sleep – your little cheeks are white with weariness.'

Rhian nodded. 'I do love you, Father, and you too, Charlotte.' She leaned across the bed and kissed Charlotte's cheek. 'And I won't believe any wicked lies again.'

When Rhian had gone Charlotte held the quilt up to her chin. 'What wicked lies is she talking about? What has she heard?'

'I don't know.' He turned his back against her. 'Put out the light, will you?'

For a long time Charlotte lay awake, but at last sleep claimed her and, in her dreams, she was dancing in Justin's arms, loving him, kissing him, laughing and happy. When she woke in the morning, she was alone. Justin had gone.

CHAPTER TWENTY

She had slept with her husband in that arid, loveless bed and told herself she could cope and not be silly and emotional about it. But she had seen him naked, in all his glory, and in spite of her determination not to be affected by his nearness, she had wanted him.

It shamed Charlotte, now, to have such foolish, hopeless desires. Yes, she had been so close to his warmth and had experienced a stirring of her inner feelings, unfamiliar feelings, feelings she had no intention of examining. She had to remind herself it was all a sham, an act for Rhian, the poor, confused girl. As soon as his daughter had left the bedroom, Justin had turned his back and fallen asleep like a man with no conscience.

She heard the scratching of pen against paper, the shuffling of feet, the strong smell of ink, and she remembered she was in the classroom. She put down the book she hadn't been reading and faced her young pupils. Lizzie was sitting at one of the front desks, her fair head bent over a piece of scrap paper. As Charlotte watched, Lizzie passed the now folded paper to John and, irritably, he pushed it away unread.

One of the other boys sniggered and whispered to John, who turned red and threw an angry look that seemed to encompass the whole class of children. He got to his feet and asked to be excused, and Charlotte nodded, understanding.

As she watched his gangly, coltish gait crossing the room before her desk, she realized once again that he was fast becoming a man. He was near enough for her to see the darkening along the line of his jaw, the shadow of his first facial hairs. Soon, he would need to shave.

He didn't seem happy or comfortable. He didn't even look up as he passed her, he looked fixedly at the door and, if she hadn't known better, she would have said he was off to have a smoke behind the lavatories, the way the other boys did. He was worried about something, guilty almost, and Charlotte wondered if it was school work. He shouldn't be – all his essays were gems of creative thinking, his grasp of the use of adjectives was good, he didn't lard his work with them. His spelling left a good deal to be desired and his grammar was less than brilliant, but he had the intelligence and a burning desire to learn the proper use of the English language.

Charlotte left her desk and, swishing the back of her long skirts aside, stepped down into the body of the classroom. She made her way between the desks, enjoying the acrid smell of ink in the little white pots, hearing the scratch of nib against paper and watching her students begin to bloom under her tuition. Surely that was enough to compensate her for a loveless marriage?

But she couldn't lie to herself: the relationship with Justin, if there was one, was on her side only. Charlotte felt a quickening in her heartbeat. She loved him so much, this husband of hers, and sometimes she even thought he cared a little about her.

She stood at one of the long windows, looking out at the fields beyond the school. They fell into a pattern of patchwork and looked so peaceful but it was an illusion. All the steaming, sulphurous works were at the rear of the building, out of sight. The only sign of the industry nearby was the thin trail of sulphurous smoke that drifted over the roof of the school, thinner today than usual because of the fair wind that was blowing.

Charlotte fought the little wriggles of unease that teased her brain and asked herself what Justin was really getting out of their sterile marriage. Surely she could have remained at Thornhill to look after the girls as their governess, housekeeper, anything – so why had Justin decided on marriage? Shortly after their marriage, Justin had sent the girls to boarding school, to receive a good education elsewhere. True, Charlotte was there for them when they came home, a permanent feature in their lives, but that couldn't be enough inducement for their father to marry a woman he didn't love, so there must be another reason. What was it?

The door opened and Charlotte turned to see John return to the classroom. Head bent, he slouched his way to his desk, and Lizzie, her eyes large, watched his every move. As he dropped into his chair, scraping the legs noisily against the wooden floor, the girl gazed at him adoringly.

Charlotte drew a sharp breath, her own troubles forgotten as she watched the silent interaction between them. He was as far away from her as he could be, even though their desks were close together. Lizzie, her small face puckered in anxiety, tried to attract his gaze.

Oh, no! Surely John couldn't be so foolish! And Lizzie – after her terrible experience of giving birth to an unwanted baby, surely she wouldn't fall into the same trap again? She prayed she was wrong, and it was with relief she heard the bell ring for dinner break.

'File out slowly and keep in line as you make your way to the dinner hall,' she said. 'I don't want any unruly behaviour, I want my pupils to show a good example to the new children.'

A few weeks ago she wouldn't have needed to say anything of that sort – the total number of pupils in the school had been thirty. Now the school was blossoming like a flower opening its petals and a wooden building had been hastily built to accommodate the new pupils. That thought was a source of satisfaction to Charlotte. She recognized that the load of responsibility on herself and Luke Lester was becoming unwieldy and soon she might have to take on another teacher.

As she made her way to the dinner hall, Charlotte caught sight of John's gangly frame at the far side of the building. She couldn't be sure, but the girl with him looked like Lizzie, and her heart sank. It seemed her fears were well grounded: the two were together again.

She felt a spurt of anger. John was a fool!

Hadn't he had enough trouble? And the girl, foolish little Lizzie, she probably loved John in her own innocent way, just as Charlotte loved Justin, hopelessly, pointlessly.

As she helped supervise the meal of thin soup and slices of hard, coarse bread, Charlotte pushed the tantalizing uncertainties of her own position out of her head. She was here, in her school, looking after her pupils, teaching them, nurturing them, hopefully generating a new future for them. More than that she could not do.

Justin was unsettled when he left his office on the edge of his huge nickel enterprise and stepped out into the sunshine, too weak to warm the nip of cold with the approach of winter.

He went to his horse and trap. So far, he had ignored the early advent of the motor car and opted for what he knew and loved – his animals. He smoothed the soft nose of his grey mare, and she looked at him with large eyes, her soft, thick mouth nuzzling his hand. His mare loved him, unconditionally. Would that he had a woman who felt the same.

He would take the rest of the day off and go home to see his children. The girls loved him, of course they did, and yet there was an emptiness, a longing in him, that his daughters couldn't fill.

Once seated in the trap, he flicked the reins as though to outride his thoughts of that night, of Rhian standing in his bedroom, and the farce of he and Charlotte pretending that their marriage was a loving, happy one. And they had to keep up the pretence.

It was a pretence, of course – how could it not be? They had made a bargain. And, in the future, what? Perhaps Charlotte would want to move out of his house when she knew the full extent of his duplicity. How would the girls feel about that? Rhian, in particular, would know he'd lied, that the marriage had been a sham.

The previous night, for a brief time, Charlotte had been close to him, physically, at least. He'd felt her warmth and, when she slept, she had moved closer to him and he'd felt her soft hair against his cheek. Her closeness had moved him not only to desire for her but to something far more tender.

When he arrived home, the girls were thrilled to see him. Morwen ran across the lawn to fling herself into his arms. He hugged her close and tried to put the problems of his marriage out of his mind, but the feel of Charlotte, the scent of her, stayed obstinately in his thoughts.

CHAPTER TWENTY-ONE

The pantomime of going up to bed with Justin went on the whole time the girls were on holiday. Charlotte became used to the closeness. The knowledge that he was beside her in the bed was disturbing, though he never touched her, but also comforting. Sometimes it felt as if she really was married and, somehow, that closeness was reflected in a daytime warmth towards each other.

On sunny afternoons, when Charlotte's school day was over, the four of them would go out to Victoria Park, opposite the slip, and have a picnic. From there Charlotte could hear the soft sound of the waves eagerly sucking back the small pebbles along the stretch of Swansea Bay.

The girls seemed happy. Morwen was like a young puppy, laughing and dancing, feet bare and pink on the softness of the grass. Rhian was more subdued, she was growing up, but she too seemed content to bask in the warmth that was encompassing the small family.

That day was laundry day, so Rhian and Morwen kept out of the way. Charlotte was helping the maids to sort out the clothes ready for washing in the small laundry room at the back of the house; there, for a little while, she could dream she was a happily married woman.

She picked up one of Justin's shirts and held it for a moment. She breathed in the scent of him, the smell of soap mingled with his own smell, masculine, so familiar now, and lovable.

Charlotte became aware that Polly, the most senior of the maids, was looking at her strangely. Polly was a widow, with no children, and when her husband had died in an accident in the Clydach nickel works she had been left penniless. Now, she lived on the premises of the big house, was hard-working and fiercely loyal to Justin, who had paid for the funeral and treated her with a kindness and consideration that was rarely shown by any of the higher classes to their servants.

Hurriedly, Charlotte handed over Justin's shirt. 'I was daydreaming again, Polly,' she said, and Polly smiled sadly.

'I know that look, Mrs Harvard.'

'What look?' As soon as the words were out of her mouth, Charlotte regretted them. She had opened the way for Polly to enlarge on what she had to say.

'A lady in love with her husband, content with her lot – I felt like that once, before it was all taken from me.' She paused. 'If I can give you a bit of advice, Mrs Harvard, make the most of this time, the very most, because no one knows when your happiness will be snatched away from you.'

Polly bent over the huge china sink, plunging her hands into the hot water. She rubbed at the soaking clothes with tears rolling down her cheeks. Charlotte made a tentative move towards her and then stopped as Polly's shoulders tensed; she would find any physical contact, however kindly meant, embarrassing.

When two of the other laundrymaids came into the room carrying arms full of bedding, Charlotte murmured that she had other business to see to and left the steam and the heat of the laundry and returned to the house.

Justin was sitting with his daughters, and he looked up at Charlotte as she came into the room and smiled. 'What have you done to your hair? It's all curly and wild.'

Morwen jumped up from her place on the floor and ran to embrace her. 'But you're still beautiful, Charlotte, isn't she beautiful, Father?'

Justin put his head on one side and pretended to consider his younger daughter's words. 'Well...' He hesitated, and Morwen clung more tightly around Charlotte's waist.

'Come on, Daddy!' she said impatiently.

'Charlotte is indeed very lovely,' he said

slowly, and for a moment a shadow seemed to pass over his face. 'Your mother was very beautiful, too, girls.' He stood up, suddenly brisk.

'I'd better do some work today, I suppose.' He kissed his daughters, and Charlotte saw him hesitate before touching her cheek lightly with his lips. She felt a thrill of happiness run through her, even though she knew he was simply putting on a show for his girls.

She watched his retreating back, the broad shoulders and the crisp hair that curled on the back of his neck. How she loved him. Charlotte couldn't deny her feelings for him, and she couldn't hide them either, at least not from Rhian.

'I'm sorry, Charlotte,' Rhian said suddenly.

'Sorry for what?'

'For being unfair to you, doubting you. I can see you really care for my father and he cares for you.' Her shoulders slumped, and suddenly she looked like the child she really was. 'I've been disloyal to you and...'

Charlotte put her arm around Rhian's shoulder and was encouraged when the girl didn't pull away. 'It's all right. We just had to take our time, get to know each other.' She was warmed by Rhian's words, wishing it was true that Justin cared for her. Perhaps he did, just a little.

Morwen, anxious not to be left out of things, hugged Charlotte even more tightly.

'Will you take us to the park, Charlotte?'

Charlotte looked out at the dull clouds gathering over the rocky prominence of Mumbles Head. 'I think it's going to rain. What a shame, and it's washing day too.' Now the washing would hang like the shadows of ghosts in the dimness of the laundry room. Polly would be upset; she'd told Charlotte that it gave her a sense of satisfaction to see the washing billow and blow on the line in the garden at the back of the building.

'Morwen, perhaps we'd better stay in and, if you like, I'll read to you.'

'Yes!' Morwen jumped up and down, her bare toes curling in anticipated enjoyment. 'Will it be a fairy story or a ghost story or what?'

'We'll see. Let's go upstairs and choose a nice book.'

'"Cinderella" is a good story,' Rhian said. 'It's about a lady who is poor and has to rake the ashes from the fireplace, but in the end she marries the prince.' Her eyes met Charlotte's. 'That's something you did, Stepmother.'

Suddenly Rhian's expression changed, and her countenance was guarded and wary as she said, 'My mother brought Daddy a fortune when they married.'

'How do you know, Rhian?' Morwen had sensed the hostility in her sister's voice. 'You wasn't even born then.'

'Weren't even born,' Charlotte corrected, absentmindedly, her thoughts on what Rhian had just said. Her happiness fading, Charlotte led the way up the stairs to the girls' library room. Her euphoria of earlier had vanished. She had been put in her place, and by a girl who seemed now to be her enemy.

Justin sat in his office and fiddled with his pen. Inadvertently, he squeezed the nib and ink spilled out on to the papers in front of him. 'Damn and blast! Why can't I get that woman out of my mind, out of my blood?'

In his mind he saw Charlotte again, coming in from the laundry room, her hair damp and curly, her face flushed with the steam. He wanted her, by God, how he wanted her, but that had never been part of their bargain. Each night as he lay with her in bed, he longed to turn to her, to take her in his arms and make love to her.

But she didn't want that; all she wanted was her damned school. Still, he made an effort to console himself, she was good with the girls, good *for* them. Morwen, in particular, loved her, needed her, she was a mother to come home to in place of the mother she had never known.

He looked through the grimy window of his office. It had begun to rain, a thin drizzle that misted everything outside. It was depressing; it matched his feelings exactly. Why couldn't he have met Charlotte in a different time, a different place, where he could have courted her, won her, made her love him? But, he reminded himself, their paths would never have crossed.

Impatient with his thoughts, he pushed aside his chair and got to his feet. He had work to do, money to earn, he had ploughed a great deal into the Harvard nickel works and he would plough much more into it. His inheritance was safe: that's what marriage had given him. But somehow that wasn't so important any more.

The girls' holiday was over. Charlotte saw them on to the train and nodded to Polly, who was taking the journey with the children to see them safely back to the college. 'Take good care of them.'

Morwen, predictably, was in tears and, as the train wound its way out of the station, Charlotte felt her own eyes burn. It would be empty in the house without them. No more nights sharing a bed with Justin. Would their new-found closeness vanish now? She glanced at her watch, she'd better get back to school – Luke would be hard pushed to cope with two classes, his own and hers, and she didn't want him to be in a bad mood. These days, it seemed as if he was always in a bad mood and she, of course, was to blame.

Luke was a born teacher; he had the magic some teachers had to hold the pupils rapt. Charlotte envied him that. She wondered how life would have been if she'd married him as planned. But then there would be no school. And the school was everything. Wasn't it?

The classroom was empty. Charlotte looked around at the empty desks in bewilderment. Where was everyone?

Faintly, through the slight opening of the windows, she heard the sound of children's voices. She looked out, her hands grasping the sill. She could see the boys running about on the playing field next to the school, chasing a ball as though their lives depended on it. On the perimeter of the field stood the girls, their attitude and stance showing how bored they were with the whole thing.

The door opened, and John Merriman came to stand beside her.

'What's going on, John?' Charlotte turned, making an effort to quell her sudden feelings of anger.

John shrugged. 'Mr Lester's decided to take them all outside for an hour every day,' he said, not meeting her eyes. 'Suits most of them, they love it when there's no hard brain work.'

'But not you?'

'I want to study, to get on in the world,

Mrs Harvard. I'm a man now, and I should be making my own way.' He moved away from her and sat at his desk, flicking through one of the books he'd brought with him. Charlotte bent over his shoulder, curious about his choice of reading. It was a history book about the Tudors and Stuarts.

'I didn't know you liked history, John.' Most of the pupils thought history boring, irrelevant to their everyday lives.

'I like anything that helps me to know more, Mrs Harvard.' John didn't look up and Charlotte noticed that his hair needed cutting. It was straight and fell over his eyes as he read his book.

Charlotte sat in the seat beside him. 'If you have any questions, anything you would like explained...'

He looked up slowly and his eyes were shadowed.

'Why is Mr Lester trying to upset you?'

'I meant questions about history, John, not about my private life. In any case, why do you think Mr Lester is trying to upset me?'

He shrugged. 'I dunno, the way he looks at you, the things he does, like taking the boys out to play football when they should be in class. He knows you wouldn't like it, you think it's a waste of time, don't you?'

Charlotte answered carefully. 'Football is very good for young people, fresh air and exercise play a part in all our lives but, of course, I think time at school should be spent in proper lessons, English, arithmetic–' she pointed at his book '–history perhaps.'

John looked directly into her face. 'I think he means you harm, miss, I've seen him watching you like a cat with a mouse.' He blushed. 'Begging your pardon, I don't mean you're like a mouse.'

Charlotte put her hand on his shoulder. 'That's all right, John, it's good of you to warn me, but I'm sure you're wrong. Mr Lester is a gentleman.' She smiled and moved away from the boy. 'Did you know that you used a simile in that sentence?'

He shook his head. 'What's a simile, Mrs Harvard?'

'It's when you say something is *like* something else, "like a cat with a mouse", for example.'

She watched him digesting the information. 'We'll learn more about similes later on.'

By the time Luke brought the children back into the school, Charlotte was ringing the bell for the end of the day's lessons. She scowled at Luke and he paused beside her.

'Anything wrong?'

'I'll talk to you in my classroom.' Charlotte's voice was firm. She watched the children push noisily through the doors, and then silence descended on the school. Luke followed her obediently and, when he came into the room, Charlotte sat at her high desk and stared at him. 'Well?'

'Well what, Mrs Harvard?'

'Why are you wasting valuable time running the boys around the field chasing a ball with the girls standing by shivering in the cold? The children have little enough time to study as it is.'

'It's good for them to exercise, isn't it? You say yourself how important it is.'

'They get enough exercise at home, bringing in coal for the fires, fetching potatoes from the market.' She was exasperated. 'Don't you think it's better to exercise their minds?'

'Both are important,' Luke said. 'Look, Charlotte, I know we don't see eye to eye on many things but–' he shrugged '–the children need fun as well as work.'

'But only the boys were having fun, the girls were standing on the sidelines, and they looked cold and miserable to me.'

'Well, if you'd been here, you could have taken care of the girls. Can't you see that?'

Charlotte was aware he was trying to put her in the wrong and she sighed in exasperation. 'I was just seeing Rhian and Morwen on to the train. I wasn't exactly wasting time, was I?'

Luke sighed in turn. 'I suppose you have to keep your husband happy, or he might stop funding the school. That would never do, would it?'

'How dare you!' Charlotte tried to control her anger. 'It wouldn't be in your interest to see the school closed, would it?'

Before he could reply she walked to the door. 'All right, once a week the boys can go out to the fields, and I'll take the girls, though I don't know what I'm going to do with them.'

'Teach them household management, how to budget the money, that sort of thing,' Luke suggested, and for once his voice lacked the sarcasm that had been present ever since she'd broken off their engagement.

'That's a good idea, Luke,' Charlotte said. 'I could take them to the market, teach them how to buy good cheap food.' She paused and knew by Luke's change of face that he was sceptical. 'There was a time after my father died that the whole family lived on very little money. There were five of us girls and my little brother to feed. My stepmother, Ella, had to manage the money carefully. I learned a thing or two about good cheap meals, I can tell you.'

'I know.' He sounded contrite.

'Goodnight, Luke.' He left the classroom and Charlotte sank into her chair. Perhaps, just perhaps, she and Luke could be friends after all. The thought cheered her and stayed with her as she headed for the school door.

Briskly, she set out for home. The sky was

lightening now and the stormcloud which had threatened the day with rain was gone. She turned up the collar of her coat and walked eagerly towards Thornhill.

CHAPTER TWENTY-TWO

A feeling of dread filled John's mind but he tried his best to be calm. 'What is it, Lizzie? What are you trying to tell me?'

They were standing just outside the school boundaries. Lizzie was staring up into his face. She seemed oblivious of people passing by, even Mrs Harvard, who noticed them with some concern as she left the school for home.

'I don't know how to tell you and that's the truth, my lovely boy.' Her eyes were even larger as she blinked away her tears.

He knew then it was bad news; he saw it coming but was powerless to stop it. He looked away to the horizon, the grey sky lighter as it seemed to touch the water.

'Get on with it, Lizzie, for God's sake.'

'Don't blaspheme, John, it might bring us bad luck.'

She saw nothing wrong in her words. Talking about God and bad luck in the same sentence was to show ignorance, but she probably thought she was hedging her bets. He smiled, even though he knew the sky was about to fall on him.

Encouraged, Lizzie touched his arm. 'Promise you won't shout at me,' she implored. 'I'm frightened to death as it is.'

John sighed heavily. 'Go on, say it.' He felt he already knew the worst but he had a faint hope that he was wrong.

'I've fallen for a babba again.' The words were bald, flat, spoken in a whisper, and John put his hands over his face.

'I thought you knew how to stop that happening,' he said.

'I thought I did too.' Lizzie was on the defensive. 'Maggie Jones said if I put vinegar inside my ... before and after ... well, you know, I'd be all right.'

John gasped at her naivety. 'Lizzie! How could you be so silly as to believe such rubbish?'

She sank down on to the grass and her face as she gazed up at him was that of a terrified child, but her body was full and rounded, her breasts so good to touch, her secret place always ready for him.

'I thought she was a wise woman, John, everyone says she is. I'll have to go to her again, that's what I'll do.'

'It could be too late for that,' John said flatly. 'How far gone are you?'

She looked away from him, hugging her

knees. ''Bout two months I think.'

'What can this wise woman do now?'

'She can do things to me, make the babba come out of me now before it grows too big.'

John was horrified, but only for a moment. Lizzie was offering a way out, and she had to take it. No one would help them now, not a second time.

'Will you come with me, John, to see Maggie? I'm a bit frightened, see.'

'How can I come with you?' he said. 'Everyone will put two and two together and know that I'm the father. We might as well shout it from the top of the Guildhall. You know I can't come with you.'

Lizzie began to cry, large tears rolling down her plump face like huge drops of rain, and John felt his guts twist into knots.

'I'll wait for you,' he said at last. 'You know the hill just above the three ponds? I'll wait for you there.' It was the least he could do.

'She'll want paying,' Lizzie warned. 'I got a bit put by and I can pawn a few things.'

'What have you got to pawn?' The tone of disbelief in his voice made Lizzie blush.

'A few things, I'll find something,' she said defensively. 'Here, help me up, John, I feel fat as a cow already, even though I'm only a couple of months gone.'

Absently, John held his hand out to her and drew her to her feet. She rested against him for a few moments, soft as a kitten, her face damp with tears. He felt like a traitor, he had done this to her with his recklessness, he should control the need that sometimes burned in him, his body clamouring for something he shouldn't have.

He needed to talk to someone – Mr Harvard perhaps, or Luke Lester, ask an older man's advice. He wasn't sure that Lizzie should be going to this woman, Maggie, it seemed wrong somehow, though John didn't know why.

'Will it hurt, Lizzie?' He spoke softly. She burrowed her face into him.

'I don't know, but I'm having nightmares about it. Got to be done, though, can't have another bastard child, can I?'

John fumbled in his pocket and drew out some shillings. 'Here,' he said, 'perhaps that will help a bit.'

Lizzie looked at him in amazement. 'Where did you get that, John, you haven't been thieving, have you?'

He shook his head. 'Mr Harvard gave it to me, said I could buy some books with it if I needed any.' There would be no books now. 'Come on, I think it's going to rain.' As soon as he spoke, forks of lightning lit the sky and thunder cracked overhead. Lizzie squealed in fear and began to run towards the dilapidated wooden shed that stood on the boundary of the field. Once inside, John drew

Lizzie towards him, and she clung tightly around his neck, her eyes squeezed shut.

He held her close, feeling her breasts press against him. She sensed the change in him and wriggled nearer, tantalizing him. John tried to pull away but Lizzie held him fast.

'Come on, this last time, can't do any more harm, can it?'

John tried to resist but the need was strong in him. Lizzie lay on the straw spread across the floor and reached her arms towards him. With a groan he sank down beside her and her hand reached out, rubbing at his hardness. He was lost. He gave up the struggle and let Lizzie pull him into her soft, willing flesh.

Charlotte sat at the dining table making an effort to smile at the guests Justin had invited to dinner. She was annoyed he hadn't spoken to her of it until the last moment.

'Put on some nice jewellery–' his voice had been neutral, as if he were talking to a casual friend '–we're having guests to dine with us.'

The change in him was marked: ever since they had said goodbye to the children he'd been short with her. And of course he had spent the nights sleeping alone, leaving Charlotte feeling abandoned and lonely. She became aware that the Honourable Mr Morris was talking to her.

'I'm sorry.' She gave him a smile and his face relaxed. 'I was wondering what Cook was serving for pudding, a woman is always careful that she does her duty in an effort to please her guests.'

Mrs Morris leaned around her husband. 'I'm surprised, my dear–' her tone was edged with ice '–being the daughter of a theatre manager, you mustn't have had many dinner parties to arrange.'

'Hilda!' Mr Morris said. 'That's not very polite of you.'

'Sorry, dear.' Mrs Morris's voice showed she was not sorry at all. 'I hear your step-mother used to clean the floors of the Palace before she married your father.'

'Yes, you are quite right, Mrs Morris, my family never had much by way of wealth, but I think we made up for it with the good manners we were taught.'

Mrs Morris drew sharply away, a snail disappearing into its shell. Her words had stung and it brought home to Charlotte that the so-called affluent gentry in the town would always think of her as a usurper, a gold-digger who had feathered her nest very well by marrying a rich man.

She looked to Justin for support but it was not forthcoming. He must have heard the exchange between Mrs Morris and his wife but had no intention of becoming involved.

The pudding was served, a rich, sumptuous summer pudding, which Mrs Morris pushed away with a look of distaste. She turned round to Charlotte and fixed her with a steely expression. 'You just can't get good cooks these days. Oh, they're all right for ordinary fare but give them a sophisticated dish and they throw a tantrum.'

Charlotte ignored her and directed her remarks to Mr Morris. 'Your grandson is doing very well in school,' she said. 'I think Michael has the intellect to get right to the top of the tree, perhaps go to one of the big colleges, Oxford or Cambridge.'

Mrs Morris flapped her napkin to get attention and the other diners looked at her in surprise. 'Actually, Mrs Harvard–' her voice was hard '–our darling Michael will be leaving the school shortly. It was only a temporary measure until we secured a more appropriate place for him.'

Charlotte was dismayed. 'Oh, why, Mrs Morris? Why take him out of the school where he's learning so much?'

'Your school caters for all sorts of ghastly people. Just look at that John Merriman, getting a girl in the family way, at his tender age. I think it's disgusting.'

Charlotte saw Justin direct his gaze on to Mrs Morris. 'I admire your father greatly,' he said, and Mrs Morris looked startled. 'He is a self-made man, is he not?'

Mrs Morris stared at him, her mouth

hanging open, but she seemed incapable of speech.

'He rose from the ranks of the poor, a simple steel worker, to become one of the richest men in Swansea. And all that without an education, I believe.' He paused, waiting for Mrs Morris to speak, but she just shook her head and remained silent.

Justin smiled politely, but the smile didn't reach his eyes. 'We're hoping that John Merriman will make good when he's older, he's certainly quick at his lessons. Quicker even than your grandson.'

Mrs Morris found her voice. 'The wretched boy is quick at everything, even bedding a no-good little servant.' Her face was red now, the beads of sweat forming along her top lip caught in a moustache she had done her best to camouflage. 'I've decided I don't want my grandson taught in the same school as such riffraff. I'll take him out from his class right away.'

'That's your privilege and your grandson's loss,' Justin said smoothly, 'though I must add that you won't find such excellent teachers anywhere else in Swansea. Now–' he rose to his feet '–we have an evening of entertainment for you, a vocalist and four musicians. I think you will all enjoy listening to them.'

Mrs Morris tugged at her husband's arm. 'We have to leave early, I'm afraid.' She ignored her husband's look of surprise and walked like a ship in full sail from the dining room and into the hall.

The maid was not ready to send off departing guests so soon and there followed a fluster of activity, accompanied by grumbles from Mrs Morris at the lack of good servants, and then the couple was gone and the door closed against the cold.

Justin had led the other guests into the music room. The singer was standing by the grand piano ready to perform for her audience. Justin made way for Charlotte to sit alongside him and, when she did, he put his arm around her and smiled encouragement. Charlotte was surprised he was being so kind and supportive. He bent towards her, his mouth close to her ear.

'Mrs Morris has come up from the gutter, I could have embarrassed her further if I'd a mind to, so don't let her attitude worry you. The school is doing well and I respect your dedication to it.'

Although gently said, his words reminded Charlotte that their marriage was just a bargain, yet she saw only kindness in his eyes as they met hers.

Cheered, she gave her attention to the lovely voice of the singer. The young woman was sumptuously dressed in a beautiful gown of silk and lace beaded with tiny pearls. Her slender arms were bare except for a gold bangle that shot flashes of light.

For a time, Charlotte held herself erect under the weight of Justin's arm but, after a while, she relaxed against him, enjoying the show of affection, even if it was only done to impress his guests.

When the musical entertainment was over, people began to drift away and Charlotte was happy about that; she was tired and all she wanted to do was sleep. Her mouth ached with the effort to smile and she still smarted as she remembered Mrs Morris's scorn.

She and Justin enjoyed a nightcap of hot brandy sprinkled with spices and sat for a while in companionable silence, the only sounds the ticking of the clock and the shifting of coals in the fire. Not wanting to break the spell, Charlotte remained quiet. At last Justin rose to his feet.

'Time to go up, I suppose,' he said, almost regretfully, 'we both have work in the morning.'

They walked side by side up the broad, elegant staircase and, though Charlotte's eyes were almost closed with the effects of the brandy, she stood for a moment on the landing, waiting.

'Charlotte.' Her name burst from his lips and his mouth was very close to hers. They stood for a moment together just looking into each other's eyes, then Justin straightened his shoulders.

'Goodnight, Charlotte, thank you for being the perfect hostess this evening.'

She turned away, her heart thumping. What had he been going to say – that he cared for her? How foolish she was even to think that.

In her room, she sank on to the bed. Loneliness engulfed her as she looked around the large bedroom, beautifully furnished but empty. She put her head in her hands, wishing she'd never been such a fool as to enter into this marriage. But she had made her bed, as her father used to say, and now she must lie on it.

School was over for the day, and Charlotte stopped ringing the bell, holding the clapper between her fingers. John Merriman had been absent and, worriedly, Charlotte remembered seeing him talking to Lizzie. Were the pair in trouble again? She sincerely hoped not. One mistake might be forgiven, but two?

Luke came through the school doors towards her. 'Mrs Harvard,' he said, 'just the person I wanted to see. It's John Merriman. It seems he's run off. None of his classmates has seen him since yesterday.'

Her heart sank. 'Perhaps he's not well.'

'And perhaps he's given into his carnal desires again and got that girl in trouble.' His voice had taken on a bitter, judgemental tone. 'If so, he's an arrogant fool and doesn't

279

deserve our support and the effort we've put in to educate him.'

'Do you have to look at things from the worst sort of angle?' Charlotte asked. 'Who are you to take the moral high ground anyway?'

Luke's colour rose. 'I'm the man you promised yourself to, I was meant to be your husband. Instead, you sold yourself to the highest bidder. You're as bad as the whores walking the streets – they're at least honest about what they do.'

'And you could be out of a job if I told my husband what you just called me.' Charlotte's voice rose in anger, yet she knew that Luke's bitterness was justified: she'd betrayed him.

'Tell your husband,' he said, and his voice was loaded with venom. 'It's about time you knew the true facts about your marriage.' He looked down at her disdainfully. 'Justin Harvard needed a living wife to claim his inheritance from his father; as a widower he didn't qualify, so he made a bargain with you.'

Charlotte swallowed hard. 'How could you possibly know that?'

'I heard it from your stepdaughter, no less. It's the truth, however unpalatable it seems; you were just a woman he could buy and toss away when he'd finished with you, and finish with you he will, as soon as he's good and ready.'

Charlotte had to get away from Luke's

sneering face. The world was rushing in on her and she felt she might faint. Gathering her wits, she pushed him aside and blindly made her way through the gates of the school. How silly she'd been, how stupid, to think a man like Justin Harvard could care about her. His closeness, his physical nearness as he slept in the same bed had meant nothing. No wonder he had never reached for her in the night: he didn't want her, never had.

It began to rain, beating down on Charlotte and soaking her coat and her hat, but she didn't even feel the chill of it seeping through her clothes. She walked blindly on, not knowing where she was going or what she was going to do. All she knew was she couldn't spend another night under Justin's roof.

CHAPTER TWENTY-THREE

Charlotte woke abruptly. The light of early morning poured in through the window. For a moment she wondered where she was, and then she remembered. She was in her own bedroom, and it had been the rustling starch of the maid's apron as she set down the breakfast tray that had woken her. She looked up sleepily as the maid vanished through the doorway and sighed. So much for promising herself she would never sleep under Justin's roof again.

For hours Charlotte had walked the streets of Swansea in the rain, wondering what she should do. She had no money for lodgings, she was cold and wet and, at last, in despair, she had gone back home.

But it wasn't her home. The big, gracious house belonged to Justin; the school she loved, which she'd worked so hard for – it and everything else belonged to Justin, and she did, too, the wife he'd bought and paid for.

Justin had been out the previous night and she had been thankful that she hadn't had to face him. She'd crept up to her room and sat shivering before the fire, which had been tamped down by one of the maids, so there was only a faint glow to warm her. She shivered now in the chill morning air. Perhaps a hot cup of tea and some food would make her feel better.

The silver tray held a rack of hot toast, scrolls of butter and a dish of honey. There was a tap on the door and the maid came in with a cup and saucer.

'Sorry if I woke you, Mrs Harvard.' She looked curiously at Charlotte. 'I took the master his breakfast, but he's not in his bed.'

'Perhaps he's gone out for an early morning ride.' Charlotte didn't know why she had to excuse Justin's absence to the maid but, as he was probably with his mistress, what else could she do?

She felt better when she'd eaten a few pieces of toast, or at least that's what she told herself. Propped up on the pillows, she tried to think rationally. If she left Justin, the school and everything behind her, she would have nothing, no work to do, nowhere to live, and she would never see the girls again.

She sighed. Morwen relied on her and so did Rhian, after a fashion, even though she'd made mischief, talking to Luke and telling him about the inheritance, giving him the chance to gloat. Rhian was sorry now, but it was too late, the damage had been done and, to be fair, Rhian hadn't realized that by blurting out the truth about her father's marriage, she had given Luke a weapon to use against Charlotte.

And now Charlotte couldn't wait to confront Justin with the truth: how could he have used her in such a cold-blooded way? Had he no humanity in him? She shook her head. If she reproached Justin, he could retaliate, condemn her for doing exactly the same thing.

She glanced at the clock on the mantelpiece. She needed to get up; she was due at school in less than half an hour, but she'd never felt less like teaching in her life.

She pushed aside the bedclothes and took a

deep breath. She had work to do, work that at one time was all-important to her, but now? She pushed her doubts away. Teaching the poor was her dream, without it, her life was empty. The sooner she faced that cold, hard fact, the sooner she could pull the pieces of her life into some sort of order.

Luke was coldly polite when she saw him in the schoolyard. 'Good morning, Mrs Harvard.' He avoided looking directly at her. 'I see our star pupil is missing again this morning. I wonder what's happened to our teacher's pet? Perhaps he's decided to be a real man and get a job of work.'

Charlotte knew he meant John Merriman. Because the boy was older than most of the children attending the school, Luke had singled him out for special attention, giving him lessons after school. Charlotte knew Luke got on well with the boy and agreed with her that he should be given every encouragement to get on in the world, but now he was prepared to use John as a weapon against her. Was everyone in the world against her, even John, her star pupil?

She didn't speak to Luke. Instead, she ushered the children indoors out of the needle-like darts of rain. As the children took off their outer coats, which smelled of wet wool, Charlotte blew her whistle for silence and, gradually, the talk subsided.

'Neatly form a line,' she said. They obeyed and followed her quietly into the schoolroom.

Charlotte's class consisted of children, some of them nine and ten years old, who would normally be at work in the wool mill or the nickel works. She looked around. Her pupils were sitting obediently still. All of them had white faces in the early morning gloom; the lack of fresh air and sunlight and the proximity of the evil pall of smoke from the works chimneys bleached the colour from their cheeks just as it bleached the few hardy camomile flowers that dared to show their face above the poisoned soil. And yet the children in her school were fortunate to have parents willing to make a sacrifice to pay for their children's education, and Charlotte made sure they were aware of the privilege they had been granted. Old before their time, the pupils knew education was a path to a better life than their parents had had.

The morning session was difficult. Charlotte felt she was walking through a swamp, feet dragging, making no headway. At last she set the children a task they found enjoyable, writing a story about a subject of their own choosing, and there was peace as Charlotte tried to make sense of her own life. Except for the scraping of nibs against paper and now and again a hasty whisper which died away when Charlotte raised her head, the pupils were engrossed in their work.

Charlotte became worried as the morning dragged on with no sign of John. She wondered if he was sick. It was not like him to miss school. She pushed it out of her mind; her own problems seemed insurmountable. She sighed with relief when she heard the harsh ringing of the bell to signal dinner time. Charlotte put away her books, glad to have survived the interminable hours during which teaching had become a chore rather than a dedicated need to impart knowledge.

Luke was waiting in the dinner hall. He looked genuinely worried. 'Do you think we should look for John?' he asked.

Charlotte warmed to him. Angry though he was with her, he still cared for the welfare of one of the children. Charlotte was thoughtful; with a lurch of fear she remembered the look on John's face as he spoke with young Lizzie.

Justin was sitting in one of the deep armchairs in the dark-panelled lounge at his club staring into the fire as if the warm shimmer of the coals could give him answers. The previous night he'd been tempted to go to the bed of some willing woman. His thoughts were confused but his body cried out for relief. Justin found he was no good at celibacy, his body clamoured for a woman, and yet the only woman he really wanted was out

286

of his reach. She was beautiful, intelligent, burning with ambition, and she was his wife.

Impatiently, he put down his glass. He'd slept in the same bed with her, for God's sake, he'd listened to her gentle breathing. Occasionally their bodies had touched in sleep, bringing him abruptly awake so that, lying beside her, wanting her so badly, caused him physical pain. For a time she had seemed to warm towards him but now, as Luke Lester had last night delighted in telling him, she knew the truth about the terms of his inheritance and he could imagine what her reaction would have been.

At one time he had thought her not worthy of him; a suitable wife would have been one of the high-born ladies of the town, the well-brought-up daughters of the rich and successful. Now it was he who felt unworthy. He had to remind himself that Charlotte, too, had married out of expediency, she had never loved or wanted him or taken any gifts from him. Her only concern was for the school, a worthy cause in anyone's eyes. Her motives, however, were altruistic, his merely financial. He needed the money if he was to provide a good living for his girls and, later, to give them a good dowry when they left home to marry.

'All alone?' The voice was craggy and thick with smoke and alcohol, and Justin was jerked sharply out of his reverie. 'We both drank our fill last night, you took one of my bedrooms over without as much as a by your leave, and then you buggered off at first light of the morning. What are you up to, you young sprog, haven't fallen out with your lovely wife, have you?'

'Cummins, you old sea dog, sorry to have left your house without a word, but you were fast asleep.' Justin forced a smile. 'I must say, you look the picture of health, considering you too had a skinful last night.'

'I took a brisk ride on my horse and the fresh air brought the colour into my cheeks. A good gallop might've done you good – you look bloody awful, if *I* may say so.'

Captain Cummins took the seat opposite Justin and sank into its depths with a grateful sigh. 'You look as if you spent your night in heavy seas, old chum, and I know for a fact there was no lovely lady on board to disturb your sleep.'

Justin looked affectionately at his friend, he was more like a benevolent uncle than anything else. He would never change; his life had been spent at sea, a life of freedom, travelling the world, revered and trusted by those who looked to him for leadership. Had Cummins ever faced a dilemma over a woman? Justin doubted it. The old man would have had a woman in every port, no time to put down roots.

Cummins leaned closer. 'What is it that

bothers you, my son? Money? No, hardly, you've got a fat inheritance to keep you going for many a year yet, and that bugger of a nickel works must bring you in a small fortune.'

Cummins wasn't to know that the nickel works was draining his money like a drunk drains a bottle of spirits. It would pay, one day, there was no arguing with that, and yet, at the moment, the factory was a weight on his shoulders.

Cummins didn't believe in giving up. 'A woman then.' He leaned back in his chair, his smile jubilant. 'That's it. I can see by the look on your face. Marriage isn't always a bed of roses, as you must have found out for yourself. It's not the first time I've sheltered a married man seeking solace from a nagging wife. That's why I've never been tempted to indulge in a marriage myself.'

Justin didn't know what to say so he remained silent. Cummins kept on talking and probing. ''Bout time you found a new lady friend, Justin, my lad. That last one you had was just a light breeze, she would never have blown any real love into your life.'

Justin looked carefully at Cummins, wanting badly to confide in someone older, wiser, someone who was unbiased, someone he trusted.

'I've fallen in love with my wife.' The words came out flat, without a hint of the passion Justin was feeling. He half-expected Cummins to laugh, but he didn't.

'Ah, expediency has turned like a shark and bit you on your beam end, my boy. Well, so long as the good lady doesn't know the reason for the marriage, I see no ruffled waters to hamper the relationship. Just tell your good lady the truth.'

'She knows exactly why I married her.' Justin's voice was heavy. 'Luke Lester took great delight in telling her, or so I believe.'

'How the hell did he know?'

Justin shook his head. 'It doesn't matter. Sufficient to say, he found out the truth and blurted it out to my wife out of spite and pique. She broke off their engagement to marry me, you see.'

'You could deny it. After all, no one can prove what your reasons for sailing into the deep waters of matrimony are, can they?'

'Charlotte's no fool.'

'All women are fools when it comes to love, you should know that by now, my boy.'

Justin shook his head. 'Not Charlotte. I'd better get home. I'll need to change for work.' He forced a smile. 'I expect my absence last night has been noted and the wrong con-clusions drawn.'

Cummins raised his shaggy eyebrows. 'Don't go wallowing in self-pity, Justin, you're too much of a man for that.'

Justin nodded, acknowledging the truth of

the old man's words. 'Thanks for last night, Cummins, and thanks for stopping me wallowing in self-pity.'

He left the club with a feeling of reluctance. It was warm and cosy there, no complicated decisions to be made. The pale sunlight slanting through the trees on to the pavements was chill with the remnants of winter still crisping the air. Justin paused for a moment, tempted, in cowardice, to rush back to the warm womb of his club. He knew he would find it hard to face Charlotte. He could hardly excuse himself by saying he hadn't spent the night with a woman.

Charlotte would not care either way, and that was the worst part of it all. His wife was happy with her school and her big ideas for helping the poor of the town. And she may well be right, self-sacrifice for the sake of others was a laudable path to tread. He could only wish she was happier with her lot than he was with his.

Charlotte sat at her desk that afternoon and looked at the bent heads of her pupils. The silence was broken only by an occasional cough and sounds of her pupils writing. Her gaze drifted to the window and to the streak of light shining through the grime of the glass. No matter how often the windows were cleaned, the all-pervading dust from the manufactories could not be banished.

Where had Justin been last night? She'd lain awake listening for his footsteps on the stairs although she knew he would not come to her room but would sleep in the master bedroom as he always did now the girls were back at school. She was distressed that he'd stayed out all night. For a time she'd believed he'd given up his mistress – after all, when the girls had been home, he had not stayed out a single night. They'd lain in bed together, she awake listening to his soft breathing, wishing and longing for things to be different, for him to love her as a husband should love his wife. She'd hoped that, in time, he would come to love her, but the foolish illusions she had harboured had been shattered now. The real reason for the marriage was money, plain and simple. She was a means to an end, that's all, and the knowledge lay heavy in her heart.

The classroom door opened and Luke came towards her, watched by the curious children who were glad of the distraction. He didn't look at them, and Charlotte felt herself tense, something was wrong – very wrong.

Luke stood close to her, his back to the children. 'I don't know how to say this, Charlotte.'

'What is it?'

'I've been asking around about John. It seems he's vanished. No one has seen him.'

Charlotte felt the hairs on the back of her neck rise with the sudden fear that filled her. 'He must be somewhere.'

'Obviously,' Luke said shortly. 'But where?'

Charlotte felt the heavy weight of responsibility on her shoulders: all this was her fault, everything was her fault. She seemed to have made a complete mess of her life and the lives of all those around her.

CHAPTER TWENTY-FOUR

John Merriman woke to the soft sound of a horse whickering. He sat up, pulling straw from his clothing, and stared around him, wondering for a moment where he was. And then he remembered Lizzie and was swamped by a feeling of dread. Lizzie with another baby inside her.

His feelings dipped still further: no more school, no more being taught, no more education that would make him fit for a bright future. By lying down with Lizzie he'd spoiled all that, he couldn't face the shame of it, not again.

He went to the door of the barn and peered out. Dawn was bathing the earth in the colours of early spring, yellow daffodils hidden in verdant grasslands. The fields around the barn were lying fallow, resting before the next crop of vegetables was planted. Soon the brightness would be torn up, the earth ploughed into colourless furrows.

Where was he? He didn't know. The morning after his talk with Lizzie, he'd left Swansea with nothing but the clothes he stood up in. He'd walked for most of the day and night until, at last, exhausted, he'd found the barn, dropped gratefully into the warm straw and slept.

John realized he'd taken the coward's way out, he'd run away, leaving Lizzie to face her troubles on her own. What would she do? Had she been to see the 'wise' woman Maggie?

Lizzie might die. That would be such a guilty burden to carry. Perhaps, if she decided to have it, the baby wouldn't survive – many didn't, in the unhealthy environs of Swansea, where the copper smoke dominated the poor streets, curling through open doors and into lungs. The thought somehow comforted him: no baby, no blame; he could go back to Swansea and take his place at the school again, no one any the wiser about the folly he'd committed.

Immediately, he felt shame burn in him, hot and fierce, then, overriding everything else, a physical hunger so painful that his very guts ached. How could he be so shallow, thinking of his belly at such a time?

He left the comfortable closeness of the barn and, feeling exposed under the bright morning sky, he made his way to a road. Where did it lead? He didn't know, he couldn't know; this part of Wales was unfamiliar to him, and yet it was only a few miles from Swansea and all he held dear.

Charlotte sat at her desk, high above the pupils, and stared at the unopened book in front of her without seeing it. John Merriman was gone, run away to London, or so the gossips said, but Charlotte knew John would be lost in the great big world outside Swansea. He'd never travelled outside the boundaries of the town, never even visited the surrounding villages.

The children in the class were talking more loudly now, taking the inattention of their teacher as an invitation to discuss the momentous news of the day: John Merriman had disappeared, and the talk was of Lizzie – poor, foolish Lizzie had fallen for a baby again.

Charlotte's reverie was shattered by a loud burst of laughter from the back of the room. She looked up and briskly called the children to order. 'We will carry on from yesterday's reading of *Our Mutual Friend* by Mr Charles Dickens. Open your books at page fifteen, if you please.'

A hush fell over the children. The classroom was dark and gloomy and the panes of glass at the tall, narrow windows seemed pressed inwards by the heavy clouds outside. The morning had started off brightly enough – the dawn had been lovely, colourful, promising a happy, sunny day – but now the sun had been elbowed aside to give way to an overcast greyness, a mistiness which met with the smoke and fumes from the copperworks and blanketed the entire east side of the town.

'Now,' Charlotte said, 'I want you to read to me, starting with Ruby at the back of the class.'

'Can I read the bit about the body in the river, miss?' The girl spoke with relish, and Charlotte hid a smile. 'All right, Ruby, read the bit about the river.' She walked over to the window and stared out, only half-listening to the young girl's softly singing Welsh tones as she read about the huge river, the Thames, which threaded its way through the heart of London.

Swansea had its own river, the Tawe, its waters coppery and turgid. What was it about Swansea that she loved so much? If she'd moved away, perhaps to teach in London, she would have been free, not married to a man who thought of her as a gateway to an inheritance. The thought raced bitterly through her mind and then she pulled herself up sharply: she'd given up her freedom for the sake of the school and for all it meant for the poor of the area, a means for them to shake off the smothering oppression of the copper and nickel works. And had it been worth the sacrifice? Perhaps not. Tired of her own arguments, she felt like crying to the empty sky that all she really wanted was for her husband to love her.

'Shall I stop now, miss, 'cos I don't know this word by yer?'

'It's "here", Ruby, not "by yer".' Charlotte dragged her thoughts back to the lesson in hand. 'You may sit down, Ruby. I'd like all of you to write a little story in your own words about the girl in the boat – who she was, what she was doing there and anything else you can think of.'

Her mind settled, she began to give all her concentration to her class of pupils, each of them trying hard to make sense of the written word, the capturing of a time and place unknown to them. Her heart lifted as she saw their heads bowed low over their exercise books. They would benefit from the school, they had to – otherwise her life meant nothing at all.

Dusk clothed the hills as she made her way home that evening. Charlotte paused on the high ground, staring up at the impressive stones and dimensions of Thornhill. Then, she looked back at the town laid out beneath the folding hills; lights were beginning to glow in squares of windows like a pattern on a patchwork quilt. And beyond the buildings, the sea, its beautiful expanse signalling freedom. This evening the sea was calm except for the flecks of white foam still visible in the near-darkness, washing over the humped back of the Mixen Shoal, the sandbank a few miles offshore.

Dinner was a silent affair and as soon as the food had been eaten, Justin made a mumbled apology and disappeared into his study. Foolishly, Charlotte felt deserted. She pushed away the rich pudding served with hot custard and put down her linen table napkin. What should she do now to while away the long evening? Perhaps she should follow in her older sister's footsteps and begin writing, perhaps a novel, as the Brontës had done alone in their lonely parsonage on the moors. But she knew she didn't have the talent for writing, her life was built around teaching and, now, she felt, she was failing even in that.

Luke was a good teacher, a gifted teacher who could breathe life into the coldest of mathematical problems and yet still put his heart into explaining the correct use of the English language. He cared about the children almost as much as she did. He enjoyed feeding young minds, watching the seeds of knowledge find fertile soil. Suddenly, she missed him. They had been good friends. Sometimes they had talked all evening about the children, discussed plans for the future – never a personal future as a married couple, that was a foregone conclusion, but working out ways to develop and shape the children in their care. They'd shared those dreams, and now she missed sharing them.

She looked around the empty dining room. The furniture was heavy, glowing with polish. The table was long and gleamed in the candlelight.

Restless, she decided to go for a walk. She pushed back her chair and got up. Her mind was troubled, she felt weighed down with regrets and missed opportunities and suffused with worry about John Merriman. Where had he gone?

In the hall she took up her coat and let herself out silently. The breeze was fresher now, whipping her hair free from its pins. There was the promise of rain in the air and Charlotte felt the cold clutch of fear. Was John crouching in some cold shop doorway lonely and afraid, running away from yet another situation he was too young to deal with?

She made a decision. She would swallow her pride, try to make friends with Luke; he had an excellent rapport with John and might have some idea where he would run to. She set out down the hill towards the town.

Luke saw her when she was still a long way off. He'd been walking the streets, trying to clear his head, to shake off the love he still felt for Charlotte, his Charlotte, now out of reach. She was tied to Justin Harvard and his fortune for good or ill. Could he help it if he sometimes wished for the ill? If she fell, he knew he would be there to pick her up. He loved her, damn it!

Luke could almost taste his bitterness and tried to tell himself she was nothing but a gold-digger, selling herself to a rich man. And yet as she drew nearer, all he knew was the urge to take her in his arms and hold her close. He felt guilty, wishing he'd never taunted her about Justin's reason for the marriage. He remembered the stricken look on her face with a sweep of anger. Why did she love a selfish oaf like Harvard?

'We need to talk, Luke.' Charlotte's lovely, luminous eyes met his, and he almost flinched at the pain of the memories of when she was his, when she'd agreed to be his bride, when he had the right to hold her hand in his, to have her walk beside him as they talked in easy companionship, sharing like minds, sharing everything.

'I suppose this is about John Merriman.' The words came out like an accusation. She lowered her eyes.

'Yes,' she said softly.

'I thought so – that's the only reason you

have to talk to me at all. Shall we walk?' he suggested. She nodded and he swallowed hard, resisting the urge to grab her and shake her and make her say she was still in love with him. 'We don't know where he is, so what can we do?'

'We at least know why he's run away.' Her tone was soft but edged with fear. 'It's because of poor little Lizzie: she's expecting another child and he can't face the scandal, not again.'

'He should have thought of that before he lay down with her.' That was the common-sense attitude Luke held to, but what would he do if Charlotte were willing? He would be just as weak as John had been. 'I don't think he will have gone far,' Luke said. 'He's on foot. He'll probably be heading for Cardiff, or even London.'

'Surely he wouldn't walk all the way to London?' Charlotte said, and she glanced up at Luke with her wonderful eyes, so beautiful that his stomach tightened and he had to keep a rein on his emotions.

'The cattle drovers of old did just that – walked with their herds all the way from Wales to London,' he pointed out, in what he hoped was a reasonable tone.

'You're right, of course. Which way would he go? Perhaps we can follow and find him.'

Luke shook his head. 'There are many routes leading out of Swansea, but John might just follow the roads the cattlemen took. He's an intelligent boy and I've just been teaching the class about the trails made by the drovers before the railways came.'

'Will you go and look for him?' Charlotte's voice shook. 'I can stay and manage the school while you are away.'

Luke looked doubtful. 'I'll think it through, Charlotte, but I can't promise anything. John has run away from a serious problem. I can't see him agreeing to come back to Swansea, even if I did manage to find him.'

He saw Charlotte nod. 'You're right, Luke. It was a foolish suggestion and, in any case, I need you at the school.' She paused and glanced up at him again, and he felt her look, as though it were a loving touch.

His throat constricted. 'Come on, I'll walk you home, to your husband.' How he hated saying that.

'There's no need to see me home,' said Charlotte quickly. He held up his hand for silence, much as he did with the children in school and, like a child, she obeyed him.

'I will see you home.'

They walked in silence, leaving the lively streets of Swansea behind and making their way across the grass hills in the velvet darkness. At the gates of Thornhill, Luke stopped. 'There, now I know you're safe. I'll see you in the morning. Perhaps we will have news of

John by then.'

He bent and, on an impulse, kissed Charlotte's cheek; it was soft and smelled of roses. Charlotte tried to move away, but he reached out and drew her against him, his lips hard and demanding on hers. She tore herself out of his arms, but not before he'd had the joy of feeling her mouth beneath his.

'How dare you!' she said, her voice harsh. 'How dare you take such liberties, Luke Lester?'

'I dare because we were once promised to each other in marriage.' He heard the breathlessness in his voice. 'I'll just say this, Charlotte: if your marriage turns out to be a mistake, I'll be waiting for you.'

He moved away. 'We'll talk more about John in the morning.'

Charlotte was a small figure in the darkness, arms folded about her as if for protection. 'I'll go to see Lizzie, find out what we can do to help her,' she said gently.

The gates behind Charlotte were pushed open, and Luke saw Harvard holding a lantern high and staring at him with fury, his eyes burning more brightly than the candle ever could.

'Get away from my wife before I horsewhip you.' Justin Harvard's voice was low with menace. 'You,' he said to Charlotte, without taking his eyes from Luke's face, 'go indoors. I'll speak to you later.'

Luke shrugged his shoulders. 'If you're at all worried about your wife, you shouldn't let her wander about town in the darkness, should you?' He was concealing his anger well, though his fists were clenched. He would like nothing more than to beat Justin Harvard to a pulp, but that was not the rational act of a civilized man and, more than that, one who should set a good example to the children in his care.

'Goodnight, Mrs Harvard,' he said, 'and goodnight to you, Mr Harvard.' Even as he walked away he could feel the other man's anger burning a hole in his back. He half smiled in the darkness – at least he had achieved something tonight: he'd shaken Harvard's composure and, more, he had kissed the mouth of his beloved Charlotte.

CHAPTER TWENTY-FIVE

Over the previous few days Justin had taken to staying out late at night again and Charlotte had reached the painful conclusion that he must have gone back to his mistress. She'd got used to him being with her; they'd reached what she hoped was an amicable state of affairs, where they could at least talk civilly together. Of course sometimes he attended events concerning business, and to these he went alone, but he occasionally took her to a concert or for an evening elsewhere, treating her like a beloved wife. Now, at home, he had reverted to his usual habit of abruptly avoiding her.

Tonight, though, he was at home, and Charlotte fervently hoped they could talk about Luke; they needed to clear the air. She would explain that the kiss was none of her doing. She guessed that this was the reason he'd been so remote, his tone icy when he did speak to her, which was seldom. He was worried she would make a spectacle of herself and drag him into some sort of scandal.

Tonight, like an old married couple, they sat on either side of the fire. Justin was reading his paper and Charlotte was belatedly marking an essay written by John Merriman.

'This boy has a fine brain.' She surprised herself by speaking out loud. Justin looked up and folded the paper in his lap.

'I suppose you're talking about John?'

Charlotte nodded. 'It's so worrying – goodness knows where he is. I hate to think of him sleeping under a hedge somewhere, especially now the weather's so bad. All it's done lately is rain.' She looked up at him. 'I suppose that's why you're not out with your...' She stopped, appalled at what she had been about to say. She'd no right to chastise him, even to question him, and she felt the hot, mortified colour flooding her face.

'My what, Charlotte?' She glanced at the window. The heavy curtains were drawn but, still, the sound of rain drumming against the panes, though muted, was insistent. Justin shook his newspaper into neat folds. 'Were you about to accuse me of something?'

She avoided the icy glint in his eyes. 'No, I have no right...' Her words trailed away into a miserable silence.

'No,' he agreed, 'but I do have rights, Charlotte. We made a bargain: for better or worse, I took you as my wife, and I expect you to behave with a little dignity, at least to keep up the pretence that we are a respectable married couple.'

Suddenly Charlotte was angry. 'Just as you do, I suppose.' Her voice was heavy with sarcasm. 'Anyway, what you saw was nothing of my choosing. Luke was foolish and impertinent, he had no right to kiss me but...'

'There is no "but".' Justin threw down the paper and stood over her, the line of his jaw knotted, his muscles taut. Every word seemed ground out of him. 'You are no common kitchenmaid yet you act like a harlot. I feel like horsewhipping Lester and you, too, if it comes to that.'

Charlotte stood up and faced him. 'If you ever dare lay a finger on me, I'll kill you.' Her voice rose on a high note of anger and frustration. 'I'll kill you, do you hear?'

He raised his hand and, instinctively, she caught his forearm and then they were grappling with each other just like quarrelling children.

Justin was strong, and Charlotte, tripping over the pages of the newspaper, fell and clung to him, dragging him to the floor. He was on top of her, his breathing ragged. The fire in his eyes had changed subtly. She felt his body harden against hers and a fierce passion tore at her. She wanted to hold on to him, to kiss his mouth, so close to hers, and she was angry with her own weakness.

'Do men of your sort rape their wives then, Mr Harvard?' Her voice was hoarse, but her words were distinct and cold. He moved away from her and was on his feet. He stared at her rumpled skirts with disgust, though at her behaviour or his own it was difficult to tell.

He reached out a hand to help her to her feet and, as her fingers twined in his, they stared at each other. And then Charlotte saw the funny side of things; she began to laugh. A wry smile lit his features, and then they were both laughing, hands still entwined, breathless and speechless. Suddenly they were sober, laughter fled and Charlotte looked up at him.

Slowly, he bent towards her, his mouth tantalizingly close, and she tasted him, the sweetness of his breath mingling with her own as the scent of the man filled her with desire. What sort of woman was she, desiring a man who would use her just like he used his mistresses? It was she who moved away.

'Thank goodness the girls are not here to see how childish we are.' Her voice was brittle. She brushed at her skirts with little effect and, picking up John's essay from the floor, stood for a moment, wondering what to do next.

She did not look at Justin as he poured himself a drink. She could hear the soft swish of liquor in the glass and sensed Justin's need to return to some sort of normality, distancing himself from her, the only way he could keep up this sham of a marriage.

She would go up to bed shortly, the sooner she was away from him the better. She could still feel his body against hers, see his mouth poised above hers and taste his breath as if it were her own.

Charlotte returned to her chair and tried to concentrate on marking the essay, but she just couldn't put her mind to it. She heard the rustle of Justin's newspaper and she sensed that he too was finding it difficult to return to the mutual, guarded politeness they usually employed when they were together.

She murmured an excuse about a head-ache, retreated to her room and sat on the bed wondering once more if she could keep her side of the bargain. Could she live a love-less, celibate life without children of her own? It was beyond her imagining. The years stretched ahead of her, empty and arid.

She heard the front door close and she knew with a plummeting heart that Justin had gone out. By now he would be heading into town to find comfort in the arms of his latest mistress. And then, quite suddenly, she began to cry.

Lizzie was frightened. She stood in the pour-ing rain staring at the train rushing past her and wished she was on it, safe behind the windows of the noisy, shadowed carriages, leaving Swansea and all her troubles. Her hand rested on her stomach, feeling the soft swell of her body, half in hope and half in fear. She didn't want the baby taken away from her, John's baby, John whom she loved, John who had run away from her, letting her face the music alone again.

Heedless of the wet mud sticking to the edge of her skirt, Lizzie began to walk towards Thornhill. Mrs Harvard had shown her nothing but kindness, even when she had fallen with the first baby and most people she knew had scorned her, looking down their self-righteous noses at her.

'Dear God, please help me.' Lizzie spoke in a whisper. Pausing, the mud sucked at her boots; there was nothing but the beating of the rain to answer her.

Perhaps there would be room enough for Lizzie at Thornhill, even with a baby to keep and love. She could be useful: she could sew nicely, mending sheets and patching torn clothing with fine stitches which were almost invisible. Surely Mrs Harvard would find her a job.

In the streets of the town, she stopped as an old woman with a sack covering her head came stumbling towards her. 'Can I help you, love?'

'I'm on my way to Thornhill.'

The woman looked at her strangely. 'Bit late to go out visiting, isn't it, girl? Ah, I know who you are, you're that little girl who got herself in a heap of trouble. I doubt if you'll be welcome at the house where those rich folks live.'

She was silent for a minute, then she swung the sacking from her hair and placed it round Lizzie's thin shoulders. 'Poor child, you're soaked through. Now, listen to old Nora – stay away from the boys, they're nothing but trouble, as you've found out. God go with you.'

Lizzie felt tears in her eyes at the unexpected kindness. The old woman put her hand on Lizzie's shoulder. 'If you gets no answer there, come to me. I'll put you up, but just for one night, mind. Number five, I am, in Brickyard Lane.'

Lizzie nodded and, almost running, made her way out of the town towards the darkness of Mount Pleasant Hill.

To her relief, the lights were still on in the big house with the iron gates. Although it had stopped raining, droplets of water fell from the overhanging branches of the trees that lined the drive, mingling with the tears on Lizzie's face.

She went round to the back door and knocked timidly. Almost at once she heard footsteps click-clacking on stone, and then the door was opened cautiously.

'What d'you want?' The pale round face of the young girl peering round the door was filled with curiosity. 'They're all abed at this hour 'cept me. I banks the fires up ready for the morning.'

'I wanted to see Mrs Harvard,' Lizzie stuttered. 'It's very important.'

'Come back tomorrow, she might see you then, but I don't dare get her out of bed.'

'What's going on out there?' The man's voice was slurred, as though he'd been at the drink.

'It's all right, Willy, it's time you was going home.' She looked at Lizzie. 'Him and me are walking out together, but he's not in a good mood right at this minute.' She paused. 'It's all right, Willy, just a girl here looking for work. I've told her to come back in the morning.'

Lizzie heard heavy steps approaching along the flagged passageway. She turned and ran back down the drive, diving through the gates as though the hounds of hell were after her. She knew how men could be when they were in their cups, reaching out, touching, stroking – wanting to do things that weren't right.

Breathless, Lizzie slowed to a walk. A watery moon peered down at her through the clouds. She didn't know what to do now: if she were to go to number five Brickyard Lane, there would be questions, questions she couldn't answer.

She climbed over the fence surrounding the park and sat on a bench staring at the lonely water of the lake, which in the daytime was busy with birds and young boys fishing for tiddlers; now, all was quiet – even the ducks didn't want her company.

She rubbed her stomach, trying to erase the stitch in her side, and thought of her baby in there, curled up, waiting to grow big enough to come into the world. The baby, the only good thing in her life except for John, but then he didn't want her, he'd made that plain when he'd run away.

She heard a rustle in the bushes behind her and turned quickly, her heart pounding. Were the ghosts that lurked in the night after her? A boy about her own age appeared, and she sighed with relief.

'Brian Jones, you gave me a scare.'

He was joined by another boy and another, until four of them stood around her, leering, their faces in the moonlight white and waxy like those of the dead.

Lizzie saw Brian open the buttons on his trousers. The other boys jeered and joshed him about the size of his beezer. Lizzie tried to run but stumbled and fell. Brian crossed the small space between them. 'Lie down on the ground.' His voice was gruff. She knew what he wanted, what they all wanted, and she felt sick. The only one she wanted inside her was her lovely John.

'Please don't hurt me.' Lizzie's voice was shaking. 'I'm carrying a baby, see?'

The boy laughed. 'Same old story, Lizzie, you can't keep your legs shut, can you?'

'I don't want you to touch me, Brian.'

'Why not? It can't do much harm, can it, Lizzie, not when you have a little package in there already?' He put his arm around her. 'Come on, be friendly, Lizzie. It'll go more easy on you.' His hand traced the outline of her breast.

'No!' She pushed his hand away.

'You like it rough, do you?' He caught her and dragged her on to the grass, pushing her skirt up around her waist, dragging her underclothes aside and tearing the cloth in his haste, and then he was on her, in her, pushing and shoving his hateful thing time and time again into her unyielding flesh, laughing while he rode her. When it was over he stood upright, lazily doing up his flies. Lizzie was crying. Silent, bitter tears ran down her face and she could taste the salt of them in her mouth.

'Who's goin' to be next?'

So it was not over. Lizzie screamed as one of the other boys climbed on to her, putting his hand roughly over her mouth so that she had to fight for breath. The others lined up behind him, jeering encouragingly and making coarse remarks about her body. Lizzie stopped struggling. She knew it was useless to protest: they would all have their use of her whatever she said or did.

And then it really was over. The last one drove his seed into her and stood away, buttoning up his trousers. 'You're not the best bitch I've ever had but, as the sailors say, any port in a storm.'

Laughing, they went away, leaving her lying in the muddy, wet grass, her skirt still up about her waist, her undergarments torn to shreds. She didn't know how long she lay there; she was beyond feeling anything but a deep disgust at the wetness left between her legs.

At last, she dragged herself up and walked to the lake, staring down at the dark waters. No man would want her now, not even her precious John. She had loved him; he had been the only one to treat her properly, gentle as he kissed her and touched her and took her. John was the only good thing to happen in all her life. And now he was gone and she knew she would never find him.

The water was cold as it lapped around her legs. The moon cut a swathe of light through the deep darkness, and Lizzie walked towards the glow of it as though it were a beloved friend.

Then the water was up to her breasts and her chin and the ground below her spun away. For a moment Lizzie panicked as the water closed over her head. She wanted to struggle, but only for a brief second. She felt weeds tangle around her like gentle hands reaching out to her. She would be hurt no more; she was going to heaven and taking her unborn baby with her. Her last thought before giving herself up to darkness and oblivion was of John.

CHAPTER TWENTY-SIX

Charlotte stood in the cold, clinical room of the mortuary and swallowed her fear. 'I'm ready.' She felt Justin's arm around her. He might only be making a show of being concerned, but she was glad of his nearness.

A man, draped in a glossy black apron, pulled back the sheet from the face of the young girl on the glistening slab, and Charlotte drew in a sharp breath.

'It's Lizzie.' She was unable to take her eyes away from the drowned face of the young girl. Around Lizzie's neck was a thick scar, and it continued down between her breasts. The marks from the rudimentary examination looked almost like the fastenings of a jacket, the proud scar burned so rawly against the whiteness of the surrounding flesh.

'We found her in the deep lake in the park.' Sergeant Denholm, who was standing beside Charlotte, spoke almost apologetically, as if he were personally responsible for Lizzie's death. 'If you'll pardon me speaking frankly, Mrs Harvard, the girl had been attacked by some persons unknown.'

'Attacked?' Charlotte asked in bewilderment. Then the meaning of the word became clear. 'Do you mean Lizzie was raped and then murdered?'

It was the man in the apron who answered. 'No. We think she went into the water herself after the attack.' He cleared his throat. 'There are bruises around her belly and her thighs but not on her upper arms and neck. No, the attackers had their way with her and left her alive.' He hesitated. 'And there was a baby on the way, too. It must have all been too much for the poor girl.'

'Why did you need my wife to come down here, Sergeant Denholm?' Justin's voice held more than a touch of indignation. 'Surely Lizzie's last employers should have been the ones to identify the girl.'

'She'd been dismissed from her position, and her employers said they wanted nothing to do with the matter,' Denholm replied.

'But why me?' Charlotte repeated Justin's question.

'The girl was seen late last night asking the way to your house, Mrs Harvard, and, as you know, we spoke to your maid. She was the last one to see the poor girl alive – except for the boys who attacked her, that is.' Charlotte shivered and the policeman took pity on her and led her and Justin, who still had his arm around her, out of the coldness of the mortuary.

'There's another reason for us coming to you: John Merriman – you took him under your wing, didn't you, Mrs Harvard?'

'You don't think he's done this to Lizzie surely?'

'We have to look at all sides of the incident, you see.'

'Then you do?'

'To tell you the truth, we just don't know. We believe there was more than one attacker. Her injuries are such that–'

Justin intervened. 'My wife has been upset

enough.' His voice was mild, but the command in it was clear.

'I understand. Sorry to trouble you with this terrible crime, Mrs Harvard, but there was just a chance you could shed a little light on the investigation.'

Charlotte shook her head, bewildered. 'Poor little Lizzie, poor child. She didn't deserve this.'

Justin hugged her and for a moment there was genuine sympathy in his eyes. He cared, of course he cared: he was a kind man, a compassionate one. She glanced up at him, grateful for the warmth of his arm around her shoulders, and she read the horror of the situation in his eyes. For a brief moment, they were united, and she rested her head on his shoulder.

'I can see you're upset, Mrs Harvard. Shall I fetch you a cup of tea?'

Justin answered for her. 'I'll take my wife home, thank you, Sergeant Denholm.' He led Charlotte out of the grim surroundings of the mortuary and into the fresh air. But even the sunshine did nothing to wipe away the memory of Lizzie's dead face, or the thought of what the girl had suffered before she died.

John was worn out. Hunger gnawed at his belly and his clothes were damp and muddy, clinging to him like an encasing layer of cold and misery. He'd been accustomed lately to hot water and cleanliness, to good food eaten in comfortable surroundings and, most of all, to reading his books and studying. He yearned for all that, and to have it back he'd have to take responsibility for his actions. Lizzie needed his support; he'd been a coward to run away.

He turned back towards the only home he knew – Swansea, the hills surrounding the town like protective arms; the sea, the golden beach, even the stink of the works to the east of the town – these were familiar to him, the town was his home, it was where he belonged.

He walked the lanes hedged by trees and shrubbery, dismal in the pouring rain. Even the spring flowers were drooping, submitting to the rigours of the heavy weather. He heard the sounds of the cattle in the fields beyond the trees, the mournful mooing of the cows in the wet grass. They sounded as miserable as he felt.

He raised his head to look at the grey skies, and he felt closed in, claustrophobic, longing for the sight of the sea stretching into the distance, offering unending horizons, a gateway to other lands. He lifted his fist and pummelled the air.

'I'm going home!' he shouted at the skies and, for a brief moment, the clouds parted and a finger of sunlight, watery and pale, shone down on him. It was as if God, way there beyond his skies, was offering him a blessing.

Luke Lester looked at the bedraggled figure of John Merriman and, after a moment, held the door wide.

'Come in, John.' He led the way into his sitting room, where a good fire burned in the hearth. 'Take off those wet clothes and I'll find you something of mine to wear.'

As Luke opened the immaculately kept wardrobe where his clothes hung in orderly fashion, he felt a dart of pity. Yet within it was pride: he was glad the boy had chosen to come to him for help and not Harvard.

He returned with the clothing – a pair of trousers and a warm shirt – and then uncertainly he offered the boy some underclothes. 'If you want to wash, the bathroom is on the landing,' he said. His eyes were fixed on the boy's naked body, and a spasm of feeling that was foreign to him caused him a moment of pain. He felt paternal, loving even, towards this thin, guilt-wrought boy.

'You'll need to wash off the dirt and grime.' His voice was rougher than he'd intended. 'You're absolutely filthy, John.'

He sank into his chair, a drink of good port in his unsteady hand, and wondered if he'd ever be a father. He loved Charlotte – well, he *had* loved her once. He'd had disturbing urges when he was with her, he'd wanted to touch her, make love to her, to be everything she wanted and needed in life. But that was all gone now, his dreams of home and family, and it was all Charlotte's fault.

John returned from the bathroom fully dressed, and Luke smiled at the too-big shirtcollar standing away from the boy's slender neck. John stood in the doorway, uncertain and vulnerable and, unaccountably, a lump rose to Luke's throat. He gestured for John to take a seat, and the boy obeyed his schoolmaster at once.

'What's happened?' Luke hesitated. 'I mean, what were you running away from?'

'Lizzie,' John said.

Luke swallowed hard – so John didn't know what had happened to Lizzie.

'Where did you go?'

'I went as far as I could walk. I slept in barns or under hedges and, then, I knew I had to come back and face the music.' He flushed with shame, and again Luke felt pity and a longing to protect the boy, but the truth would have to be told. Luke would have to break the news about Lizzie's death, and he dreaded the moment.

John looked down at his bare feet. The toes were long, Luke noticed, and there were blisters on his heels.

'Are you in love with the girl?'

'No!' John said. 'The other boys call her

bug-eyes – you know the way her eyes bulge – and to be honest I wouldn't want her. She'd be like a millstone around my neck.'

Luke sought the right words. 'And yet you made love to her, got her with child. Surely you must have felt something for her, John?'

The boy sighed and hung his head, and Luke was struck by the way his damp hair stood out in tufts around his face, giving him an almost fragile appearance.

'I know she tempted me. I suppose I wanted to know – well, everything – and she made me do it, dragged me into it. I knew it was daft after what happened last time when she fell for a baby.'

'Do you want a drink, John?'

John looked puzzled. 'What, a cup of tea or something?'

'I was thinking more along the lines of a whisky or brandy to warm you up, but you can have tea, if that's what you want.'

'I've never drunk strong liquor, sir. No harm in trying it, is there?' Luke poured him a golden drink that sparkled in the lamplight.

On an impulse, Luke spoke again. 'You'd better sleep here tonight.' It was a sensible suggestion. In the circumstances, John could hardly be turned out into the night, and yet Luke knew the impulse was not generated by common sense but by a deep sense of pity, the thought that a young, intelligent mind might be damaged.

'I 'ope I won't be putting you out, Mr Lester; sorry to put all my troubles on to you – I'm a man, I should be looking out for myself. I'm sorry.'

Luke hated to see the boy's abject pain. 'You still have a great deal of growing up to do yet, John. Don't blame yourself too much for ... well, for everything.'

John was a bright boy and picked up on the strange tone in Luke's voice, and Luke cursed himself for being stupid. 'What is it, sir, what's happened?'

Luke hesitated for a moment, but John would have to learn the bad news some time, and it may as well be now.

'It's Lizzie, there's been a tragic accident.'

'What do you mean?'

'I'm afraid she's dead, John, drowned in the lake in the park.'

John's face grew pale. He was silent for a long time, staring into the fire. 'It's all my fault, isn't it, sir? I drove her to it.'

'No!' Luke shook his head – he would have to tell John all of it, the abuse, the manner of the girl's death. 'It wasn't your fault, John.' He took a deep breath. 'She was attacked by some boys. They treated her badly, she was hurt and in pain and, regrettably, she wanted to end it all.'

'Tell me all about it, sir, please. And I mean *all* of it.'

Luke could see it was impossible to fob John off with anything other than the truth. 'She was raped, John. I'm sorry, I can't put it any other way. Three or four lads had her, and I suppose she couldn't live with the pain and scandal of it all. She went into the water and drowned.'

'Who were they, the boys?'

Luke shrugged. The boy wanted the truth and he should have it. Luke saw no virtue or use in hiding anything from him. John would soon find out once he was back in school.

'Brian Jones was the ringleader. No one would have known that, except the foolish boy went about bragging about it.'

'The police got him for it, did they?'

Luke felt uncomfortable. 'Well, no. When he was confronted by the law, Jones denied everything. No one would tell on him either, so there was no proof.'

John was white. 'The bastard! I'll get him for this.'

Luke was alarmed. 'Don't do anything rash, John, you'll only make things worse for yourself. Be calm now. Try to make the best of things, get your education – be a police-man yourself, or a lawyer. Work within the law, John, if you want to punish anyone.'

He made John take another drink. He could see the boy was weary and sleep was not far away. 'Things will look better in the morning, they always do.'

Later, he looked in on John. His eyes were closed, his breathing soft and regular. There were shadows under his eyes, and the bony structure of his undeveloped face made him look young and vulnerable. Why were some children born to poverty and strife while others, such as Brian Jones, whose family were well-to-do, respectable, seemed to get away with anything? He knew the answer of course. It was useful to have powerful parents, plenty of money and the confidence such a way of life offered.

Luke took another drink and stretched out on the old, sagging sofa. In the morning, he would sort everything out – where John would live, for instance. He couldn't live in the same house as Luke, and yet Luke wasn't ready to face the implications of why this should be so.

He slept at last, a dreamless sleep, until the sound of crying woke him. For a moment Luke was confused: why was he on the sofa in the sitting room instead of in his comfortable bed? He sat up and listened. The sound of weeping was soft but insistent, beating into his brain. He tried to ignore it; John was unhappy and he had a right to be unhappy. Everything in his life had been turned upside-down.

The sobbing continued, and Luke got up and stood outside the bedroom door, uncertain of what he should do. At last he opened the door and went in. John was under the bedclothes, his face hidden, his body shaking.

A great sense of pity overwhelmed Luke. 'John, don't cry. Things will turn out all right, you'll see. No one will blame you for what happened to Lizzie.' He put his arms awkwardly around the boy and held him as close as he could, the bedding in between them. He rocked John like a baby, talking softly to him until at last he was quiet. John turned away, then, his back to Luke, who left the room, weary and drained. Well, he'd done the best he could for the boy. The rest – the pain and the guilt – was something John would have to face on his own.

CHAPTER TWENTY-SEVEN

Justin's inheritance had turned out to be more than he'd expected. He felt he should have been elated and yet, somehow, all he felt was a sense of hopelessness at the way his life had turned out. He'd wanted the money to infuse into his nickel factory in Clydach, and now the works was expected to make a good profit. He also needed the money to give his two daughters lifetime security, a worthy enough cause, but he despised that part of him that had driven him into using Charlotte. He wished he could turn back the clock. He'd married Charlotte for the worst of reasons and now he'd fallen in love with her. He was caught in a trap of his own making.

He glanced at her as she stood beside him on the platform waiting for the train that would bring his daughters home from college. He felt a thrill of anticipation, followed quickly by shame: he and Charlotte would once again share the same bedroom, the same bed, keep up the shabby pretence that they really were man and wife.

He saw the thin streak of steam rounding the bend of the railway track, heard the distant whistle, took Charlotte's hand and tucked her arm through his. 'The train is coming.'

Charlotte's reply was instant. 'Why else would you give me any show of affection?'

Her words hurt, but he couldn't blame her. His birthday had come and gone several weeks before and tomorrow there would be a formal party to celebrate the event. The rich and influential members of Swansea society would be there to congratulate him, to shake his hand. He was the man who had everything, a prosperous business and a young, beautiful wife on his arm.

It was Charlotte Morwen greeted first, she hugged her stepmother with the shine of happy tears in her eyes, then turned her face up to her father for a kiss. She still clung to Charlotte, though, clutching her hand as though she would never let her go.

'Charlotte, I love you and I've missed you so much.' Morwen, too, was growing up, Justin realized, with a small shock of surprise. The round, babyish face had thinned down and her hair was cut in a fashionable bob which, though becoming, was too old a style for a child to wear. Morwen saw his look and touched the back of her hair proudly.

'Like it, Daddy?'

'It's different,' Justin said dryly, 'but isn't it a bit too ... too old for you?'

Morwen shook her head in exasperation. 'It's the fashion, Daddy, don't you know anything?'

'Presumably not.' He glanced at Charlotte and saw she was concealing a smile. 'I suppose you like it, don't you!' he said playfully, and Charlotte laughed out loud. For a moment they seemed like a real family, wrapped in warmth and love.

'We'd better get you girls home,' Charlotte said. 'I have to teach this afternoon, or Luke ... Mr Lester will be complaining about running the school single-handed.'

'Oh, Charlotte.' The disappointment in Morwen's voice cut Justin to the quick; his little girl, his baby, loved Charlotte so very much. He tried to justify his unease. Charlotte too had made a bargain. But there again, she had been inspired not by greed but by a real desire to help the poor of Swansea make a better life for themselves. Shaking off his worrying thoughts, he smiled at his children. 'Come on then, family, let's get ourselves home.'

Charlotte felt a sweeping sensation of peace as she let herself in through the school gates: she was home. She took in the smell of damp coats and pencil shavings, the sharp aroma of ink, and felt the usual thrill at being in the school. This was what she'd sacrificed her life for – but why did she have to suffer the final indignity of falling in love with her husband?

Still, she needn't think of that now; she had escaped into a world where everything was safe and familiar, and she had the rest of the day to think of things other than her sham marriage. She could push aside the pain of seeing Justin every day, wanting him, needing him. And, now the girls were home, once again she would be sleeping in the same bed as him.

When she had left, the house was bustling with newly hired maids preparing for tomorrow's party. The thought brought a bitter taste to her mouth: this was what Justin had wanted her for, to secure his inheritance, and now he had it, would he want her out of his life? Would she be subjected to the humiliation of being put aside, pensioned off in some far-away cottage out of sight? Or worse, would Justin divorce her? It was a real fear, one she could hardly bear to imagine. Life without Justin and the girls would be barren indeed.

'John's back.' Luke Lester's voice broke into her thoughts, and Charlotte turned sharply, staring at him uncomprehendingly for a moment.

'John's back home! Thank God for that!'

'He came to see me last night. He was cold and miserable and I took him in. He was so pale and sick I made him stay in bed, at least for today.'

'That was good of you, Luke,' Charlotte said warmly. She rested her hand on his, and he looked at her sharply.

'There's to be a grand gathering at your husband's home tomorrow, I understand. Naturally, I'm not invited. Could there be a happy outcome of your marriage to announce?'

She saw the speculation in his eyes as they rested on her waist. 'Of course not! Is that what the gossips are saying?'

Luke's eyes were cold. 'Is it true? Are you expecting a son and heir for Harvard?'

'No, I am not!' Anger got the better of discretion. 'As I've never slept with him, it would be an impossibility.' The moment they were spoken she regretted her words.

'I see.' Luke's voice was loaded with triumph. 'He's found himself a beautiful wife, but he cannot perform the basic function of a husband. No wonder you go round with a look of the hangdog about you; the man bought you to cover up his shame at being less than a man. I thought there was some other reason he'd take on a nobody for a wife.'

'Do you know something, Luke?' Charlotte was stung to reply. 'You have an acid tongue, and I'd have done even worse if I'd been a blind fool and married you.' She made herself walk calmly away from him, but her emotions were in turmoil. How dare people talk about her, speculate on something that was none of their business? The gossips had been chattering, wondering if she was expecting a baby and, now, through her own careless words, she'd given them real fuel. Luke would be sure to spread the word that Justin was inadequate in the bedroom. What a mess she'd made of her life.

Woodenly, she moved towards the classroom door: she must put her own feelings to one side. At least she could do some good in her life; she knew her goals, and Justin provided the necessary finance. With that she would have to be content.

John woke slowly to see the sun poking thin

fingers through the heavy curtains. For a moment he had to catch his breath: where was he? The room swung into focus. John saw the pile of books to be marked, smelled the sharp, masculine scent of a tobacco pipe and remembered he was at Mr Lester's home.

He sat up and saw his image reflected in the long mirror that hung on the door of a thickly carved wooden cupboard. He saw a boy, a boy without a beard, a thin face that had not yet moulded into the hardness of a man's. He shivered although the bedroom was cosy and warm. The fire had been banked up for his benefit, he realized. And then he remembered that Lizzie was dead.

He felt sick with anger. She had been used by a gang of spoiled rich kids. Brian Jones, the ringleader, as he always was, hated John, and the feeling was mutual. John had clashed with him more than once. Jones had everything: rich folks, a grand house, money to buy anything he wanted – even a high-class lady of the night, if he wanted those sort of thrills. Instead he'd picked on poor, innocent Lizzie, who had no one to complain to, no one to right the wrong done her. But *he* would avenge her death. It was his fault she'd fallen for a baby again, and he must take action to get even with the bastard who'd used her and given her to his friends to use.

He got up from bed and washed quickly,

then opened the curtains and looked out at the day. To his surprise, the sun was declining, not rising, as he'd first thought. He must have slept away most of the day, but now he felt fresh, clear-headed, and as he dressed he made up his mind to think through his plan of revenge. He would humiliate Jones, publicly if possible, make him pay for what he'd done, let the whole town of Swansea know what a pathetic little runt he really was. Without his father's money, Brian Jones was nothing and soon everyone would be aware of that.

He found some bread in the larder. It was a bit on the stale side, but with a thick spreading of good salt butter it tasted good, it was the best food he'd eaten for days. He made a pot of tea and sat down to consider his options. They were not plentiful. He would follow Jones around, wait for the right moment and then strike deep and hard. Hate sucked at John's guts.

He heard the door open and stood up quickly, guiltily aware that he was eating Mr Lester's food, making himself at home without as much as a by-your-leave. He looked up when Mr Lester came in. 'I'm sorry–' he pointed to the bread '– I was hungry.'

'That's all right, John. Pour me a cup of tea, would you?'

Eagerly John did as he was told. He pushed the cup and saucer towards his teacher and stood for a moment, wondering what he should say and do. Mr Lester drank the tea in silence, gesturing for John to sit down.

'How is Mrs Harvard?' John asked at last. 'Is she upset because I ran away?' He knew that, apart from Mr Lester, only Mrs Harvard would have noticed his disappearance.

'She came in late today. The girls were coming home on holiday from that posh school they attend, and she was meeting them at the station.'

There was a touch of bitterness to his voice, and John remembered that, once, they had been engaged to be married. He realized something then: even older people, educated people like his teachers, had problems to face. It surprised him. 'A fine party is to be held tomorrow night.' Luke's face was pale and there was a hint of pain in his eyes. 'I'm not invited. She won't even give a thought to me while she's cavorting with her new, influential friends.' He sounded hurt. John was silent, not knowing what to say. He sat back in his chair, his mind whirling.

'I suppose the Joneses are going,' he said at last. 'I expect even Brian Jones will be there, showing off, trying to make himself popular with all the grown-ups.'

If Luke was surprised, he didn't show it. 'I suppose so.'

'Don't anybody care about what he did to Lizzie, him and his pals?' John asked. Luke corrected him at once, almost absent-mindedly.

'*Doesn't* anybody care is the correct grammar there, John.' He sighed heavily. 'It's all been swept under the carpet, John, the Joneses' precious son can do no wrong, and the father will punish anyone who says different.'

John's thoughts were already elsewhere. Everyone would be at the party in Mr Harvard's house, all the posh people of the town, and Jones would be patted and praised. His head would grow even bigger, he'd have people's wonderful opinion of him dripping over him like honey from a spoon. How he would strike John didn't know, but strike he would and hard.

'Another cup of tea, Mr Lester?' he said innocently and, as he watched the golden liquid pour from the brown earthenware teapot, he began to make his plans.

CHAPTER TWENTY-EIGHT

After school was over Charlotte took home the exercise books so that she could correct the compositions of the children in her class. Dinner was long over and the aroma of roasted meat hung in the air. Charlotte felt hungry and that emphasized her sense of aloneness.

The girls had gone with their father to visit friends and, though she'd been asked to go with them, she'd declined, feeling that Justin needed to spend time alone with Rhian and Morwen.

She sat in the empty dining room, the books spread out around her. A plate of cheese and biscuits had been left out for her and she nibbled at it absentmindedly while she read the compositions.

She felt the excitement grow in her as she saw how well her pupils were getting to grips with the tasks she set them. Some essays were larded with spelling errors, most of the offerings showed a lack of good grammar, but all of them attested to the fact that the children were progressing.

At last, she put down her pencil and, bone-tired, she went to bed. It was strange to be in the master bedroom again. It was a cheerful room. A good fire burned in the grate and the bed was turned down ready for its occupants. She wondered what the servants made of the strange changing about of rooms; one minute madam was sleeping with her husband and the next she'd returned to her solitary bed.

She sank on to the soft comfort of the patchwork quilt and took off her shoes. Her eyes were heavy and she was glad to slip under the blankets and rest. But sleep eluded her. She thought of Justin coming home, undressing, his muscular back turned to her for modesty's sake, and she wanted to cry.

Later she heard them come in; she'd been waiting for them, waiting for *him*. She was wide awake now, her tiredness vanished, but she wished she could sleep, forget that the man coming to her bed was her husband only in name. He didn't love her, he'd made that clear from the start.

When at last he came to the bedroom, he undressed quietly, believing she was asleep. Charlotte kept still, tinglingly aware of every rustle of his clothes. She heard the soft thump of his shoes on the floor and she tensed, waiting for him to slip into bed beside her. When he did, he turned his back, keeping as far away from her as he could, and Charlotte felt a lump rise to her throat. She knew he didn't want her, but the physical act of turning away from her brought home how little he cared.

She should be glad, her only worry when she married him had been that he might demand his conjugal rights, but nothing could be further from the truth. He didn't want her. He didn't love her. He didn't even find her attractive.

Yet she was still fairly certain he no longer visited his mistress and hadn't done so for a long time. Most evenings, he stayed in and read his papers and, if there were social occasions to attend, she was at his side. What did that mean? Nothing, except that he'd grown tired of the poor woman and cast her aside. He would soon find another willing woman to sleep with.

Eventually, Charlotte slept, and when she woke dawn was shedding a rosy glow into the bedroom. She stirred, feeling Justin's arm flung over her breasts. Cautiously, she turned to look at him. He was sleeping facing her and his breathing was soft against her cheek. Such a wave of love for him washed over her that a physical pain shot through her.

She got out of bed before he woke, afraid he would read her naked love for him in her eyes. Once she was bathed and ready, she hurried down the stairs with a forced smile to join the girls at breakfast.

'Where's Father?' Rhian asked. 'He's usually up before us. He's not sick, is he?'

Charlotte felt a dart of alarm. Justin had been sleeping heavily – perhaps she should have checked he was all right before she'd rushed from the bedroom. 'I'll go and see. You girls start on your breakfast, don't let the food get cold.'

Justin was awake now. He looked up at her as though he hardly saw her. His face was flushed, his forehead beaded with sweat. 'Are you all right?' she asked, afraid to approach

338

the bed in case he told her to get away and mind her own business.

He struggled to sit up, and she noticed his eyes were not focusing properly. He fell back on the pillow, the effort of rising too much for him. Anxiously, Charlotte sat beside him and rested her hand on his face. His skin was burning hot.

'I'm going to call the doctor.' She spoke as much to herself as to him and, though he shook his head, he began to cough and she knew she'd made the right decision. For the first time she wondered what her world would be like if she lost him.

He coughed again and Charlotte took a sharp breath and left the room. She hurried down the stairs and sent one of the maids to fetch Dr Brand. 'Be quick!'

Startled by her tone, the maid rushed to collect her coat.

The proposed party was postponed until Mr Harvard had recovered from his sickness, though the good news was that he was already much improved and up from his sick bed. John was agitated, anxious to put his plan into action. He had thought long and hard how he would punish Jones for hurting Lizzie. The time to strike had been decided: he'd wait for the party and catch him afterwards.

He was walking back to Mr Lester's house

when the subject of his thoughts approached him.

Jones was swaggering, smirking in the sly, patronizing way he did with those he considered beneath him. 'Well, look – if it isn't the "poke anything ape", you even did poor frog-eyed Lizzie, you must be desperate.' The older boy stood directly in front of John, his face full of spiteful mirth.

'But then Lizzie wasn't good enough for you once you became teacher's pet.'

John stepped closer to Jones, who didn't back off. 'What is it, Merriman, got the gripes for the schoolmistress, have you? Well, she's not a bad choice – she married for money, didn't she? No better than a whore selling herself to the highest bidder, that's our Mrs Harvard.'

John's hands bunched into fists. 'Shut your dirty mouth, Jones, before I shut it for you.'

Jones smiled slowly. 'You and whose army, Merriman?' He shrugged in disbelief. 'Come on then, if you think you can lick me I'll be generous and give the first punch to you.' He stuck out his jaw, and John was sorely tempted to smash the grin from Jones's hateful face.

John forced himself to be calm. 'Not just now, Jones, I'll pick my time and place and then I'll teach you a lesson you'll never forget.'

'Scared gutless, I thought so.' Jones moved away. 'Keep to your own slums, Merriman. All the teaching in the world won't make a gentleman out of scum like you.'

Cockily, he walked away, and John seethed with anger hearing his laughter. Jones was in for a big surprise, a very big surprise.

Justin's recovery was swifter than Charlotte had dared to hope. After three days his temperature was down and the red flush of his skin had paled to a healthier colour. She sat beside him with a bowl of chicken broth and coaxed him to eat as though he were a child in her charge.

'Just try a little, please,' she said, holding the spoon to Justin's lips. Obediently he opened his mouth, and she fed him. Charlotte felt the warmth and comfort of the closeness they had shared over the last few days.

Justin had almost finished the soup when Charlotte began to laugh. She put down the bowl and leaned back in her chair, still laughing.

'What?' Justin asked, bunching the pillow up behind him so that he could sit straighter. 'What's so funny?'

Charlotte pointed to his face. 'You've got a white moustache with bits of chicken sticking to it. You look like Father Christmas without the white beard.'

She held a mirror for him to see his reflection, and he began to laugh too. 'How would I look with a real moustache?' he asked. 'Perhaps I'd be the evil baron in one of the fairy-tales the girls are so fond of.' He pretended to twirl his non-existent moustache, wiping away a bit of the soup as he did so.

Charlotte laughed harder and, without thinking, wiped his mouth tenderly. He took her hand and kissed it, and her laughter stopped abruptly. As though embarrassed by his actions, Justin sank back on to the pillows.

'Thank you for caring for me while I have been sick.' He almost mumbled the words. The soft moment of humour and closeness between them was gone, and Charlotte wondered if she had imagined it, Justin now turning his face away from her and looking through the window.

'I expect to be up from bed by tomorrow.' His tone was formal. 'There's no need for you to be burdened with me any longer. In fact, I'll be strong enough to get up for dinner tonight.'

She wanted to say that it had been a pleasure, not a burden, but the words wouldn't come. She was reminded by his cold tone that they were playing a part, and now there was no need for the pretence to continue.

'All right,' she said. At the door she paused. 'I'm happy to see you feeling so well. I was worried for a while.'

'No need to worry,' he said. 'If I shook off this mortal coil, you'd be the chief beneficiary of my will. I've seen to it that you and the girls will be well provided for, whatever happens to me.'

Of course he would only consider leaving her his fortune to ensure she looked after his girls, but she was pleased that he trusted her, for all that.

'Thank you for that, but I'd look after the girls whatever happened. I love them.'

'I know you do, and they love you.' The softness was in his voice again. 'And, what's more, you could keep the school open. I know how important that is to you.' The softness had given way to bitterness now, and she understood why. She had given up her freedom for a school and now he thought it the only thing she cared about. It just wasn't true, not any more, but she couldn't humiliate herself and tell him so.

Downstairs, the girls were seated in the hall, dressed in coats and hats. 'Come on, Charlotte, you're supposed to be taking us to the park.' Morwen slipped her hand into Charlotte's. 'I know Daddy's better, I heard you both laughing.' She smiled happily. 'I know you love Daddy as much as you love me, and he loves you, too, he shows it all the time.'

Charlotte took a deep breath, wondering if

Rhian would burst her sister's bubble of happiness with some cutting remark but, surprisingly, the girl remained silent.

It was Sunday. The bells of the church rang out and in the pale light of the day, the park was full of parents and children. A group of older boys were monopolizing the swings, and Charlotte saw that the Jones boy was throwing his weight about. He pushed a small girl on to the grass and took the swing himself, clinging to the chains as he swung himself higher and higher.

Morwen watched in fascination. 'Look, Charlotte, see how high he's going, he must be able to see over all the houses to where the beach is. Can I have a go?'

'Of course you can.' She moved across the grass to where the boys were laughing and joking noisily.

'Excuse me, could you give up the swing and allow someone else to have a go?' The Jones boy took no notice, but one of the other boys pushed her aside with his shoulder, without even turning his head.

Charlotte was angry. 'Move!' she said icily.

'Or what?' Jones was jerking the swing even higher, his boots almost crashing on her head. When he swung towards her again, Charlotte caught his ankles in a firm grip and he was almost pulled from his seat and then the momentum of the swing dragged him back.

When the swing came to a stop, Jones kicked her hands away and jumped off. He stood staring menacingly, eye to eye with Charlotte. 'Who the hell do you think you are, ordering me about?' He jutted his chin forward, trying to intimidate her. 'I'm not one of your slum kids, so show me respect, understand?'

For a moment Charlotte was speechless. It was Rhian who saved the moment. She poked Jones in the chest. 'If you don't clear off from the park I'll be telling my father and your father about the sort of things you and your gang of idiots get up to. Now push off. Understand?'

'Oh, shut your clanging cakehole, Rhian Harvard, you've got the biggest mouth in Swansea. I'm not afraid of you.'

In spite of his words he backed away, but before he went he threw Charlotte a look of such malevolence that she shuddered.

'Come on, boys,' he said. 'We don't want to hang around with kids and old witches anyway.'

Charlotte tried to compose herself. 'What a horrible boy,' she said, looking gratefully at Rhian. 'Thank goodness you put him in his place.'

'Come on,' Rhian said. 'I've had enough of this play-acting. You're not my mother, however hard you try, and this park is for babies.

I'm leaving.' She strode away, and Charlotte, exasperated, took Morwen's hand and followed the older girl towards home.

CHAPTER TWENTY-NINE

The day of the party was bright and sunny, tipping the waves in the bay with diamond lights. White wavelets kissed the golden sand and, in the dunes, sharp spikes of grass bent towards the shore, driven by the soft breeze.

But Charlotte knew there was little time to stare out of the window, not today. Cook and the extra maids hired for the party were busy preparing the menu for the night-time festivities. Charlotte's heart lightened. She had more to rejoice about than a mere party: Justin was fully recovered, the fever gone, the healthy colour back in his face again.

Her love for him was almost incandescent; tonight she would be treated like a beloved wife, a role she wished fervently would be hers for ever. Rhian came into the room and stood beside Charlotte. 'We need to talk.' She sounded very grown-up and very modern.

Morwen shouted from the doorway. 'Charlotte, Cook wants you in the kitchen, she says it's urgent.' Charlotte put her hand on Rhian's shoulder.

'We'll talk later, all right?'

'I suppose it will have to be.' Rhian's eyes were suddenly cold. 'Well, perhaps I won't bother then.'

Charlotte was flustered; she had half-turned away but did not miss Rhian's cold stare. On her way to the kitchen, Charlotte sighed heavily; she just couldn't please the girl, all she got from Rhian were glowering looks. She'd been more difficult than ever since she'd come home from school this time.

Perhaps she should have kept Cook waiting for a moment and let Rhian have her say, but it was too late now.

In the kitchen Cook was standing over the table, sobbing into her spotless apron. Charlotte went to her and pulled her hands away from her eyes. 'Cook, what on earth is wrong?'

'It's my mother, Mrs Harvard, she's ill with a fever. One of her neighbours just came with the news. I've got to go to her, see? She's old and frail now, she might even be on her death bed, for all I know. I'd be with her all the time if I could afford to give up my work.' She shrugged her plump shoulders in despair. 'But that's not likely, is it?'

'Don't worry about money,' Charlotte said at once. 'Go to your mother; you shall have your wages as usual.'

A look of relief spread across Cook's face, and then the tears came again, flowing unchecked down her rosy cheeks. 'But there's the party, Mrs Harvard, how are you going to manage without me?'

'It will be difficult, but that's not your concern. Now get your coat and whatever else you need. We'll manage, we'll jolly well have to manage. Are any of the maids good cooks?'

Cook shook her head. 'No, sorry, Mrs Harvard. They cut veg and stoke up the fire, but they can't cook.'

'All right. Just give me your menu before you go.'

'It's consommé first, and that's done. It's to be served chilled tonight, because of the fine weather, see? Then there's fish fresh caught this morning, it's prepared, boned and filleted, it just needs to be lightly steamed.'

'And beef and poultry?'

'The beef should be stuffed with peppercorns and cloves, then put it in the oven to cook slowly – the meat will take a bit longer than the bird, but you tell that to whoever takes over from me, won't you, Mrs Harvard? The kitchenmaids will do the veg, as I said, but I haven't done nothing about the pudding.' She hesitated. 'I doubt you'll get anyone to do the cooking, not at such short notice.'

'Just go to your mother and stop worrying about us, we'll be just fine. We'll miss you, of course, but your duty is to be at home just now.'

When Cook had gone, Charlotte looked round the busy kitchen. There were six maids, including the temporary girls. All of them were looking at her, waiting for instructions.

'What veg are we doin', Mrs Harvard?' Bessie, one of the full-time maids, was prompted to ask by a poke in the ribs from one of the new girls.

Charlotte tried to gather her thoughts. She had helped to cook meals at home when Father died and left the family penniless; then, she'd sometimes made bread-and-butter pudding. Surely with all the maids to help she could manage that? But doubt assailed her. This was a dinner party for twenty guests. How could she cope with servings for that many people? She sighed. She would ruddy well have to cope, there was no option.

'What are your names?' she asked the bolder of the two new girls.

'I'm Annie Evans, miss, and this–' she pointed to the girl who was standing behind her chewing her nail anxiously '–this is Dolly Potter. She's not very bright, see, but she's a good worker.'

'Right then, Annie, you and Dolly can start by peeling the potatoes. Allow four roast potatoes for each guest, and a good potful of potatoes to be mashed.' She took a deep breath. 'Then do the turnips and cut up the carrots, all right? Just fill the pots to the top.' She turned to Bessie. 'Fetch me all the stale bread in the larder and plenty of eggs. If we haven't got enough eggs in the larder, raid the henhouse.' She smiled at the girl. 'I'll make bread-and-butter pudding, I'm famous for it.'

Bessie looked doubtful. 'But that's common food, Mrs Harvard. Cook usually does some lovely steamed puddings, and the loveliest meringue.'

'Well, tonight it's plain pudding, it's the only dish I can make and, Bessie, you'll be serving the dinner. You're used to that, aren't you?'

'I am, Mrs Harvard, but I'll need Mr Squires to help me.'

Charlotte looked around. 'Where is Mr Squires?'

''Cos he's the butler, he don't need to be with us in by yer, I 'spects he's in the back kitchen reading his paper till the guests arrive, then he'll be needed to take the coats and things.' Bessie smiled. 'He's partial to a drop of sherry, to "set him up", as he calls it. He reckons it will be 'ard work tonight, what with all those folks to serve.'

'Well, he could be right.' Charlotte rolled up her sleeves. 'Find me an apron, Bessie, there's a good girl.'

'What you goin' to do, Mrs Harvard?'

'I'm going to roast some meat, Bessie, so I'll need you to prepare a few of the potatoes as quickly as you can. They'll go into the dish with the beef.'

The next few hours passed quickly and Charlotte found that, in spite of her initial sense of panic, she was enjoying herself. The dinner was almost ready.

'Charlotte. What on earth are you doing?' Justin had come into the kitchen and was blinking as if he didn't believe the evidence of his own eyes. The maids stopped working, and Bessie poked Dolly. 'Stop gawping,' she whispered, 'you're like a fish there with your mouth hanging open.'

Charlotte became aware of her hair coming loose from under her linen cap. Her apron was stained with blood from the meat and her face must be as red as a beetroot, no wonder Justin was staring at her as though he'd never seen her before.

'Charlotte–' his voice was stern '–have you gone mad? You should be getting ready to greet our guests.'

'Cook's had to go home, so I'm seeing to the dinner. You do want your precious guests to eat, don't you?'

His face softened, and a smile twitched the corners of his mouth. 'I see, you've come to the rescue. You're a sterling worker as well as a beautiful woman. You have hidden depths, Charlotte.'

It was the first time he'd ever compli-
mented her, and her face became even hot-
ter. 'I'm doing my best, Justin.' She shrugged
her shoulders. 'You'll just have to make my
excuses to the guests, say I'm indisposed –
anything. I just can't leave the kitchen. Bessie–' she looked at the girl '–soon you must
change your apron and cap, you will be
serving the food in about–' she glanced at
the large clock on the kitchen wall '–in about
an hour and a half.'

Justin shook his head in bewilderment. He
took a few quick strides, closing the gap
between them, and bent and kissed Charlotte's unsuspecting mouth. She started back
in surprise, trying to think of something to
say, but he had turned away and was headed
for the door, chuckling to himself.

Charlotte took a deep breath and tried,
unsuccessfully, to be calm and still her flut-
tering heart. Justin had just been showing
his gratitude, that was all. She didn't dare to
read too much into it.

She was once again engrossed in the
business at hand, leaning into the heat of
the oven and trying to decide if the meat
was properly cooked, when the clip-clop of
horses' hooves and the grinding of carriage
wheels on the gravel drive made her realize
the guests were arriving.

The sound of voices and the occasional
burst of laughter in the hall made her panic.

After a time, Mr Squires came into the kitchen. He frowned when he saw Charlotte in a cap and apron.

'Where's Cook?' he asked, and Dolly giggled.

'If you hadn't been sipping sherry all evening you'd know Cook 'ad to go home, her mammy's sick.' She glanced anxiously at Charlotte. 'Begging your pardon for bein' so forward, Mrs Harvard.'

'It's all right. Serve the consommé, if you would be so kind, Mr Squires.'

The butler looked as puzzled as Justin had done earlier. 'Can you cook then?' He apologized at once. 'Sorry, Mrs Harvard.' He smiled at her and, for once, there was a surprising warmth in his voice. Usually the butler treated her as an interloper, a mere teacher, not the sort of woman the master should have married. Charlotte knew how his thoughts had run, but now there was an element of respect in his voice, and he bowed to her as he took up the first tray of consommé and left the room.

After that, Charlotte was too busy to think of anything other than getting good food to the dining table. She moved quickly from oven to table, loading vegetables from cooking pots on to the pristine porcelain serving dishes. When the last dish, the bread-and-butter pudding, all golden and brown, was carried from the kitchen, Charlotte flopped into a chair. 'Make me a pot of strong tea, Annie, I'm worn out.'

Mr Squires returned to the kitchen, a wide smile on his face. 'All the guests made compliments about the meal, Mrs Harvard. The pudding was a triumph, second helpings called for all round. No wonder, too, folk are growing tired of new fancy dishes, and good old-fashioned cooking is a rare treat.'

He bowed and picked up the teapot. 'May I pour, Mrs Harvard?' His smile was wide, and Charlotte realized he was offering her something rare – a butler who normally would be serving only the illustrious guests was ready to take a hand in the kitchen.

'That would be very kind, Mr Squires.' Charlotte kicked off her shoes and wriggled her toes in ecstasy, suddenly aware that her feet were aching as they'd never ached before. But then, she'd been standing for several hours without a break.

Justin popped his head into the kitchen. 'Come along, Mrs Harvard.' Justin's eyes were twinkling. 'The guests want to see you.'

'But I'm not dressed for a party, I'm full of flour and my apron is stained.' She made to remove her apron, but Justin caught her hand. 'I want my guests to see you as you are: a clever woman who can rise above any difficult situation.'

He drew her inexorably towards the large

drawing room and, as they entered, the chatter of many voices trailed away, the guests turning to look at her in surprise, disdain even.

'May I present my wife?' Justin's voice carried around the room. 'My clever, beautiful wife.'

No one spoke, and Justin raised his voice. 'Charlotte has saved the occasion by her quick thinking and excellent organizing skills. I hope you will all join me in a toast to my wife.' He took a glass of wine from a tray and raised it. 'To Mrs Justin Harvard.'

Most of the assembled guests did as they were told, but one woman with steely eyes stared at Charlotte as if she had just been dragged in from the gutter.

'What can you expect from the daughter of a common theatre-owner? Her place should be in the kitchen, not mixing with people of our standing.'

Justin lowered his glass, his voice, dangerously calm, rang around the room. 'My wife is too much of a lady to comment, Muriel, on your spiteful, petty remarks.'

'Oh, come along, Justin, we all know you had to be married to get your inheritance.'

A babble of voices broke out as guests tried to cover their embarrassment with laughter and chatter, but the words had been said and they struck at Charlotte's heart. Her marriage to Justin had been gossiped about at dining tables all over the town. She realized how low she was in the eyes of Justin's so-called friends.

Her face flaming, she squared her shoulders and left the room, her head defiantly high. But once in the kitchen, she sank down into a chair and began to cry.

CHAPTER THIRTY

Charlotte sat in the kitchen drinking a cup of tea with a good measure of brandy in it. The servants gathered round her as if to protect her, but it was Mr Squires who came to her and rested his hand briefly on her shoulder. The gesture showed how concerned he was.

'The guests have all gone now, Mrs Harvard, that awful madam Muriel Larkman was last out the door. I felt like putting my boot in her fat backside to help her on her way.' He turned pink to the end of his nose and, in spite of her tears, she smiled.

'I would have liked to have been there to help you, Mr Squires!' Charlotte looked up at him. 'What happened after I left the room? Was Justin ... Mr Harvard embarrassed?'

'On the contrary, Mrs Harvard, the master

was very jolly and all the guests rallied round him. It was Miss Larkman who was left with the proverbial egg on her face.' He smiled and took his usual chair at the head of the table. 'She tried to apologize but no one took any notice of her, especially not Mr Harvard.'

Charlotte felt her pain fade away. Justin had defended her mightily, his loyalty was beyond question. Perhaps she ought to thank him, but her heart quailed: her courage was all gone, drained away by the arduous tasks of cooking and then her humiliation at the hand of Muriel Larkman.

The door was flung open and Cook came rushing into the kitchen, followed by the sounds of high winds and heavy rain.

Charlotte was on her feet in moments. 'Cook, what's wrong? Is it your mother, is she worse?'

Cook shook her head and, gasping, took her usual seat beside the butler. 'No, Mrs Harvard, my mother is over the worst, her fever has broken. It's the boys, John Merriman and Master Jones.'

She held her hand over her chest in an effort to control her breathing. 'They're heading for the school. Young Jones is threatening to burn the place down.'

Charlotte felt fear ripen and grow hard inside her. 'My God! There are oil drums stored alongside the school – they'll go up like a bomb if they're ignited. I must get down there at once, stop this dangerous nonsense.'

'Please get a coat,' Cook said hastily. 'It's cold and wet outside.'

Wet, Charlotte thought, the weather might be of help tonight – but not if the oil drums went up. No amount of rain would help extinguish the flames or lessen the effects of the blast. She pulled on the coat Bessie handed to her and the girl followed Charlotte to the back door.

'What are you doing, Bessie? Why have you got your coat on? You're not going anywhere.'

'I am, begging your pardon, Mrs Harvard.'

'I'm coming too,' Mr Squires said firmly. His words were followed by cries from the rest of the servants. They were all going to help her stop the boy burning down the school.

Charlotte felt a lump in her throat. 'Bessie, I would deem it a great favour if you stayed behind to look after the master. You know more about the master's needs than any of the younger maids. And Bessie, don't tell him what has happened.'

'I can't promise that,' Bessie said, but her voice was kept deliberately low so that her mistress couldn't hear.

And then Charlotte was out in the driving

rain, her staff of servants coming behind her like a flock of birds. Through her fear, Charlotte felt a great sense of pride in them and knew each and every one of them would be loyal to the last.

'You killed Lizzie, you scum!' John stood face to face with Brian Jones. 'You raped her and let your friends rape her, and then you probably watched her drown just for the fun of it.'

'Don't try anything stupid.' Jones's voice was full of scorn, though he was pressed up against the wall of the school with no way of escape. 'You'll have my father to deal with if you lay a hand on me.'

'You can't hide behind your father now, can you? What if I kill you? Drag you down to the river and hold your head under the water – see how much you wriggle and beg for your life.'

'For your information,' Jones said easily, 'I didn't see Lizzie drown, she was daft enough to do that all by herself. She had more between her legs than between her ears.' He laughed at his own witticism.

John threw a punch and, taken by surprise, Jones fell to the ground. 'Aye, but you haven't got friends with you now, have you? They've all run away like the scared rabbits they are.' John saw Jones reach into the pocket of his expensive jacket.

'Ah, but I have these.' Jones held out a box of matches, lit one and threw it in the direction of the oil drums.

'You ruddy fool! The whole place will go up like a fireball, us included.' John made a dash for the match, which glowed briefly on the top of one of the drums and was then extinguished by the rain.

He turned and saw his error: the lit match had been a ploy to get him away from Jones. He stood behind John now with a large plank of wood in his hands. Before John could move, the timber crashed against his skull and he fell into a well of darkness that had no bottom.

Charlotte was out of breath, her side ached. She had what her father would have called a stitch, but she ran on, knowing that she might be too late to prevent a disaster.

As she approached the school building everything seemed normal, the building stood stark and solid as always. And then she caught sight of two figures, one limp and apparently unconscious being dragged inside the school by the other.

She saw the oil drum against the wall and sighed with relief, but then it struck her: there should be two oil drums, not one. She turned to see who was with her, but only Mr Squires had kept pace.

'The oil – move it away from the school.'

She didn't wait for his reply, but ran to the end of the building where the big doors of the school creaked and banged in the wind. 'John!' she called, but there was no reply, and she knew then that John was the boy being dragged, unconscious, perhaps dead, inside the building.

There were only a few rooms to search and, in any case, she heard the rumble of metal on wood and realized the oil drum was being rolled across the wooden floor of the classroom. She pushed open the door and saw John lying dazed against the wall on which, incongruously, the coloured pictures made by the younger children were displayed.

'Jones, what do you think you're doing?'

'I'm opening the lid of the drum so I can get at the oil and set it alight. What do you think I'm doing, woman!'

'You'll kill us all, you fool!'

The lid clanged against the floor and Jones stared at her hard. 'Get out of here, if you value your life,' he ordered. He struck a match and held it aloft. 'As for me, I can run faster than a hare. I'll not get killed, I'm too clever for that.'

He kicked out at John and the boy uttered a soft moan.

'Leave him be, you bully!' Charlotte crossed the room and bent over John. Blood ran from a jagged cut in his head, and when she prised his eyes open they were unfocused, unseeing.

'He needs to see a doctor.' She felt like screaming at Jones, but she knew aggression would get her nowhere. He had a wild light in his eyes, and she knew he meant to blow up the school, whatever the cost in human life. She had no doubt that Jones could outrun the flames.

'How are you going to explain all this? My servants will arrive here any moment. My butler is just outside. There's no escape.'

He smiled, a shark showing his teeth. 'I'd better act straight away then, hadn't I?'

Deliberately, Jones dropped the flaring match into the slick of oil and at once a sheet of flame raced like a monster across the room. Jones ran past, pushing Charlotte aside and knocking her head against the door frame. She sagged against the wall for a moment, trying to shake the mist from her eyes. She must save John, she must.

Smoke was filling the classroom now as she crawled to where John was stirring, rubbing his eyes.

'Come on, John, wake up!' Her voice was urgent. 'We have to get out of here.' Unsteadily, he got to his feet and, her arm under his shoulder, she half-dragged him towards the door. There was nothing she could do about the oil now; once the flames spread the whole thing would go up like a giant fire cracker. The school would burn,

362

there was nothing surer than that. All that was important now was to save John's life.

They'd almost reached the door when Charlotte heard the noise. It started like a train crashing at speed then became the roar of an animal sighting its prey. With all her might, she surged forwards. She pushed John outside. There was another ear-splitting blast, and Charlotte fell to the floor. Before her vision was obscured by smoke and falling debris, she saw John tumble down the bank. Charlotte tried to rise, and then the entire world seemed to explode. Flames, a terrible heat. She heard her hair sizzle, and then all was darkness as the building crashed down on her.

For a moment she was dazed and then she tried to get up once more. The fire hadn't touched her body yet, but soon it would devour the planks that now pressed against her, pinning her to the ground. Like a slow-moving poison, the smoke spiralled towards her, and she closed her eyes, waiting for the inevitable flames to devour her.

Above her, something moved, and then, with a gasp, fighting for every breath, she felt the planking that held her being shifted, easing the weight on her back. She began to cough. The smoke was getting thicker and the heat from the flames was reaching its threatening hands towards her. She felt like giving up the struggle for life.

'Mummy! Charlotte!' It was Morwen's girlish voice, thick with tears. 'Don't die. You promised you'd never leave me.'

Another voice, Rhian's, called urgently. 'Charlotte, I'm sorry I treated you so badly. I want you to live, I want it so much.'

The children's voices ringing in her head, the urge to live sprang afresh in Charlotte's heart. She helped push against the wood. Another plank was moved and, then, gratefully, she felt the rain beat down on her face.

She heard the clang of the fire engine but she knew it was too late to save the school. All she could concentrate on now was getting away from the heat and smoke that was choking her.

It seemed to go on for ever. Bit by bit the planking was being lifted away from her. Near her face, some of the wood was alight and, desperately, she hid her head in her hands. She was going to die, after all, and she didn't want to, she wanted to live. She was frightened, more frightened than she had ever been in her life. She kicked away the burning wood nearest to her and felt the rain-fresh air fill her lungs. She coughed again, expelling the heat and smoke from her tortured body. She was going to live!

She was lifted then, in strong arms which folded around her, holding her close.

'My darling, my sweet girl, you're going to be all right now.'

Was she dreaming or was it really happening? Was Justin holding her in his arms, calling her his darling? She began to cry, her sobs loud and uncontrolled.

'Don't worry, my darling Charlotte,' he said, 'I'm getting you out of here. John is safe, Squires has taken him to our house.'

He pressed a kiss on her lips so she couldn't speak. She hung round his neck, feeling the warmth of his skin, and smelling smoke that clung to his hair. She loved it all.

'Don't worry, the Jones boy's been taken into custody. As for the school, I'll build you a new one.'

Charlotte tried to speak, but her throat was raw. Everything was unimportant except that Justin was telling her such sweet things.

'I was stupid,' he admitted. 'I married you for money and then I didn't know what to do with it when I had it. It came between us, driving us apart, so I couldn't tell you how much I loved you.'

'Tell me more,' she croaked. Justin had carried her away from the burning inferno of the school, and they stood near the river. The moon was shining, silvering the water, and for once it looked beautiful. But everything was beautiful – the river, the sky, the humble way Justin was pleading with her.

'I love you so much, Charlotte.'

She wound her arms around his neck, her face close to his. He kissed away her tears.

She looked up at him and, with the moonlight shining in her eyes, her love for him was plain enough for him to see.

'Charlotte, will you marry me?' he said softly against her mouth.

'We are married, my Justin,' she said.

'I mean, will you be my wife?'

'I am your wife.' She was showing him no mercy.

'I love you, Charlotte, and I want you and need you, and I've been a fool to take so long to tell you how I feel. God, I could have lost you in the fire, then my life would have been desolate.'

She put her hands on his face and looked into his eyes. It was an effort to talk, but the words needed saying. 'I love you, too, Justin Harvard. I want you and I need you and I can't wait to be your wife.'

As he pressed his lips against hers, parting the softness of her mouth with his tongue, she heard the cheering that rose from the servants as the fire brigade doused the flames. And then she forgot everything except her love for this man who held her, the man who was her husband.

'Till death do us part,' Justin said. And she repeated, 'Till death do us part.'

The publishers hope that this book has given you enjoyable reading. Large Print Books are especially designed to be as easy to see and hold as possible. If you wish a complete list of our books please ask at your local library or write directly to:

Magna Large Print Books
Magna House, Long Preston,
Skipton, North Yorkshire.
BD23 4ND

This Large Print Book, for people
who cannot read normal print,
is published under the auspices of

THE ULVERSCROFT FOUNDATION